THE FASHIONABLE SPY

Emily Johnson

CHIVERS

British Library Cataloguing in Publication Data available

This Large Print edition published by BBC Audiobooks Ltd, Bath, 2010.
Published by arrangement with Robert Hale Ltd.

U.K. Hardcover ISBN 978 1 408 47778 6
U.K. Softcover ISBN 978 1 408 47779 3

Copyright © Doris Emily Hendrickson, 1992, 2009

Printed and bound in Great Britain by
CPI Antony Rowe, Chippenham and Eastbourne

THE FASHIONABLE SPY

'Where on earth are you, you wretched man?' Victoria muttered.

She stamped her foot, shivering from the damp. It was to be so simple. A pause in Dover, pick up a packet at the castle from her contact, then on to London. She brushed back a wet tendril of chestnut hair that had somehow escaped from beneath her hood, then looked down, blue eyes ablaze with annoyance, at her faithful companion.

Rain dripped from the end of Victoria's nose, now pink with cold. She gave it an impatient wipe.

'I have stubbed toes on rocks, searched everywhere in these miserable ruins, and now I'm near frozen with this horrid June weather. June! More like March, I say. But I shan't give up just yet,' she murmured to her friend. The wind tugged at the hood of her sturdy gray cloak, seeking entry beneath its protective folds. Cold mist tingled against her skin. The dim roar of an angry sea could barely be heard, but she knew the tide was wicked. Victoria shivered again. She stared across the bay that curved along the Dover coast. Where was he? Why was he late?

The snap of a branch caught her attention. Again she searched about her. 'Not a soul around. Silly girl,' she scolded herself. "Twos the wind, most likely.' Merely because the hour grew late and the light became dim because of this blasted drizzle was no reason to be missish. But her heart began to beat faster.

Another growl. She whirled about, staring into the gray mists in vain, her hand clutching at her cloak. Nothing, no one to be seen. The black dog at her side bristled, head lowered as though ready to charge at a foe.

'What is it, Sable?' she whispered, although there was not a soul to hear her. Or was there? The lowering gloom concealed others as well as herself. Her gloved hand steadied her against the cold stone wall as she willed her heart to cease its foolish pounding.

The shadows grew longer; pinpricks of light began to show in the town below. Across the bay, the undulating hills swept inland from the sea, a slash of black above the pale gray of the cliffs. Never had she felt so alone, so vulnerable as today, this moment. A few minutes more and she would leave, regardless.

Sable growled once again, and Victoria hastily dropped to her knees to reassure him, threading suddenly nervous fingers through his fur. As her hand touched the enormous black poodle, an object whistled past her shoulder, clattering against the stone wall behind her.

The dog tore off into the darkness like a shot. Snarls punctuated by muttered curses

2

rooted Victoria to the spot. The sounds faded as her pet pursued whoever threatened his owner's life. It couldn't be her contact, because Sable knew him. But there were others, menacing unknowns who could wish her gone.

Her mouth grew dry as she stretched trembling fingers to pick up the object. A knife. The blade glittered in the dim light. It was a short, lethal-looking weapon. She could feel carving incised on the rough handle.

'Oh, Sable!' she whispered, quite relieved as he trotted up to her. He looked enormously pleased with himself. 'Good dog,' she whisered as she rose from where she crouched.

She silently darted from her waiting place, the knife still grasped in her left hand, cloak billowing about her, rapidly slipping down the steep hill through the trees and scrubby brush that covered the slope. Her pet kept pace with her, staying as close as possible, showing her the way when necessary. Shortly she was enveloped in the mists below the castle.

'You came at last,' she softly exclaimed to the dark figure who emerged from the first alley to confront her. For a moment their figures blended, then parted. Victoria thrust the packet of papers inside her cloak as he melted into the shadows. She was alone again. At her side, Sable growled.

She glanced behind her, up the hill to

where the castle sat obscured from view. Nothing could be seen moving but a solitary gull, who complained his state with a mournful cry as he wheeled about through what was now a steady rain. Nonetheless, she suspected there was someone out there, possibly watching her even now.

'Come, Sable. We must hurry. There is not a moment to lose.' She gathered her cloak tightly about her while the pair slipped along the deserted cobbled streets. At first she ran, skirts lifted slightly, dashing from street to street, staying on the lea side for protection from the rain, her heart in her throat at every sound, every shadow. When they entered the more populated area, she slowed, fearing curious eyes at such unseemly haste.

Afraid of what she might see, yet knowing she must look, she risked a glance behind her. A tall lean man, his battered hat tilted forward, paused beside a tavern. No one else was fool enough to be out and about this rainy night. The man seemed not the least interested in her, so she ran on her way, her delay having been but seconds.

At last she and Sable reached the small neat house where she rented a room. She had been warned to leave, and leave she must. At once.

*　　　*　　　*

4

Across the street from the house, a tall lean man blended into the shadows, patiently waiting, biding his time. When he saw the girl leave, he followed her to the mews where her coach was kept. Not close enough to overhear her instructions, he surmised her destination. He knew her well.

Leaving the mews, he returned to the neat house where the girl had stayed. It was a simple matter to rent the same room. Once he closed the door behind him, he searched every corner, hoping for a snippet, a clue.

'Damn and blast,' he grumbled, as not one shred could be found. She had picked the room clean.

*   *   *

'Bless you, Sam,' Victoria said in a low voice as she clambered into the traveling coach, nudging Sable before her. 'London, with all possible speed,' she commanded before he closed the door.

'Aye, Miss Dancy, I suspected as much,' the portly man replied as he climbed to his perch with an agility that belied his years.

In short order the coach was headed north and west on the Dover Road, the driver skillfully making his way along the darkening path. The lamps were lit, the horses prime goers, but Sam had made it evident he didn't relish the journey. Those snapping eyes had

5

told her all. Her pity for Sam warred with the need to reach London as soon as possible.

Victoria peered out of the window, then turned to her pet. 'The rain is growing worse. 'Tis not the best of times to be making a dash for the city.' Then she reflected a few moments. 'I wonder who it was that found me out. Where did I make a slip? Worse yet, what does he do next . . . and why? Have we a traitor in our midst, as they fear?'

The dog whined in seeming sympathy, rubbing his head against her sleeve as though to comfort her.

'Aye, Sable, what's to be done?' Her fingers smoothed the packet resting in her lap. One never knew what might happen, and she could take no chances. Her own life aside, it was important to the security of England that these papers not fall into the wrong hands. The portmanteau she always carried with her sat on the opposite seat and she reached for it.

In moments she removed the carefully wrapped head, then dumped the chisels and sculpturing tools in a tumble on the opposite seat. She secured the packet in the false bottom of the case before restoring it to its previous untidy state.

Smiling at the dog, she said, 'I doubt if anyone will be interested in that clutter, eh, Sable?'

The dog gave a friendly growl, if one could say there was such a thing, then placed his head on her lap, seeming happy to have the matter bothering his mistress settled.

Victoria sensed the storm was worsening, with rain pelting the coach in ever-increasing strength. When the coach slithered violently about on the road, she rolled down her window to peer into the gloom. Nasty. She drew her head back inside, shaking the water from her hood with annoyance. Lurching to her feet, she thumped hard on the roof. Shortly Sam picked up the trap to peer down at her.

'Sam,' she called out as loudly as she might, 'best stop at the next inn, wherever it might be. No sense in killing ourselves.' There was a wave of a gloved hand, then the trap fell closed once again.

'At least,' she murmured to the dog while sinking down to the seat, 'there is no one else fool enough to be on the road.'

*　　*　　*

Sir Edward Hawkswood swore fiercely while he attempted to retain control of his bays as his traveling chaise tore south along the Dover Road. 'Bad going,' he shouted to his groom.

Higgens, a spare little man with a long, thin nose, shouted back, 'Aye, sir,' his eyes alight with admiration for the skill of his master's driving.

'This road is abominable, the weather

worse. Why did I think I had to reach Dover as soon as possible?' Rain streamed down Edward's face and soaked his many-caped greatcoat. 'Should have stayed at the inn in Canterbury.'

As it was now, he wondered if he might survive the trip. His leg ached horribly, the pain piercing, eating at him with relentless intensity.

'Pity we had to be pressing on.' Higgens glanced at his master as though to see if he might divulge the point of this harebrained trip.

Edward grimly thought of the information he'd received. Spies, traitors—fantastic stuff indeed. He couldn't rest until he'd investigated the matter. The tip he'd received had offered information. Now, if he'd but get there in time.

And then he caught sight of a post chaise coming toward him. At first he thought it to be a phantom, a figment of his imagination rising from the gray mists.

'Who in their right mind would leave Dover on a day such as this?' he wondered to Higgens.

The groom, looking worried at the sight of another coach on the appalling road, exhaled, 'Aye.'

Edward fought to guide his team on the slippery highway. He had a chance, though a near one, that he might safely skim by the other vehicle. The other man looked to be a skilled driver, for he held his team well.

Then a clap of thunder rolled across the sky and a crack of lightning flashed. The horses took violent exception to this terror, plunging wildly, and were nigh impossible to control.

'Good God!' Edward exclaimed. There seemed no way he could prevent a collision.

The sound of dreadful smashing of wood and grinding of metal, horses in distress, and the cries of men reverberated across the valley, and in concert with this, another rumble of thunder.

The other driver jumped to escape the brunt of the crash, landing on the back of the near wheeler. The front-right corner of Edward's chaise had come off the worse in the encounter between the two carriages. The other chaise had been snapped off its springs, and now tilted crazily, with its occupants surely in a heap.

'Best see what we can do,' Edward observed as he clambered down, ignoring the pain in his leg. Obviously the last thing the other man wanted was to have the horses panic and bolt, thus dragging the damaged traveling coach through the mire.

Hawkswood handed the reins to his groom, knowing the man would have the team under control in a trice. He limped over to the other driver, wondering how anyone in the other coach had managed in the crash.

'Here, let me lend a hand,' he offered.

9

'Best see to Miss Dancy, what's inside,' replied the other man as he tended the horses.

Ignoring his painful leg, Edward made his way about the vehicle, and, seeing that the coachman had now attained control of his animals, he wrenched open the coach door.

About at his knee level lay the figure of a woman garbed in a plain gray cloak, strands of dark chestnut hair trailing down from beneath her hood. She was ably guarded by a black poodle of formidable size. Its intelligent eyes studied Hawkswood with disconcerting thoroughness.

'Easy now, fellow, be a good dog and let me have a look at your mistress. She's in a bad way, make no mistake about it.'

Hawkswood knelt, ignoring what the mud would do to his fine coat and breeches. A cursory examination of the woman revealed that she was likely concussed, with a possible bruise where the case had struck her. A small lump had formed on her brow. Even in the dim light he could make out her lovely features, delicately shaped face. They both needed a warm, dry spot in which to recover from their collision, but where?

Glancing about, he could see no sign of any houses, and knew it had been some time since he had passed one. No farm buildings were near, with the exception of a windmill off to one side, up the hill. He couldn't recall an inn on the remainder of the Dover Road either.

10

There'd most likely be no doctor to be found, worse luck.

Blast it! He needed to get to Dover and quickly. Even now, it might be too late. Yet he was in no condition to drape her across a horse for a ride to town. He suspected she'd not thank him for such a jolting ride, either. When concussed, the patient needed quiet and rest. Rain swirled about him into the coach, turning her cloak dark with wetness.

Reaching a swift decision, he approached the coachman.

'I'd best get her to a dry haven. Sooner the better,' he said tersely, not wanting speech in the rain. 'Hawkswood's the name.'

'Aye . . . Sir Edward,' the coachman said slowly, 'I've heard tell of you.'

'I'll take care of her,' Edward assured him. He was relieved at the man's acceptance of him.

'We can each ride a leader, taking the others in tow, to Canterbury and find help there,' offered Higgens to the coachman.

'Me name's Sam, and that's the best to be done, I reckon.' The coachman looked over Edward's groom, nodding his concurrence.

The two men began a crisp discussion of who would go first and what to do with the coaches. Neither seemed worried about the possibility of another vehicle on the highway.

Edward knew he could endure little more of the cold and wet, and doubted his companion could either. He scooped up the young woman in his arms and staggered across the field until he found a stone path to the front of the mill. Her cloak fell open and her gown rapidly became soaked in the downpour as he struggled up the path. He leaned against the building until he managed to open the door, then stumbled inside, the black dog trotting at his side, whining from time to time.

In the faint light of the windmill interior, Hawkswood made out a crude bed, and he carefully deposited his burden on it, first pulling her gray cloak aside, then off. His chilled fingers fumbled with the barrel-snap fastenings, yet she didn't stir.

With the large black dog beside him, he made a hasty perusal of the miller's room with the help of a candle and tinder he discovered on a ledge. A fire was the first order of business, and he blessed the unknown miller who had left a pile of kindling and wood in a rough box to one side of the hearth. Within moments the warmth of the fire began seeping through the room. A chill would do neither of them any good.

The shape of the room was peculiar to a windmill, with its circular outer wall of brick, and the staircase winding upward in the center of the structure. Not all windmills had living quarters for the miller, and Edward was most thankful this one did. This place had not been vacant for long; there were signs of habitation.

Edward was grateful he need answer no questions, nor that their identity would be known by another, at least for the present.

A rapid search resulted in the find of a cache of food—slightly stale bread, dry sausage, and a half-keg of ale. They could be warm and dry, and not want for sustenance. Now, if the lady could be persuaded to revive . . . .

Shedding his greatcoat when the warmth of the fire seeped through, he turned his full attention to the woman on the bed. She hadn't stirred since he had placed her there. God willing, her injury would not be overly serious. She was soaked, though. He'd done his best, but when the cloak had fallen open her gown had absorbed water like a sponge. There was naught to do but peel the damp clothing from her body, get her dry, so as to fend off an inflammation of the lungs, or worse.

What a coil to be in, trapped for the night with an unconscious but beautiful and very shapely miss. He had noted the supple grace of her form when he carried her. The damp gown clung to her body, revealing a great deal to his appreciative eyes. Was there someone who would step forth to demand he do the honorable thing after compromising her by his actions? He'd meant to save the chit, and hadn't thought about the ramifications of his deed. She looked innocent, vulnerable. He glanced at the dratted dog, who looked for all the world as though he laughed.

'Aye, laugh you might, I'm the one to pay the price, my fellow.' The thought did not cheer, in spite of her beauty.

He wasn't experienced in this sort of thing. Not being in the petticoat line, he limited his knowledge of the fair sex to conversation at dinner, casual chat at a party, and silent communication at the gaming table. A twinge of his leg was a grim reminder of just why he maintained the discreet distance. His first experience with rejection from a lady, when the extent of his injuries was revealed, had prompted a reluctance for repetition of the same. The other sort of woman never revealed her reaction.

He proceeded to strip the spice-brown gown from her, trying not to tear the opening at the neck. Buttons and tapes were alien to him, and more than a bit daunting at this moment. At long last he had removed all but her shift and stays, and left them on, even if faintly damp, for what he was certain would be her modesty. She looked to be the virginal sort.

About to cover her with the faded wool blanket that had been folded at the foot of the narrow bed, he paused. She had shifted slightly, an encouraging sign for all that she had been as limp as a dead frog while he removed those damp garments, and something caught his eye. The woman wore a

14

necklace, not an unusual thing as a rule. However, her movement revealed the design of an iris on the locket at the end of the chain, a blue iris done in lapis lazuli in an instantly recognized style. He knew it well.

Intrigued, he bent closer. Could it be possible she was associated with *that* group? A dangerous association, if so, and he examined her face again.

In the language of flowers the iris meant 'I have a message for you.' It had been adopted by a ring of spies as their secret identification, a fact few people, other than members, and a number in the government, knew.

How could any woman who looked as innocent and angelic as this one be a part of such a group? His instincts told him she was what she first seemed to be, innocent and respectable. But appearances could be deceptive. She might be selected for her part for that very reason. He touched the edge of the locket, and the top sprang open, revealing two miniatures, a man and a woman. Parents? There was a resemblance.

He tucked the blanket around her, then stood thinking. Rather than attempt to revive her again, he examined her garments. They might be plain, but they were of the highest quality. Delicate embroidery decorated her petticoat. Her footwear bespoke a fine bootmaker, and the unusual gold ring on her finger, while oddly shaped, was exquisite.

15

He turned again to study her face. Long dark lashes fanned over porcelain cheeks. He wondered if that straight little nose was the inquisitive sort, and bet that it was. Was she perhaps the one he sought? No one in her right mind would have set out on such a day . . . unless she had very pressing business. And what might be hers?

He raised a skeptical brow and limped over to the fireplace. He added wood to the fire, then turned to contemplate his companion and her guardian. Odd, how the dog had permitted her garments to be removed, not objected to his presence in the least. What did that say for his mistress? 'Here, old fellow,' Edward said, snapping his fingers.

The dog obeyed. It rubbed a curly head against Edward's good leg, establishing a friendship of sorts, and the two settled down to hold watch on the young woman.

'Elizabeth? Julia?' Victoria murmured, turning her head from side to side. 'My head hurts.' Then her eyelids fluttered before she opened them wide and stared, utterly dismayed, at the stranger. He was a handsome man, one with a fascinating face. Tall, perhaps? But who? She knew she had not seen him before.

'How do you feel? A cup of tea, perhaps?' His gentle offer revealed a cultured background, proper upbringing.

'Sam and the horses? Are they all right? I

16

should have stopped before. . . .' She went still, suddenly aware of something most significant. She moved slightly, then stiffened as the enormity of her predicament reached her befogged mind.

'You . . .' she sputtered, unable to do more than glare at him, for she felt as weak as a new chick. He might look like a gentleman, but surely no true gentleman would undress a helpless female! She transferred her gaze to the dog. 'How could you, Sable? I thought you would defend me.'

She closed her eyes. This man had stripped her of most of her clothes, wooed her dog away from her, and now had her in his complete power. No man should have her in such a position. Yet here she was. Helpless. She fingered the ring she always wore and amended that thought to: almost helpless.

'Your coachman took the horses to Canterbury, as did my groom. The vehicles will be tended to as soon as possible, I have no doubt. The weather is so nasty I question whether anyone will attempt to use the Dover Road tonight, so there is little worry for the coaches. I fear we are stuck in this windmill, but it could be worse.' He gestured to the fireplace. 'We have a rousing fire, there is bread and ale, and possibly tea. I thought you'd not take kindly to a trip through the rain back to Dover. Was your trip so pressing?' he probed.

She evaded his gaze, taking refuge in peeking at the fire, then looking about the room revealed in the dim light. 'I need to get to London as soon as possible.'

'Impossible.'

You spoke with Sam.' She digested the curious fact that Sam had spoken with this man and entrusted her to him. 'And you are...?'

'Hawkswood,' he replied, looking as though he might swoop down upon her. His dark eyes crinkled slightly as though to smile, and beneath an aristocratic nose, a sensual mouth twitched faintly.

'I'll fetch you a bit of sausage and bread. Unless I can locate that tea, I fear your beverage will have to be ale.' He rose and went across the room.

Victoria took note of his faint limp and wondered how he had managed to carry her. She was not a featherweight, as tall as she was.

'Where are my clothes?' she demanded, then winced at the sound of her own voice in her aching head.

He bestowed a glance on her from the pantry door. 'Drying. Your gown is over the chair—the one upon which I sat, so as not to crowd your narrow bed. The rest are draped here and there near the fire. I have no designs on your virtue.'

Not in the least amused by his words, nor completely reassured, for that matter, she

18

stretched out a hand toward her dog and was rewarded with his eager nudge. He would remain close by her, of that she was determined. A chestnut curl fell across her shoulder as she shifted beneath her blanket. Oh, she was totally undone.

He returned with a plate and mug in hand, pausing before offering them to her. 'By the bye, Hawkswood is preceded by Sir Edward. We ought not dispense with the formalities.' His eyes glittered, but with what, she couldn't say. They were a deep brown, and did not reveal his thoughts in the least.

'Indeed.' She had heard his name, but couldn't remember where. Stretching out one hand, while managing to retain a hold on the blanket that kept her modestly covered, she accepted the fare.

'I suspect you are concerned over our, er, involvement . . . that is, the forced intimacy of the situation,' he said, then appeared annoyed when she frowned at him. 'You have, I repeat, no need to mistrust me, young woman.'

Well,' she said with asperity, 'you are not in your dotage, and there is no one else with us. What the polite world might make of our predicament, I dread to consider.'

'You would be compromised, I suspect.'

'In truth? Or malicious conjecture? One is as damning as the other.' She sighed before nibbling at her bread.

'Your family will be worried about you

when you are late in arriving.' He dropped down on the chair, then sampled his food.

'True,' she replied after taking another bite. 'But you know how it is with traveling, one is forever running into unexpected obstacles. And this was one of the more unexpected ones.' In a burst of honesty she added, 'The road was terrible. I fancy neither my coachman nor your groom could help the crash.'

'I was driving, not my groom,' he replied tersely, then countered, 'Why are you alone? No maid, no outriders. 'Tis not proper.'

'With Sable I have always been safe.' She glared at the dog, who looked innocently from the man to his mistress.

Sir Edward picked up her stockings and petticoat. 'These have dried out now. I shall absent myself so you may be a bit more comfortable.'

He was as good as his word, walking off with that faint but distinct limp. Victoria quickly pulled on her stockings, shaking her head to clear its fuzziness. Then she slipped on her petticoat and absurdly felt better.

'All clear?'

'You may come back. I daresay it's chilly in there.'

He returned carrying the sausage in one hand. 'More sustenance.' She watched as he prepared bread, then sliced off a few pieces of sausage for her. 'Hungry?'

Victoria held out a hand. She ought not have been so starved. The girls in the Minerva novels always managed to survive without food—fainting frequently, sighing sadly, and being bird-witted in general. She was more earthy, needing her primitive comforts of food and shelter.

'Your belongings are still in the carriage, my dear.' He studied her with a disconcerting gaze and she shifted uncomfortably under his look. She doubted he had been out to investigate the contents of her portmanteau, but that look of his made her wonder what was in his mind.

'I suppose we had best get some sleep and hope that morning brings better weather,' was her slurred comment, evidence that she was still not quite herself. The dreadful ache in her head refused to subside.

'Aye,' he said, sounding dubious about the possibility.

At last she drifted off into an uneasy slumber, wondering how this ticklish situation could be resolved.

*   *   *

The following morning brought no relief from the storm. Rain still pelted the windmill. Victoria listened, curled beneath the blanket, wondering at the silence. 'There is not the sound from a windmill.'

21

'The sweeps have been disconnected, I would wager,' Hawkswood offered.

'Oh.' She continued, 'My head does not ache quite so much this morning, although the lump on my forehead is most tender.' She peered warily at him as he sat by the hearth. In spite of what must have been a tempting circumstance, he had remained the gentleman, and she should be grateful. He intrigued her not a little; she longed to ask questions. A frown furrowed her brow, and she winced. He caught her curious look at his leg stretched out before him toward the fire.

'Stupid accident,' was his terse comment.

She gave him a startled glance.

'No, you did not need to ask me. I expect whenever anyone sees someone with a limp, interest is aroused. I fancy the fellows who come home from the Peninsula experience it frequently.'

'My brother is over there fighting.'

'Who is he? I may have encountered him.' Sir Edward spoke with an absent manner, as though more interested in building up the fire than her answer.

In the quiet intimacy fostered by the flickering of the flames and the pattering of the rain, she replied to his question in the same vein. 'Geoffrey Dancy.'

He flicked her a surprised glance, then returned his attention to the fire. 'Lord Dancy? I met him several times while in

Portugal. Fine man. Elizabeth and Julia are your sisters?'

'How did you know? Did my brother mention his family?' She tried to conceal her alarm at his question.

'You spoke their names yesterday. Although you did not call for your parents.' There was a question in his voice.

'My parents were murdered by the French while on an innocent visit, one with written permission from Napoleon himself. They were scholars,' she added at his look.

He paused a time, then cleared his throat. 'You know that we have a bit of a dilemma here. I have the ideal solution. We shall marry.'

2

Elizabeth stared out of the bare windows of the workroom, considering the falling rain with concern. 'I thought Victoria would be home ere now.'

'As did I,' Julia replied from her chair near the fireplace. She turned to the man who sat quietly at her side, adding, 'There have been so many coach accidents of late, one cannot help but feel anxious.'

'Dear lady, have you not assured me that your coachman is highly skilled? Still, it is a wonder that your sister is off alone, without a companion.'

'Victoria has her dog, and he is as fierce as any guard,' Elizabeth flashed back from where she sat at her desk, her pen in hand.

'As long as he is alive, I fancy.' At their shocked gasps, Mr Padbury shook his head. 'What ails me? I am utterly thoughtless to put such a notion in your heads. Dear ladies, I feel certain that the . . . Dover Road, did you say? . . . is quite passable. Doubtless the reckless driver is ensconced at his club on such a day.'

Julia's warning look at her younger sister came too late when Elizabeth blurted out, 'The Dover Road is well enough, 'tis the road along the coast that gives one pause.'

'True,' murmured Mr Padbury. 'However, I feel certain she will arrive safe and sound later. Most likely she has sought sanctuary in a cozy inn with all amenities. Even now she may be seated by a fire, cosseted by a genial landlady.' He beamed a reassuring smile on the young ladies, and they both relaxed a trifle.

*　　　*　　　*

'What utter rubbish,' Victoria exclaimed. 'I have no desire to wed, you or another. Who is to know we tarried here? Sam and I shan't say a word, and I doubt you have any desire to be leg-shackled to a stranger either.'

'Perhaps you have the right of it,' Sir

Edward replied, although sounding most dubious.

A gust of wind rattled the windowpanes, and the fragile mood broke. Victoria shifted uneasily beneath her covering. 'My gown ought to be dry.'

'I shall absent myself so you can change. Perhaps if I check the carriages, there is something you would wish to have in here? The men have not returned to take them for repair.' He looked out of the window toward the road. 'I fear your coach may not be salvageable.'

She pulled the blanket about her shoulders, then crossed to peer out of the window through the falling rain. This delay was intolerable, but she would have to make the best of it. He must not uncover the truth. 'I have two cases in the coach. I would appreciate a change of clothing, to be sure. But should you go outside in this nasty weather?' She turned to look at him with concern.

'I wish to change garments as well, Miss Dancy.'

He seemed to mock her with his eyes, and she dared not argue with him as she longed to do. She merely nodded in understanding, then watched while he shrugged into his greatcoat, clapped his battered beaver on his head, and dashed through the rain—an irregular gait — down the hill to where the two vehicles sat in

25

forlorn dejection.

Sable had slipped out the door after Hawkswood before she could stop him. He gamboled along beside the tall man, ignoring the wet. Her gaze narrowed as Sir Edward wrenched open the door to her coach, then pulled her two cases from the interior. He struggled back up the slope, dumped them inside the door, then took off again before she could say a word, his limp more pronounced this trip.

She felt guilty for causing him to make two trips. She'd not remembered his injured leg, or considered the difficulty in bringing several cases. While he was yet gone, she hastily grabbed the case with her clothing and rushed into the pantry. Pulling out a warm gown, she hurriedly struggled into it, accustomed to doing for herself when on these special trips. Fortunately, it buttoned up the front, and she was completing that task when the door slammed once again. She heard him stamp his feet and she opened the pantry door, peering cautiously around the corner.

'I shan't bite you, especially when you wear such a depressingly respectable gown, Miss Dancy.'

Those dark eyes of his seemed to tease her, even if his voice did not. Victoria took no notice, but walked over to place her case by the narrow bed where she slept. The bed was close to the door, a factor in the plans beginning to form in her mind.

'How comforting. I'd not wish to think I cast out lures, Sir Edward.' She reluctantly smiled at the small joke she'd made.

He tossed his hat on the deal table by the wall, then took his greatcoat and shook it well before hanging it up on a peg near the door. 'I believe that if we are to spend another day in close company we could dispense with formalities, do you not?'

He arched one of those dark brows and smiled. Victoria wished he hadn't, for it gave him such an endearingly warm quality, dispelling that air of cool aristocratic aloofness she had first viewed. She had hoped to avoid any familiarity. Yet she supposed it made little difference at this point. 'Granted. My given name is Victoria.'

'Victoria Dancy?' He paused in the act of placing a log on the fire, staring at nothing for a moment. 'I have heard that name before, but cannot recall just where. Why would I know of you and not your sisters? Elizabeth or Julia Dancy do not ring a bell in the least.'

'Julia married Lord Winton several years ago though she styles herself as Mrs Winton as she is not on terms with her late husband's family. She is now widowed and paints miniatures.' Victoria waited, holding her breath.

'Ah,' he said, 'you are also an artist, a sculptress. I have heard something of your

27

work.' The searching look he gave her made Victoria wonder precisely what he'd heard. By the expression on his face, it was not to her credit.

She was most piqued. Why did he not say something? She watched and waited. His deep brown eyes gave nothing away, but his sensual mouth twisted into a grin, and she jumped as he spoke.

'Perhaps we had best get something to eat.'

'I spotted a tin of tea and there is still some bread. I shall tend to making tea while you change out of those wet garments.' Glad to have something to occupy her hands, she turned to get the tea and wavered a bit. She shook her head to clear it, annoyed at the momentary weakness.

His hand at her elbow guided her to the chair by the fire. 'I doubt if you are quite as stout after your injury as you may think. I shall bring you the tea and fetch the water in the kettle. I trust you can handle the rest.'

Edward took the kettle and filled it from the pump, then hung the kettle over the fire. He wished he knew something of her parents. What had been the purpose of that supposedly innocent trip to France? With Napoleon's blessing? His eyes narrowed with his conjectures. Then he took his portmanteau into the pantry and proceeded to make a change of clothing.

She was full of contradictions. While she

pretended to be so prim, she had the laciest of petticoats. Her present gown looked to be one favored by an ape leader, yet Miss Dancy was young, too young to be on the shelf, although certainly not just out of the schoolroom. He wondered about the other items of clothing in her bag, then shook his head in disgust. Surely he had more necessary things to consider. In spite of her brave words, he knew what had to be done. After all, she was of the gentry, and a lady.

He had met her brother. Would she demand he consult with him, since Lord Dancy was the head of her family? That might make it difficult, as he doubted that young man planned to return to England in the near future.

When Edward joined her before the fire, it seemed as though she had conceded their predicament, for she gave him a hesitant smile and appeared to relax when he returned it with a smile of his own. Accepting the mug of tea from her, he picked up a slab of bread and sausage from the cracked plate, while seeking the words to convince her of their fate. Once settled beside her, he brought up the subject he knew he could not avoid.

'You are well and truly compromised by this stay with me,' he began. 'Surely you cannot dismiss our situation, unplanned though it might be?'

'Nonsense,' she answered with an indignant

29

sniff. 'Who is to know about it?'

'In my experience, someone is bound to find out. Your coachman and my groom are in Canterbury, most likely together. Even if they keep mum about the accident, surely someone will take note, and gossip spreads with amazing speed.' He gazed at her over the rim of his mug, trying to assess her emotions or reaction to the truth of his words.

'That I *have* noticed,' she answered with a wry tinge to her voice.

'I see.' Had she been gossiped about? He imagined she might be, as an artist. He had heard things, vague rumblings, nothing concrete, but enough to make him wonder. He wished he could remember what more it was he had heard about her, and where.

'However,' she continued, ignoring his silence, 'I fancy I shall survive it. After all, the Polite World expects bizarre behavior from one who is an artist, you know.' She sketched an affected and rather amusing gesture in the air, and then smiled. Her eyes were truly an amazing shade of clear blue and seemed fathoms deep as he gazed into them.

'However,' he countered, '*I* am not an artist. My conduct is above reproach. I insist you accept my offer for marriage, Miss Dancy.' He waited, gauging the impact of his words by the little gasp that escaped from her lips.

Victoria studied the aristocratic lord for

several moments, then dropped her lashes down, thus concealing her eyes and the expression in them. 'Your sacrificial offer is quite unnecessary, Sir Edward, although I appreciate the gesture more than I can say.'

Julia and Elizabeth would shake the stuffing out of her if they knew about this situation and her rejection. Not that Victoria hadn't received propositions. She'd had them flung at her, she'd had them slyly thrust at her, and they'd been written to her by the score. Alas, they were also most improper, as she supposed she might expect under the circumstances of her peculiar life. But to have a suitable offer of marriage at this point in time was advantageous. It was also dangerous to them both. She had come to admire Sir Edward, and had no intention of involving him in her perils.

'I believe we deserve better, sir. Certainly I have no desire for a forced wedding to one who would rather be elsewhere, wedded to someone other than myself. I trust you have a cherished lady?' Victoria darted a glance at his face before returning her gaze to the flames. It made no difference to her whether he had a lady he esteemed, did it? She'd not wed him regardless. 'I do appreciate the nobility of your gesture, however.'

'There is no one,' he replied, and Victoria thought his voice a trifle grim. She wondered about that even as she leaned back against the chair.

'You are tired,' he said. 'Your head is undoubtedly still aching a bit. Why not take a nap? When you awake, I shall challenge you to a game of cards. If we cannot do anything more interesting, it is best to keep occupied in something that is innocent.'

She felt a blush heat her skin as she considered his teasing. More interesting, indeed. And how would he pass the time? Thoughts of kisses from that sensual mouth, of being held close to his tall lean frame, entered her mind, and she hastily turned from him, seeking the bed and the worn blanket with determination.

She stumbled on her path across the room, and marked the agility with which he came to her rescue. Although he had brought a cane with him on his second trip, she suspected he used it only when necessary. She wondered when he had been wounded and how, then reminded herself that it was no business of hers. She had rejected his generous offer, made from a kindly motive. Surely he had nothing to lose. Society expected gentlemen to be more free in their behavior than women, who were truly circumscribed. But she had broken through that barrier with her work, and had no need for his protection. Protection. Ah, it was a lovely-sounding word, not to mention concept.

Murmuring polite nothings, she settled

down beneath the blanket, feeling oddly tired and a little woozy in her head. It was most likely the result of her accident, and she hoped the sleep would help to ease it.

Edward watched as Victoria drifted off to a restorative sleep. Strangely enough, he was not surprised that she had rejected his well-meant offer of marriage. She seemed far more independent than most women he had met. What had prompted her to take up sculpturing? Then he recalled where he had seen her work. Victoria Dancy had already established herself at a young age as a premier artist, employed by a great many politicians to create their images. Edward had viewed one of her busts at the home of an acquaintance not too long ago. She was incredibly skilled at her craft, the likeness being a duplication, even offering an insight to the character, of the sitter.

He turned to stare at the sleeping young woman. Why? Why did she primarily seek politicians to model? Rumor had it she was working on a life-size statue of the king. Not that there was anything wrong with that.

A movement outside caught his eye, and he hurried to the door, quietly opening it while keeping the dog silent by holding its muzzle. He stepped out, remaining in the shelter of the small porch while he waited for his groom and Miss Dancy's coachman to present their assessment of the damage to the coaches.

33

'Miss Dancy is sleeping, the effects of the knock on her head, you know. What is it you have to report?' Then he noticed a cluster of men, horses, and a dray along the road. The Dancy vehicle was being hauled atop the low dray for transport. Two men stood by his own carriage, inspecting the damage to it.

'Both the coaches are going in to Canterbury, sir,' Higgens replied. 'Yours can be fixed in a day or two, at least well enough to proceed. Miss Dancy may well wish to consider traveling on by post chaise, for hers is in a sorry state.'

'Aye,' Sam nodded. 'She'll not be best pleased about this. I expect her sisters will prefer a new coach to repairing this one, it's that bad.'

'Is money a problem? Has she enough to cover the costs involved?'

Traveling was expensive, and to go by post chaise and pair was the most costly. He had no idea how well-off Lord Dancy might be, nor how well-paid Victoria was for her work. It seemed reasonable to him that if she modeled busts, and received payment for them, she did so because she had need of the money. Perhaps her scholarly parents had been improvident.

'She is well enough fixed, I expect.' Sam gave Sir Edward a shrewd look, then added, 'She's an independent lass, and won't take kindly to an offer of money.'

Edward understood what the man was implying, and pulled his purse out. Several pounds exchanged hands, followed by a grateful nod from Sam.

'I'll see to it this is spent where needed, sir.'

Edward had debated over the matter of his charge. Was she well enough to make a jolting trip to Canterbury? He had yet to convince her of the need for marriage. His own trip to Dover was pointless; by now his informant would be long gone—urgency had been stressed. Besides, he found the beautiful Miss Dancy quite intriguing. Memory of the blue-iris locket returned. He needed to learn more about her, for a number of reasons.

He turned to Higgens. 'Miss Dancy is not well enough to travel as yet. It is dangerous to travel so soon after a concussion. I fear to move her. Send a coach for us on the morrow.'

And with that instruction, the men went back to the group that waited for them. Within a short time the road was empty again, the figures a distant blur through the drizzle.

The warmth of the fire was most welcome, especially to his leg, which ached from exposure to the damp. The doctor had promised it would get better in time, but Edward wondered if it actually would. He didn't have a great deal of faith in doctors.

He leaned back in the one and only chair and relaxed, waiting for the promised game of cards.

*   *   *

When Victoria awoke from her restoring nap,
she again felt that disorientation. Then she
caught sight of Sir Edward and all memory
returned. Plague take it, why couldn't the man
have disappeared while she slept? She didn't
believe he really wanted to marry with her,
and it would have offered a neat solution had
he simply gone off to Dover. Why hadn't he?
  He had a deck of cards and now pulled the
deal table over by the fire. It was a pleasant
scene: a blazing fire, the rustic brick hearth
and walls, with all manner of tools and
necessities hanging on the far wall. The tang
of wood smoke hung in the air. The man who
awaited her had best be ignored if possible.
But she doubted if he would allow that, for he
was one who compelled the eye, drew a
lingering glance. He was a disturbing element
to her hard-earned tranquillity. She watched
while he pulled forward the bed, so he might
sit.
  'Well, Miss Dancy. Shall we see what
manner of card player you are? I trust you are
not   one   to   frequent   the   gaming
establishments.'
  'La, sir, what do you think? I am as skilled
as most young women my age.'
  They elected to play a hand of euchre.
Victoria soon observed that she was no match

36

for him in this game. Before she realized it, Sir Edward had captured most of the tricks and she went down to defeat.

She wondered if her lack of concentration was due to the circumstances, or if it was merely his proximity. Determined to beat him at something, for some unknown, but no doubt complex, reason, she suggested they continue at something else. She thought his grin quite odious.

'Piquet?'

She nodded agreement, and hoped that she had not forgotten all her brother had taught her. Sir Edward dealt the cards with skill and she gathered her hand to study it. Victoria settled in her chair, resolved to best him this time around. The play began and she found she could hold her own very well against him. By blocking him out, concentrating on the cards alone, she managed to earn a respectable score.

At length Sir Edward rose to light a candle he had found.

Victoria glanced to the window, absently noting that the wind was down and that the rain appeared to have dwindled to nothing more than a mist. She prayed that it would continue to abate. While it was too late for her to execute her plan today, she would on the morrow for certain.

'What is going on in your head, Victoria?' Sir Edward mused aloud.

37

'The rain seems to be lessening. I am anxious to be gone.'

He pretended affront. 'You are tired of my company! Alas.' Then he paused before continuing. 'Your coachman was here earlier. I neglected to tell you when you woke up. They carted your coach to Canterbury for possible repairs, but he suspects it may take some time. In which case you shall require a post chaise and pair to get to London. Will that be a problem?'

Victoria sat with her jaw tightly clenched, absolutely furious with him, then exploded. 'They were here? And you did not wake me? I would have gone with them to Canterbury. I might have been halfway to London by now.'

She dropped the cards on the table and jumped up to pace back and forth in the small room, anger evident in her every step. 'Oh,' she fumed, 'I cannot believe you would do such a thing when you knew how much I wished to leave. Believe me, sir, when I say I had rather be miles from here at the moment. No insult to your company intended,' she snapped.

She glared at the arrogant tilt of his head, and realized she had indeed insulted him. 'You made an honorable offer,' she reminded him. 'I refused. Why did *you* not leave when you could?'

'And leave you prey to anyone who might come along? I perceive your regard for me is not high, but I am not so heedless as all that.'

'I have my protection, thank you very much!' She beckoned to Sable, who obediently trotted to her side.

'I noticed just how faithful he is.' Sarcasm dripped from his words as he snapped his fingers, and Sable walked to his side, beaming idiotically up at the gentleman who had fed him this morning.

'Oh,' she stormed. 'If you must know, you are the first man Sable has ever accepted in any way, other than my brother. I rely on the dog to protect me when I am in the houses of those noble politicians who too frequently desire more than just a bust to place on a stand or mantel.'

Sir Edward tossed his cards on the table and rose to go to her side. He took her chin in hand. 'Protect you?'

'Sable,' she managed to utter in a strangled voice, snapping her fingers weakly.

To his credit, Sable growled. Victoria fancied the dog was as puzzled as she over her difficulty. Why, after all this time, had Sir Edward chosen to behave in this manner?

'Sir,' she whispered as his face neared, 'you forget yourself.'

He stepped away from her, dropping his hand to his side. 'So I do.' He ran long fingers through his hair, then glanced at her again. 'I suspect this is why they keep young women secluded and under guard.'

Victoria merely nodded, and the tension in the room eased a trifle. She had not managed to avoid, quite cleverly, she thought, the amorous intentions of the various men that she sculptured without learning something. Why did so many feel she would welcome their attentions? Oh, it was true that a few were attractive and possibly tempting. But she'd no desire to become involved in a clandestine liaison. She had met only one man she had wished with all her heart was not already wed. One embrace forced her to accept the danger of her position. She'd acquired Sable as her constant guard, and the dog daunted the most assertive man.

The dog had done its job well . . . until now. Why, of all the men in the world, did Sable choose Sir Edward Hawkswood to slaver over?

The remainder of the day was spent in playing cards. Victoria tried to concentrate, so that she might avoid contemplating what it would be like to become involved with Sir Edward. She was not a little green girl just out of the schoolroom. Stolen kisses were not beyond her.

From time to time she glanced at him, memorizing his facial structure. She would sculpture him just for herself. A smile touched her lips as she thought of how silly that sounded, hiding the bust of a handsome man in her room, just to gaze upon it in idle

40

moments. It was the combination of that aristocratic nose and brow with the unexpectedly sensual mouth that drew her, compelled her to look again and again. The planes of his cheeks, the shape of his head, were beautiful in a masculine way. He fascinated her. And in that path lay danger.

At last the fading light forced their desultory card games to an end. She rose from her chair.

He gallantly returned the bed upon which he'd sat to the original position against the wall, then stood there looking down at her.

She could read his feelings in his eyes then. The attraction she felt was mutual. But what madness, to yield to a passion. Passions were so fleeting, so undependable. She turned aside to pick up the blanket with an inward struggle, looking about to see how Sir Edward would manage for the night. Then she sat down and prepared to make the best of the circumstances and get some needed sleep.

Her portmanteau, with its secret, was stowed at the end of her bed. He oddly enough had displayed no curiosity over it, and she decided not to draw attention to it in any way.

Would she remain safe? From herself as well as from him? She patted her bed, taking comfort from Sable's nearness as he curled up close to her.

'What are your virginal fears, my lady,' Sir

Edward taunted, 'that you call your loyal dog to your side? Do you fear that I might steal a kiss? Or more? I daresay you would survive the first, and I should not consider the latter.'

She sniffed, and was surprised when he leaned over to drop a swift kiss on her upturned mouth. It was over before she could protest, and she admitted to a faintly bereft feeling deep inside her. Loath to reveal her inner reactions to this now-dangerous man, she snapped, 'Keep your distance, sir. Sable *will* obey a command from me.'

Walking to the far side of the room, Sir Edward sank down on the one chair. His deep chuckle unsettled her. With great difficulty she turned to face the wall and hoped she might find a few winks of sleep this night. She needed to be rested for what she had in mind. The ache in her head subsided and she drifted to sleep, feeling secure in the most absurd way that she would have no necessity for Sable's defense.

When next she opened her eyes she could discern faint light from the window. Gingerly sitting up in bed, she discovered that her head was near normal. Across the room Sable curled up near the fire, close to where Sir Edward stretched out beneath his greatcoat on the hearth rug.

The fire burned brightly, evidence of frequent tending during the night. Victoria waited a few moments, then, satisfied Sir

Edward was sound asleep, edged from her bed. In a few minutes she had donned her other gown and the ruined half-boots.

She debated, then emptied the contents of her fountain ring into a small mug of ale, taking care not to be observed. In spite of her attempts to be quiet, he had awakened. With a deep breath for Dutch courage, she walked to where the man now watched her.

'Your breakfast ale, sir?' she said with what she hoped was a parody of a pert maid.

'How kind,' he replied with that charming smile. He finished the drink, then relaxed on the rug again while Victoria busied herself about the little room, folding the blanket, stowing her other clothing away.

'I vow, 'tis cozy in here. The rain has subsided, and I fancy we might be rescued before long.' She chattered on softly about nothing in particular, finally risking a glance at him again. He was sound asleep, albeit a drugged sleep.

Swiftly donning her gray cloak, she snapped her fingers at Sable. The dog came, reluctantly leaving the man on the floor behind.

'Sable, we cannot be sentimental.' At the door she paused, taking a long look at Sir Edward, committing those bewitching features to memory before resolutely turning away.

Together the pair slipped from the little windmill that had housed them, then began to trudge along the road to Canterbury.

3

A round-eyed Rosemary tugged at the skirts of her newly returned and dearly beloved aunt. Her babbling was, as usual, quite incomprehensible, her concern obvious.

Her twin, the more silent Tansy, sat on the floor of the morning room, staring at her aunt with a worried expression on her face. She clutched the wooden doll her aunt had brought her with fierce possession, never mind her twin had an identical one dangling from her hand.

'Aunt is quite all right, dearest,' murmured Victoria, smoothing a tangled curl back from Rosemary's forehead while wondering how much she need reveal to her eldest sister.

'Go and play with your pretty dolls, children. Mama wishes to talk with Aunt Victoria,' commanded Julia in a kindly but firm tone that the children knew better than to ignore. The twins settled down near the hearth to examine their new toys while their mama fixed her sister with a minatory expression. 'Well? I postponed questioning you until this morning, for when you returned last evening, you looked worn to a flinder.'

'It was not quite so bad as all that,' Victoria said with a bit of spirit. 'The walk to Canterbury was blessedly cut short when a farmer gave me a ride on his cart for most of the way. Once I arrived in Canterbury it was but a minor problem to locate Sam and the chaise.' She added thoughtfully, 'That is a lovely town, really. We must visit there someday.'

'But to carry those cases? And your head injured?' Julia was clearly not to be appeased easily.

'I'd a day or so to recover, remember?' Victoria hoped that her sister would not probe too deeply into the events of those two days. Not that anything had actually happened, mind you. But her sister doted on propriety, probably because the three of them skirted on the edge so often, particularly Victoria. It would not be astonishing for Julia to demand that her younger sister accept Sir Edward's proposal, never mind that neither of the two involved wished for a marriage. Julia would organize the wedding before a cat could lick its paws.

'What of the man who rescued you?' Julia's study of her sister was with shrewd eyes.

Victoria could only pray that her sister saw no more than a bland countenance. If she so much as thought that Victoria had an interest—of any sort—in Sir Edward, it would be all over.

'It was his carriage that crashed into mine. I ought to demand he replace it, or at the very least repair the damage,' Victoria said with asperity as she thought of the expenses as a

45

result of the crash. Although, to be fair, the other driver had had little chance to avoid the impact, given the weather. And, she admitted, her family was well-off, not the least purse-pinched. 'Sam feels the chaise will never be the same, and suggested we order a new one. It is possible we might find one advertised in the *Post*,' Victoria offered mildly. 'There are often carriages for sale by people who can no longer afford to keep them.'

Any hope she might divert her sister to a different line of thought was lost when Julia said sternly, 'Vicky, you spent two nights in the same dwelling with this man. Your reputation, should word of this get out, will be ruined.'

Deciding the worst might as well be known, Victoria replied, 'Actually, it was the same room. This windmill was not a particularly large one.' She prudently omitted the provocative information that Sir Edward had divested her of most of her wet clothing. It had been in the interest of her health, and this much she allowed. 'He seemed only concerned for my well-being. He did not appear attracted to my person in the least.'

Julia stared, utterly horrified, at her sister. 'That is even worse.' She placed trembling fingers against her cheeks. 'What might be bruited about Town should news of this latest escapade leak to the *ton* is beyond thinking. We already face a certain amount of censure that is mitigated only by our financial status and Geoffrey being a baron. Women who paint, sculpture, and engrave because they wish to do so are on a different plane than those who are required to earn a living. Nevertheless. . . .' She sighed.

Julia continued, 'I do not know what we shall do regarding it. Perhaps wait to see what develops with regard to the gentleman. How fortunate you are that he was a gentleman. I am surprised Sam would allow you to be carried off like that.'

Her eyes contained more curiosity than reproach. That she was intrigued at this departure from Sam's normally protective behavior was clear. Victoria suspected that Julia also wondered at her own reticence in discussing the storm-caused delay. For some reason, she was not prepared to reveal all that had occurred.

'When I encountered Sam at the inn in Canterbury, he actually seemed surprised that Sir Edward was not with me. As though I would permit such a thing. Do you know that man had the effrontery to order a coach to come for us in the *afternoon?* He knew I wished to arrive in London as soon as possible.' Victoria sniffed with disdain at the man who had such presumption.

'Interesting,' Julia replied.

'Let us put all that behind us,' Victoria begged, partly from a need for self-defense

47

and partly from the urgency of the matter in which they were involved. 'I have the packet, and may I remind you that the information is urgently desired?' That someone threw a knife at her just before she acquired that same packet she prudently omitted. Also, the knowledge that the knife bore the crude carving of an iris was not revealed. 'The weather in Dover was extremely nasty. I was fortunate to make my contact and flee the town in one piece. It is a relief to be home. I shall send in my report, then see if I can solve the riddle posed by the cipher.'

Julia nodded, apparently happy to have her sister cozily safe in the morning room. 'You are certain that Sir Edward had no idea what you possessed?'

Victoria smiled with catlike smugness. 'Not in the least. Although he carried my case into the windmill, there isn't the least evidence that he removed it from the foot of my bed, much less opened it. Indeed, he evinced little curiosity about my occupation.' She had been surprised at this, for most people asked all manner of questions. She had often wondered if the disapproval from the women who queried her stemmed from envy rather than censure.

'What a relief.' Julia glanced to where the girls sat by the hearth, undressing their dolls and amiably arguing in their incomprehensible chatter. 'They appear settled for the nonce, at any rate. It was kind of you to remember them with such pretty trifles.' Turning back to face her sister, she got to the point. 'Shall you begin work on the papers immediately?'

Victoria withdrew the oiled silk packet from her reticule and unfolded the few papers that had been tucked within. She spread them out on the table at her side. 'It appears to be a list. But what is the key to deciphering it? It is like nothing I have encountered to this point. I must say, whoever penned this had an atrocious hand,' she murmured as she picked up a magnifying glass to again study the formation of the various letters that made up the words on the first page. While en route to London, with only Sable for companionship, Victoria had pulled the packet from her case to look it over. She had hoped to pass the hours in profitable study. Instead, she found the code impossible to break.

The room grew quiet, with the gentle crackle of the fire a sweet counterpoint to the murmurings of the girls. Victoria prepared her report, ringing for Evenson to promptly dispatch it.

Then the door burst open and a slim young woman, her chestnut curls bouncing and aquamarine eyes wide with curiosity, charged into the room. 'Why did no one wake me? What happened? Did you find any incriminating evidence? How did your stay go? Why are you late coming home? And why

49

is there a court plaster on your forehead?'

Victoria rose from the table and went to reassure her younger sister that all was well. 'Elizabeth, calm yourself. I found out not a thing. And I am well enough after my wetting, thanks to the care from the gentleman whose chaise crashed into mine. Sam is taking charge of repairs, although he said we really ought to order a new chaise to replace the damaged one. I thought we had better discuss it before agreeing with him.'

'I should like one with an aquamarine interior. Mrs Biddlesby has one and I vow it is most charming.' Then Elizabeth glanced at the table and back to her sister again. 'You received papers. Are they difficult?'

Her sisters were in awe of Victoria's ability to decipher the coded papers presented to her from time to time, frequently through highly unusual channels.

'No, 'tis most frustrating. The only instruction I received was that it was extremely important to our country's security. As I told Julia, it appears to be some sort of list.'

The door opened again to admit the elderly butler who had served the Dancy family from the time he first entered service as a young boy. Evenson bowed to Victoria, then intoned, 'There is a gentleman to see you, Miss Victoria. Sir Edward Hawkswood. Shall I tell him you are not at home?' It was evident Evenson disapproved of this departure from the proper hour for social calls.

While it was not the correct hour to be paying calls, Victoria very much doubted if Sir Edward cared in this instance. Tucking the papers carefully back into the packet, and then into the reticule she hung on her wrist, she rose from the table. Stiffening her spine, she shook her head at Evenson, then brushed down her gown before sweeping from the room, saying as she left, 'I may as well see him and be done with it.' She glanced at each of her sisters, assuring them with her eyes that she would do quite well and that they need have no fears for her.

When the door had swung shut, Elizabeth turned to Julia, saying, 'I wonder if one of us ought to go along with her . . . for propriety?' Julia crossed to give the bell rope a tug, 'I think not. The expression in her eyes said for us to remain here. I have the oddest notion about all of this. I believe there is more to this situation than she is willing to reveal, and that, you must own, is most unlike our dear sister.'

The two exchanged thoughtful looks, then Julia turned to the young maid who answered the summons and handed over the twins to her to take to their nanny. It was time that Julia returned to her painting.

Even though they all insisted that the vast funds of the Dancy family made it unnecessary to be saving, Julia's pride insisted she seek a measure of independence. Hence her painting, for which she charged a scandalous fee. A smile tugged at her mouth as she considered the advice given her by a well-known artist. He had urged her to demand a high payment, for he said the more blunt they paid, the more the patrons valued the painting. He had proved to be right, and Julia felt proud she had attained a measure of autonomy. Leaving Elizabeth to seek a late breakfast, Julia retreated to the room the women shared for their artistic endeavors.

*   *   *

Evenson had placed Sir Edward upstairs in the elegant drawing room, rather than the study, rightly estimating the baronet's social position to a nicety.

Pausing on the threshold, Victoria made an assessment of her rescuer, who now stood across the room by the marble fireplace. The deep blue and light gold of the room was a perfect foil for his dark coloring. How tall and well-built he was, with that marvelously modeled head she had studied and admired before. His clothing was impeccable, his coat and pantaloons fitting his fine figure very nicely, and those boots had a mirror finish, witness to the ministrations of a first-class valet. He held his cane with a casual air.

Sable moved to her side, and she advanced to face Sir Edward, feeling more secure with her guardian pet near her.

'Good day, Sir Edward. I trust you have recovered from the effects of your journey? I was under the impression that you planned a trip to Dover?' She watched as he spun about to face her, surmising that he had not expected her home to be of this quality. Somehow it pleased her to find he was rather taken aback at her surroundings. Had he expected a penniless and unprotected lamb?

'The delay made the trip unnecessary, the time was past.' His free hand gestured toward her as he exclaimed, 'I see your forehead is not totally restored to health. I trust your injury has not taken a turn for the worse.'

Victoria frowned as she noted that he now leaned on his carved blackthorn cane more than a gentleman usually does. Normally a cane was nothing more than a fashionable accessory. It seemed to her that he required it, and she sailed into speech without thought. ' 'Tis nothing but the insistence of my overbearing abigail. You, however, appear to be more than a trifle down-pin, sir. I fear that carrying me around tried your leg severely.'

He followed her over to the tasteful striped sofa that was arranged with several chairs to form pleasant seating for a conversation group. She sensed he was not pleased with her.

'My injury plagues me less each day, thank you,' he replied in a curt manner, confirming

53

her suspicion. 'The improvement may have been delayed a bit by our accident, but I am assured that no serious damage has been done.'

'Then I must be pleased for your sake, sir.' She seated herself at one end of the sofa, turning so she faced him while he eased himself down on the far end. He seemed stiff, in spite of the elegance of his manner, and she worried that he truly had worsened due to caring for her, for that rain couldn't have been good for him, nor her weight. His cane was kept close to hand, giving credence to her impression that he did indeed require it.

'What has your family to say to the matter of our stay at the windmill?' One hand rested on his knee, the other caressed the handle of his cane. He went directly to the point. It seemed he felt no need to shilly-shally in the least.

'Very little, if you must know. My sisters recognize that I am a model of propriety, and with Sable at my side there has never been a difficulty.' Then she recalled her pet's attraction to Sir Edward and frowned. 'At least, before this.' She watched as the dog inched toward the gentleman in question. Sable's eyes gleamed with adoration, something Victoria was accustomed to having reserved for herself.

'Sable,' she admonished, and the dog surprised her by sitting down on the floor precisely between the two on the sofa. Sable placed a chastened head on the satin striped covering and gazed at Victoria with meek eyes that would have fooled anyone but her.

A smile tugged at Edward's mouth as he watched the little charade. 'Your dog appears to remember me.'

'Indeed,' she replied in a repressive tone.

'Your family?' It appeared he would not be distracted from the purpose of his visit.

'I believe I mentioned my parents have gone aloft. Geoffrey, as you seemed to know, is in Portugal. At least, I think he is there. We've not had a letter from him in an age.' She frowned as worry over her brother's safety assailed her.

Sir Edward quickly said, 'The mail is terrible, as you may know, and who can guess where a letter may languish while waiting to go on its way?'

She rewarded his efforts with a flash of a smile. 'It is kind of you to care, sir.'

'That does not alter matters between us,' he said in a firm tone. 'I find it difficult to accept that you still refuse my offer, even after having time to consider it. You are so satisfied that nothing untoward will result from your trip, not to mention that hasty flit to Canterbury? No gossip will be filtering through the *ton*? That was not well-done of you, by the bye. I had a devil of a head when I came to later that day.' The look directed at her was the sort that Julia aimed at the girls when they had misbehaved and were due for chastisement.

Victoria frowned again, considering the amount of drug she had dropped into his ale. 'It ought not have affected you so severely. I do apologize for that, but a lady traveling alone must take precautions.' Then her brow cleared, and she continued. 'I shall keep your most kind and generous offer in mind, Sir Edward. However, as there is not the least likelihood that anyone will find out about our chance encounter or the ensuing stay in the windmill, I believe you may safely plan your future without including me in it.'

'I suppose I ought to be grateful, Miss Dancy. A man can always benefit from practice at making an offer of marriage.' He smiled, a lopsided arrangement of muscles that proved oddly attractive.

Victoria resolved that she most definitely would sculpture his head. Her fingers fairly itched to get at her clay.

Almost, she asked him if he had proposed to another, then caught herself short. It would be highly improper and she was a little shocked that she might have even considered such a thing for a moment.

Then he sobered. 'Please keep in mind that should word of this escapade be made known, your circumstances will alter greatly.'

'Allow me to brood about that, sir. I suspect it would be for nothing.'

Sir Edward rose from the sofa, a bit stiff and with an awkwardness she'd wager he'd not known before. No doubt his tight pantaloons added to the difficulty of his injured leg. What a good thing he had not attempted his offer of marriage on bended knee, not that she expected such. She watched him with sharp eyes, wondering what he thought.

She walked with him to the door, then down the stairs to where the butler waited with a bland countenance.

'Good day, Sir Edward,' Victoria said with the best of manners. 'I shall inform my sisters of your gracious expression of concern. I am certain they will agree with me on the matter at hand, that you need have no fears on the subject.' She dipped a faint curtsy, enough to be proper, then bustled off down the hall to the morning room, her soft muslin skirts swishing about her legs as she went.

Edward observed that graceful walk, the charming picture she made, then turned to the butler, who waited to help him.

He donned his beaver, then nodded to the butler as the door was cordially opened for him, and he was assisted to his coach with all pleasant goodwill. Edward couldn't help but wonder what the old man would say if he knew that his cherished mistress had spent two nights with Edward in a remote windmill on a hill between Dover and Canterbury. Alone but for the dog.

*   *   *

In the next few days Edward made it his business to nose about Town, discreetly asking leading questions and hoping that no one found them to be so. He wanted to know why Victoria Dancy sculptured mostly politicians. Oh, he had seen the head of a young girl, exquisitely done, but the girl had been the daughter of a prominent member of Parliament, one active in the war debates. Most curious.

If someone had asked him why he was so inquisitive, he would have had to reply that he found Miss Dancy something of a mystery. Fortunately for him, not a soul wondered.

However, he did acquire a basket of information about the young woman. He brought her name up with the wives, and found, somewhat to his disappointment, that Miss Dancy was indeed the soul of propriety, always insisting that doors be left open and requiring things from time to time so maids or footmen were frequently in and about the rooms where she worked.

The wives confided that they found Miss Dancy to be unthreatening. Oh, they didn't phrase it in precisely those words. Rather, Edward heard them say things like, 'Miss Dancy is such a polite young woman, and dresses in such a modest way.' He took that to

58

mean that she hadn't been observed flirting and that while in residence her gowns were not the sort to be envied.

That she had that monster of a dog made her all the more welcome, oddly enough. Few cared to get close to her, for it seemed that Sable appeared ferocious and growled when anyone neared his mistress. The women felt even their husbands received a message from Sable: they must keep their distance. The smiles of delight were not missed by Edward. A few had gone so far as to purchase large dogs.

The most disturbing event occurred when he went to visit a friend known by him to be less than discreet upon occasion. A pity he couldn't make this known to his superiors, but Edward had avoided placing Haycroft in any position of security consequence.

'Edward, old boy how are you?' Robert Haycroft exclaimed as Edward joined him in the musty study where Robert had lately spent a great deal of his time poring over dispatches for the war office. The room had that look of a well-loved place, with stacks of leather-bound books here and there, an antique globe in a dim corner, and with comfortable chairs for a man to enjoy, not those spindly things one often found in the drawing room.

'Well enough.' Edward gestured to his leg with his cane. 'Had a bit of trouble with a nasty piece of road in a spot of bad weather.

Other than that, I'm as right as rain. And you? What do you find to keep busy?'

While he spoke, Edward's eyes had been caught by a recently acquired bust near the window. Upon closer inspection it was revealed to be a bust of Haycroft, a truly excellent representation. Edward strolled over to look at the bust more closely, then turned to find Haycroft as his side.

'Dashed fine work, what?' Haycroft demanded.

'Extremely so. You commissioned this?'

'Miss Dancy. All the rage, y'know, and most choosy. Won't do just anyone. Why, had a devil of a time convincing her to do my likeness.' Haycroft struck a proud pose not far from the window to ensure that his friend couldn't fail to note the splendid resemblance between the bust and his face, his poetic curls.

'Hm,' Edward mused. 'I must confess that every work of hers that I have seen has been first-rate.' He bent over to study the fine detailing that seemed to be a part of Miss Dancy's technique. Such an approach would be time-consuming and require meticulous attention to specifics. She would need to study her subject very closely indeed. 'How did you manage to persuade her? Money?'

A cagey look crept over Robert's face, and he grinned at his good friend. 'No trouble, really. Knew old Pottinger over in the war office, and had him put in a good word for me.

Worked like a charm. Helps to know someone she has done, y'see.'

'I see,' Edward murmured. It seemed that being an up-and-coming baronet would not be sufficient, nor the ability to pay handsomely for her talent. One needed credentials. He wondered wryly just what percentage of her clients had come through the war office. Well, he could satisfy that requirement fairly easily. He knew any number of people in the war office, and it ought to be a simple matter to obtain the necessary recommendation. Perhaps Castlereagh would oblige?

He smiled at his old friend, then drifted over to sit down while they covered other interesting topics, such as who was dangling after whom, which horse they favored at the next Newmarket race, and other vital Society issues.

*　　*　　*

Victoria had been busy as well. In her social life, which was nicely active, she discreetly probed, quietly questioned, and learned much that disturbed her.

'As near as I can figure,' she confided to Julia over the nuncheon table, 'he makes quite a number of quick little trips about the country, usually south into Kent. While it is true he appears to have an estate there, it seems his destination all too frequently is Dover. It is

61

amazing what can be pieced together from the artless conversation with ladies who are cast off.'

'I thought you told me he is unattached.'

'He is at the present, but there have been a number of rather attractive women who held great hopes of being Lady Hawkswood. I heard a rumor that he might be elevated to a higher rank before too long, and that always attracts a certain sort of woman. Some service to the crown, according to my source.'

'I cannot say I approve of the methods you use to extract this information,' Julia replied, her glance measuring. 'It seems to me perilously close to gossip, and so unladylike.'

'Do not be absurd. All I need to do is drop the hint, then listen. Do you know that a wounded heart heals rather quickly? But the lady never seems to forget an imagined slight.' Victoria grinned at Julia, then attacked her food with a healthy appetite.

'Do you know that I have at last had opportunity,' Julia said, changing the topic from wounded hearts to a more agreeable one, 'to read that book *Pride and Prejudice*? 'Tis vastly enjoyable. I believe I should enjoy meeting the woman who wrote that. Do you think she would ever appear at Lady Titchbourne's? I found Miss Edgeworth rather charming when she came.'

'The conversaziones? I doubt it. I have heard that the author is a rather retiring person.'

'As we ought to be, my dear.'

'How dreadfully dull.'

'What is dreadfully dull?' Elizabeth inquired as she rounded the corner of the dining room. 'Why does no one ever call me to meals?' She flounced over to the sideboard to fill a plate with a selection of food.

'You know all the servants respect our creative privacy when we are at work. We wished it so, to prevent any problems, particularly with your engraving.'

'How did it go this morning?' Victoria said, reaching out to wipe off a spot of ink from her sister's cheek.

'I do believe I am becoming rather good at duplicating French banknotes. I doubt if Napoleon himself could detect the difference.' Elizabeth grinned at her sisters.

Every stroke they could aim at bringing the downfall of the hated Corsican, no matter how small, was cause for jubilation in the Dancy household. Napoleon was responsible for their parents' death. The Dancys all nurtured an intense desire for revenge on the man, if not the country.

'Well, I hope we can continue to keep our efforts a secret,' Victoria murmured. 'Only Julia is able to paint, secure in the knowledge she'll not be asked to spy.'

Julia smiled. 'I have been invited to do a painting of a very notable person. I am to do his *eye,* no less!'

'No!' Victoria and Elizabeth exclaimed in unison, with Elizabeth dissolving into giggles.

'At least no one can accuse you of looking for secrets in a gentleman's eye,' Victoria added with a chuckle.

'I shall do my utmost to keep questions about our behavior from arising,' Julia said with a look of concern.

'As long as no one suspects a thing, we shall be fine.' Victoria gave her sisters a smug look and sat back in her chair to sip her cup of tea. 'And I doubt if anyone does.'

6

'There, now, to be done with this head,' murmured Victoria as she vigorously stirred a pot of white goo.

An enormous white canvas apron nearly engulfed her as she worked on a plaster cast of the head she had completed before stopping at Dover. How fortunate her patron was not the sort to be anxious and in a rush, but a relaxed gentleman . . . who also had proved to be quite innocent of any possible charges of spying, as far as Victoria could find out during her stay. Her report to the war office was no doubt a disappointment, but she had done what she could. Now she took a needed break from her efforts at deciphering. She'd go mad, otherwise.

She stirred the plaster until it reached the thick, creamy consistency she preferred, then began to coat the clay head, section by section, taking care to smooth the plaster right up against the shims. These formed the sections that would enable her to separate the plaster of Paris from the original model once it hardened.

'Well, you certainly have been busy,' Elizabeth commented as she bounced into the room. Taking care not to come too close, she watched as the final strokes of plaster were applied with the spatula and Victoria set the head on its stand to complete the drying process.

'Believe me, I was most thankful to see my careful packing has saved the head from any damage. I did not dare inspect it until I reached home, for fear something would go wrong. That is another good reason for sculpturing in wax—it is so tough and durable, I believe I shall do all my work in wax after this. This clay gave me anxious moments.' She gave a considering nod as she studied her efforts. 'Wait until you see the old gentleman, I think him quite handsome in his own peculiar way.'

'You flatter these men shamelessly.' Elizabeth giggled as she strolled across to study other models sitting neatly upon a shelf.

'Just look at them, so stately, all in a row.'

There were several wax busts, quite a few plaster-of-Paris heads, and one figure that had been cast in bronze and awaited delivery to the man who had commissioned it.

'Nonsense,' denied Victoria, with an answering grin. 'I merely try to bring out the best in each person. Even his friends will see a strong likeness, and by emphasizing the finer points, the patron will be pleased.'

She thought of Sir Edward, resolving to try to meet him again. Her sketches of him were lacking something. She couldn't pinpoint what it was, and it frustrated her to no end. Never would she admit that she desired to see him because she found him quite fascinating as a man.

'You have a spot of plaster on your nose,' Elizabeth offered kindly.

'I see you do not offer to remove it.' Victoria glanced at her sister before checking the clock on the mantel of the fireplace across the room. It was a plain timepiece with large, easily read numbers, the sort to be seen from a distance. She walked to the small sink at the end wall. This was the only room in the house, other than the kitchen, that had water piped from the cistern to a sink. The girls had determined that they did not want a servant in and out while bringing all the water they required for cleaning up after their various projects. They all made frequent use of it, thankful for their foresight. How lovely it would be if it might have been heated first!

'You will take care of it. 'Tis not like ink, after all.' Elizabeth walked to her desk.

Victoria turned the handle of the faucet and watched a bit of water run into a basin. Shutting off the water, she cleaned her hands and the spatula before returning to work, quite forgetting the spot of plaster on her nose. Clean hands were a necessity while working, and she hated the feel of the plaster on her hands.

Elizabeth checked the Argand lamp that sat in readiness to light her work. She demanded strong light and had magnifying glasses in several strengths. Pots of ink stood in a ragged row, with pens and nibs tumbled in a heap. Etching needles and gravers, burnishers, and other necessary items were scattered about. A copper plate waited her touch. A sheet of thin transparent paper lay atop a sketch she had done earlier. She was not as tidy with her area as Victoria. Nor was Julia, come to think of it. A casual inspection revealed her elder sister's portion of the high-ceilinged room was littered with chunks of ore for grinding to make her own special paint colors, bottles of oil and other media, small sections of canvas. Protected by placement in a cabinet were the delicate ovals of ivory, a favorite surface for her miniatures.

Elizabeth turned to watch her sister,

wrinkling her nose in distaste. 'Ugh, what a muck that is.'

Victoria tested the surface of the plaster, decided it was quite ready, then carefully separated it into two sections. 'I believe I can take this to the foundry, the caster ought to be quite pleased with it.'

'I do not see how you can go down to that awful place, Victoria. It gives me the quakes.' Elizabeth shuddered dramatically as she paused by the door.

'Then do not go,' Victoria replied with practicality. 'I shall take Sable with me, and Sam Coachman, and there is usually a footman as well. I am well-chaperoned, my dear little sister.'

Victoria took the mold over to the sink, washed it out, then returned to a small table where she put the sections together. A new batch of plaster was mixed, then poured inside the mold she had first lightly greased. She set the sculpture on the stand, and glanced at the clock again. Elizabeth had disappeared from the room, and Victoria hadn't noticed her absence. One tended to concentrate while at work.

'Excuse me, Miss Victoria, there's a gentleman to see you and he won't be put off. Sir Edward, he said to tell you it was.' The maid, quite accustomed to the clutter of the workroom, scarcely glanced at the various materials scattered about. Most likely she was only thankful that she was never assigned to clean it up. One of the footmen had that task, and a tedious one it must be, too. They were fussy about the room, and heaven help anyone who disturbed a thing.

'Oh, botheration,' Victoria whispered. Turning to the maid, she quietly replied, 'Very well, I shall be along directly. Where is he?'

'Evenson put him in the study.'

Nodding thoughtfully at the change of rooms, Victoria removed the enormous apron, hanging it on its peg. She smoothed her hair and dress with freshly washed hands, then rubbed some cream on them as she briskly walked down the hall to the front of the house. She paused at the study door.

'Sir Edward, this is indeed a surprise. I was not aware that we had reason to meet again.' She remained where she stood for a moment, waiting for Sable to join her before entering the room. The man had been expecting her, no doubt from the sound of her footsteps in the hall. She was disconcerted when he crossed the room to her side. She had wanted to study him again, but found his closeness disturbing.

'I wished to discuss your family carriage with you. I decided that it is only right that I replace your badly damaged one. Your coachman informed me that he feels it quite definitely is no longer safe. That will never do.'

'How kind of you,' Victoria murmured, giving him high marks for fairness and wanting to do the right thing. She had forgotten that sensual quality in his voice, making the most mundane words appear fraught with secret meaning.

Sir Edward stepped still closer, then reached up to flick her nose.

'I beg your pardon,' Victoria said in a faintly affronted tone.

'Plaster, I believe. Have I disturbed you while at work?' He tilted his head as though to study her better. That lazy smile of his was nearly her undoing.

She nodded, reluctant to discuss what she did at the moment. The more intriguing possibility of a new chaise appealed to her. Not that they couldn't afford one. But the thought had occurred to her that if he were to pursue the gift of a chaise, she might very well see more of him. Would he not wish to take her for a drive to test it out? And then he possibly could wish to consult with her regarding the design and color as well. She smiled at him, that dazzling smile that had stopped lesser men in their tracks.

'Back to the matter of the chaise,' she said briskly. 'If Sam has confided in you, I may as well admit I have great reservations about taking that coach on a journey again. But I should like to have a say in the style and color,' she cautioned with what she felt to be

70

great craftiness.

He leaned against the desk, studying her through suddenly narrowed eyes. 'You plan another trip so soon?'

'I frequently find it necessary to travel, as does Julia. In her painting, she prefers to have the sitter before her, rather than work from sketches. I feel the same. Sometimes this means we have to go to a distant place. It is usually worth it, however, as we achieve a better likeness.' She avoided meeting his gaze, for she found it far too penetrating for comfort.

'Why do we not plan a call on the carriage builder soon, if that is the case. Tomorrow, perhaps?'

Victoria glanced down at her hands, unwilling he should see what might be in her eyes, for she could not always conceal her thoughts. It would hardly do to let the dratted man know that she found him fascinating, and that she really wished to see more of him— only so she might make a bust of him, of course. Raising her lashes, she returned his steady gaze. 'That would be lovely. I must take my head to the foundry in the morning, but I should be free all afternoon.'

'Take your head?' He gave her a quizzical, highly amused look that drew a chuckle from Victoria.

'I just finished making the plaster cast for the head I sculptured while I was away.' Then

71

she surprised herself by offering, 'Would you like to see it?'

He stood away from the desk. 'Indeed. I have seen samples of your work, and find the idea of viewing a work in progress most captivating.'

'Come with me, then,' she responded, wondering what had possessed her to invite this relative stranger into her most private place, where she worked at what she loved to do.

Sir Edward paused on the threshold of the room, his eyes swiftly absorbing the contents.

Victoria assessed it as well, trying to see it as he must. Whitewashed walls reflected bright morning light that streamed in through uncurtained windows, sharply revealing the tables and implements used by the women in their art. His turned to the large lump of plaster sitting on a wooden stand. '*This* is your head?'

'You can be forgiven that tone of voice. It has a way to go as yet.' She slipped on the apron, then quickly tied the tapes, wishing to avoid his help.

He followed her to the stand, watching her every move. 'What next?'

She deftly knocked off the mold, leaving the perfect cast sitting on the stand for him to admire. She tossed the waste mold into a bin, then picked up the tool she used to smooth off any roughness, gently stroking it across a spot on the head that needed finishing.

'Admirable,' Edward breathed. 'It is old Chatham to a tee, unless the man has a twin.'

'You know the admiral?'

'I see Chatham from time to time, usually at the war office. Nice old chap.'

Victoria wondered at the speculative look she caught in Sir Edward's eyes.

'He is waiting patiently for this,' she said absently, returning her attention to the sculpture. 'Fortunately, people seem to understand that the sculpturing process is not one to be done quickly. This is what I shall take with me in the morning.' She removed the apron, neatly hanging it up again, then waited for him to join her on a walk to the front door. She wanted to pin down the time for tomorrow, not to mention discover the carriage builder they would patronize, before Sir Edward left.

He seemed in no rush to depart, strolling about the room, then over to the shelves Elizabeth had perused earlier. 'Ah, I believe I see a few more friends. How diverting to find them all on the shelf.'

He turned to share a quick grin with her, and Victoria felt her heart perform the oddest flip-flop. Struggling to maintain a cool voice, she replied, 'I see what you mean. I confess I had never thought of it that way, for I believe they are all active people, are they not?'

'Which makes this all the more amusing.

You are very good, Miss Dancy. Every one of these is quite like the man it represents. Amazing.' At last he turned to join her on the walk to the front of the house.

Evenson was there before them, standing by the door in expectation of assisting the gentleman to his carriage.

'Shall we say two of the clock, then?'

Victoria pursed her mouth, then nodded. 'I ought to be home by then, surely. And where do we go?'

He mentioned the name of one of the finest carriage builders in all of London, and Victoria looked up at him with increased respect. 'Indeed?' she murmured. 'You intend to do very well by us. That is a handsome offer, Sir Edward.' She held out her hand to him, after making sure that no lingering trace of plaster remained. It had been quite enough that he'd removed a spot from her nose.

He accepted her slim hand, surprisingly strong for a woman, she supposed, cradling it in his own clasp a moment before releasing it. His inspection brought a warmth to her cheeks that seemed to catch his interest, to her dismay.

Then Sable intruded, butting his nose against Edward's good leg. 'Ah, yes, your dog.' Steadying himself with the cane, he bent over to scratch the dog behind the ears, an affectionate touch, one that pleased Victoria. So many men took one look at her dog and edged away.

He straightened with what seemed obvious reluctance. 'Until tomorrow, Miss Dancy.'

'Tomorrow,' she echoed. She remained in the entry as Evenson ushered the gentleman out to the street where his carriage awaited. It was a graceful phaeton, and his groom skillfully assisted his master up and onto the seat with a minimum of fuss.

He must hate being discommoded like that, she strongly suspected. Then, aware that she was behaving in a highly unusual manner by staring after a departing guest, she fled up the stairs. Tomorrow could not come soon enough, as far as Victoria was concerned. She hummed a gay little tune as she took the last steps to the second floor, where her bedroom was located. Although normally not one to fuss over her clothes, she wished to inspect her wardrobe. All she wanted to do was present a highly proper picture, she assured herself.

*   *   *

Later, at tea, she questioned Julia about her first visit to the gentleman whose eye she was to paint.

'Evenson saw me off as if I was a girl of ten. I fear we shall never appear adults in his eyes,' she said fondly, then continued. 'Although the house I went to is rather intimidating, with an

75

elegant entrance, I presented myself with all the hauteur I could summon, much like Aunt Montmorcy does. You know how she can quell with a look. I had our footman carry in my paints as if they were the crown jewels, so as to impress his butler.' She exchanged an amused look with her sister.

'The gentleman? You never did tell me who he is,' Victoria prompted.

'I shall tell you shortly. Allow me to describe his home for a moment. The library is impressive, with leather-bound volumes and an enormous desk with one of those comfortable padded chairs you are always wishing to have. There is a window overlooking a very pretty garden to the rear of the house. My client appeared while I was inspecting the room, and I must say I felt like a silly girl.' She studied the handkerchief clutched tightly in her hands with a deceptively casual air.

'This client . . . he is a plain man? Old, no doubt, and crippled with gout?' Victoria observed, repressing a grin.

'Oh, no,' Julia replied earnestly. 'He is excessively handsome and not the least old. I shall find painting his eye not an onerous task at all.' Then she blushed like a young miss, adding, 'I found his manners most polite, and I think his desire to have a miniature for his mother most commendable.'

'I still do not know his name,' Victoria

76

reminded her.

'I thought I told you before,' Julia murmured. 'He is the Viscount Temple. And I shall paint more than his eye, you know. A few of his lovely curls, his brow—which really is quite noble—and a portion of his cheek and nose as well. Heaven knows how long it will take me,' she concluded with an absent air. Which was most unlike Julia, who usually dispatched her paintings with all speed.

Victoria sipped her tea, wondering about the man who had dazzled her usually calm sister, a widow normally immune to men. She hoped Julia would not tumble into a devastating love, one destined to be unfulfilled.

Elizabeth paused on the threshold, her cheeks ablaze with her emotions. 'May I join you? I must confide in someone or I shall burst. Oh, that odious man,' she concluded with asperity as she plumped herself on the sofa and proceeded to pour a cup of tea for herself. Then she munched a crisp lemon biscuit while her sisters waited for her to continue.

'What an intriguing entrance,' Victoria said, alarm in her voice. One never knew what Elizabeth might plunge into, for she was given to impetuous starts.

'Well,' Elizabeth said after she had drained her first cup of tea, 'I went to the war office to turn in that pile of French banknotes and

77

accept my next assignment, and whom should I literally bump into at the bottom of the steps outside the building but that frightful man!'

'Frightful man?' Julia said in her gentle way, alarm also clear in her voice.

'"Miss Dancy,"' Elizabeth said in a deep voice, 'he murmured in that way he has, and then said how charming it was to see me again after such a long time. He accused me of avoiding him! Can you believe his nerve, as though I would bother? He insists he is harmless. Bah! And after the Fenwick ball, too.' Elizabeth picked up another lemon biscuit and bit into it with ferocious energy, as if to express her annoyance with the man in question.

Curious, Victoria tried to suppress the urge to insist that Elizabeth get to the heart of the matter, and prompted, 'What did he—whoever he is—do, dear?'

'Well, to begin with, he stole a kiss—no, two—at the Fenwick ball.' Catching a glimpse of her elder sister's look of dismay, she added, 'I did not wish to upset you, for I was certain he would never look my way again. I have heard he is quite the rake, and we all know that rakes never bother with green girls. And I am certainly green,' she sighed with apparent disgust.

'And?' Victoria urged.

'I told that impossible man that I do not welcome stolen kisses and *he* had the nerve to say that he was forced to steal a kiss for he perceived I'd not give one willingly. Now, I ask you, are those the words of a gentleman? And he said it was utterly delicious!' she concluded in what appeared to be deep affront.

'What did you say then to this unnamed man?' Victoria queried, satisfied that her sister was embroidering just a trifle upon what seemed to be a reasonably innocent bit of flirting.

'Well, I told him that just because I am an orphan he was not free to do as he liked. My family will protect me, and I may call upon friends if necessary in Geoffrey's absence. And he called me a little termagant,' she recalled, pressing her lips together in annoyance.

'Oh, dear,' Julia murmured, exchanging a look of amusement with Victoria.

'And then, do you know what he had the audacity to tell me? That he does not give up easily. He intends to continue his unwelcome pursuit, even though he can plainly see I do not care one jot for him. Oh, such an obnoxious man.' Elizabeth took another sip of tea.

'He is totally ineligible, most likely as homely as a mud fence, and possessing the manners of an encroaching toad, no doubt,' Victoria suggested gently.

'Gracious, no!' Elizabeth exclaimed. 'He is tall and slender, quite handsome—if you like a

79

man with brown hair that has a tendency to flop over his brow. Those hazel eyes tease more than not, and it seems he intends to bedevil me with his presence—unless I see him first,' she added thoughtfully.

'Rag-mannered, then?' Julia said in her quiet way, quite in the same method Victoria used for obtaining information.

'No,' Elizabeth admitted, 'he has charming manners, far too charming for the good of a young woman. Although he does have a tendency to laugh at me, and I believe he just likes to tease, nothing more.'

'Elizabeth Dancy, if you do not reveal the name of this paragon, I shall be tempted to throttle you at once,' Victoria declared.

'I thought I told you,' Elizabeth murmured much as Julia had earlier. 'He is David, Lord Leighton—you know, Viscount Leighton, son of the Earl of Crompton. I recall Aunt Bel talking about him once, and it seems he was as much a rake as his son is now.'

'Oh, dear,' Victoria muttered. It appeared to her that whether she admitted it or not, Elizabeth had become fascinated with a highly eligible rake. Did such behavior run in the family, then? First, Julia and Lord Temple, for it was clear that he charmed her. Then, the attraction Victoria felt toward Sir Edward that was utterly foolish. It appeared the Dancy girls were doomed to disappointment . . . or were they? She rose to go to her room, for it was time to prepare for their early dinner. She would share her news with them at that time.

*   *   *

'You cannot fathom how surprised I was when Sir Edward offered to purchase a new chaise for the family,' Victoria revealed after the three assembled in the dining room.

'The old one is surely not all that terrible, is it? Not that I have examined it closely, mind you. But if Sam could drive it home. . . .' Julia paused in the act of sipping the last of her soup.

'All I can tell you is that Sam informed me that he'd not take us on any bumpy roads until either it had been rebuilt or we bought a new one. And you know what the rural roads are like.' She exchanged knowing glances with Julia.

'I see. I expect it might be as costly to rebuild as to have new,' Julia speculated. She placed her soup spoon down while eyeing the remove of turbot with shrimp sauce brought to her side.

'I wish I was able to travel about as you do. I'd even welcome a visit to Aunt Bel,' Elizabeth inserted in the subsequent pause. 'All *I* get to do is sit at my table and draw money. Counterfeiter! That sounds utterly horrid. I just hope that I am able to obtain a commission for a series of engravings of "Life

81

Along the Thames" or a similar subject.' She sighed before attacking her turbot.

'Why do you not take time to drive to the park and do a bit of sketching? Perhaps you could drive out to Richmond and draw a scene of the Thames from there? It is such a lovely view,' Julia encouraged her.

The adorable pout fled from Elizabeth's pretty mouth and she grinned with pleasure. 'Would one of you be able to go with me tomorrow?'

'Oh, dear, I have to be at the foundry in the morning, and then meet with Sir Edward in the afternoon.' Victoria popped a morsel of roast chicken in her mouth, then turned to Julia.

In her soft sweet voice Julia replied, 'Much as I would adore taking the girls along and making a day of it, I had better get on with my work. I wish to transfer the sketch of Viscount Temple to the ivory. He approved the size of the piece I had brought with me, so that it is all set to begin.' She gave Elizabeth a sympathetic look, then offered, 'Perhaps later in the week, if this lovely weather holds?'

Somewhat mollified, Elizabeth gave a gusty sigh, then turned the subject. 'What are we going to see at the theater tonight? Something educational, I suppose. Opera, perhaps?' She grimaced. 'I do not care for the screaming of the singers in the least. Music is most definitely not one of my interests. I much prefer a good comedy.'

Victoria chuckled. They all agreed Elizabeth had a tin ear. 'No, dear. No opera. Although I should think you would enjoy the costumes.'

'Not enough to compensate for all that squawking. Stuff and nonsense, the lot of it.' Elizabeth speared another piece of her favorite vegetable, freshly picked asparagus. They ate in silence for a time, then Elizabeth inquired, 'What about the coach? Will you ask for an aquamarine interior? I thought the one Mrs Biddlesby has worth emulating, as I believe I mentioned to you once.'

Her hopeful gaze pleaded with Victoria. Since each of the girls had eyes that reflected green as well as blue, Victoria considered this might be an interesting scheme. She suffered a twinge of embarrassment at accepting such an expensive gift, but she also desired to see Sir Edward again, and that had easily won out over her scruples.

'Do you know, I believe that might be a good idea. Do you have any suggestions, Julia?'

'Only that it be as comfortable as possible. Pockets to hold books for the children might be a nice addition. They do so love to bring things along when we travel, and little items tend to get lost so easily.'

'How did your meeting with Lord Temple go?' Elizabeth studied her sister while the

83

rhubarb tart was placed on the table after the remains of the chicken had been removed.

'Well,' Julia said hesitantly, 'he seems quite nice. He wishes the painting for his mother. Is that not commendable?' Her gentle smile curved sweet lips, her eyes misty with admiration for so good a man.

'And you believed him?' Elizabeth cried. She made a rather rude sound, then subsided before her sisters could scold.

'Elizabeth has a point. People are not always what they seem.' Victoria spooned a dollop of custard over her rhubarb tart. 'Do exercise care, my dear.'

'Ha,' murmured Elizabeth. At her sister's look of inquiry, she added, 'Well, Julia is a widow; *she* ought to be able to handle gentlemen.'

Victoria gave her younger sister a sharp glance. 'I would insist upon an explanation regarding that remark were we not pressed for time. Hurry, so we shall not be late. I detest the throng of people in the entry to the theater. Regardless of what the *ton* does, I think it far better to arrive with time to spare so one can settle comfortably before the production begins. And by the way, Elizabeth, there will be a farce this evening. That ought to please you well enough.'

Elizabeth said nothing in reply, but looked relieved.

The girls strolled to the entry to accept

their cloaks from Evenson with their charming grace.

'Well, I shall instruct the carriage builder to use aquamarine in the interior,' Victoria announced while they bumped along to Drury Lane. 'I believe Elizabeth has the right of it, that color would be lovely.' She sat back, then exclaimed softly, pulling a folded paper from her beaded reticule. 'Oh, a letter came for you, Elizabeth. Here, you may read it now, if the light is sufficient.'

Elizabeth opened the letter, her cheeks tinting an interesting shade of pink as she scanned its contents, then tucked it deep in her reticule. 'Just an invitation to drive with a friend,' she murmured.

Victoria knew of no friend who would bring a blush to her sister's face, yet she said nothing, trusting Elizabeth to use her common sense. She might have a tin ear, but she was uncommonly practical.

5

All three young women remained oddly silent on the drive to the theater. Tickets had been most difficult to obtain. The gothic drama *De Montfort* might have been around for years, but it was still enjoyed, all the more for being a favorite. It was doubtful that any of the three was thinking of the tragedy that was to befall the hero.

Elizabeth gave a furtive glance about them as she exited the carriage, then relaxed.

'Come, do let us hurry to our box,' Victoria urged.

Even though it was early, there were many people filtering into the theater, particularly those who could not afford the luxury of a box and had to sit in the pit on hard benches. They sought a good spot, in hopes of seeing and hearing something of the play.

'I, as well, do not care to be pushed about in a horde of people,' Julia added. 'Were it not for the obvious, that more patrons are to be found in London than elsewhere, I should prefer to enjoy a quiet life in the country.'

Flashing her a look of concern, Victoria replied, 'Why do we not visit Aunt Bel after the Season is over? When nearly all of the *ton* leave Town, there are few commissions for any of us. Perhaps by then the war office will have less need for our talents.' She gave Julia a hopeful look, then observed the calculating expression on Elizabeth's face.

'What is it, Elizabeth? I know that look all too well.' She opened the door to their box and fixed a steely look on her sister as she sidled past her.

'Nothing, really. It merely occurred to me that if one wished to avoid seeing another, the country would be an excellent place to retreat.

That is, if one were wishing to avoid another person, which I am not necessarily wishing to do, that is.' Elizabeth gave her sisters an airy smile after this confusing speech, and settled in her chair to watch in apparent fascination as the crowd gradually filled the theater.

Behind her, Victoria and Julia exchanged bewildered looks. 'What on earth do you suppose she meant by that peculiar bit of nonsense?' Victoria whispered to Julia.

'Heaven only knows,' Julia whispered in return from behind a large fan painted with delicate yellow roses. The fan was a particular favorite of hers, coming from an unknown admirer. Tonight she elected to wear a silk gown the identical yellow, with a dainty matching satin hat on her head. Elizabeth had declared that Julia looked like a buttercup and Victoria had agreed that she did.

Elizabeth wore her favored aquamarine in a soft mull with rows of fine lace, while Victoria had dressed herself in a flattering shade of melon, and thought the gown, with its panel of delicate embroidery down the front, most becoming.

It was sometime later that Victoria caught sight of a now-familiar face almost directly across from her, one tier below, and in a slightly better location.

'There he is, Julia,' she whispered as she nudged her sister with her fan. 'Second box over and down one. He is the one who collided with our chaise, and now has generously offered to replace it.'

'I dared not peek when he visited the house, but what a handsome man, as well, Vicky. And you say nothing happened? What a pity.' Julia twinkled an amused look at her sister.

'What are you two whispering about?' Elizabeth demanded to know in a quiet voice.

Julia explained, quite discreet behind her painted roses.

'Well, I never,' breathed Elizabeth as she studied the man she had dubbed the Dull One. 'He scarcely fits the image you gave us. I thought him to be much older, and far less good-looking. Why, my dear sister, you have been hiding things from us.'

Victoria swallowed carefully and smiled as though nothing were amiss. If her dear sisters knew the extent of Sir Edward's actions, they would be in his box demanding he wed Victoria, their fans pointed at his head like two pistols.

The interval relieved the necessity for whispers, and Julia leaned back in her chair, a bemused look on her face. 'I must say, this is a fatiguing drama—all that melancholy sighing and agony of mind. I find it hard to believe that anyone could stand about to deliver such a long speech in the midst of terrifying apparitions. *I* would flee for my life!'

'Julia,' scolded Elizabeth, her eyes crinkling

88

with mirth, 'you simply do not understand. He is expressing the deep passion of hatred.'

'Oh, pooh.'

Then Elizabeth fell silent as she caught sight of someone not seen earlier.

'What has turned you to stone, Lizzie?'

She absently replied, 'You know how I dislike to be called that. I just saw someone I could learn to hate, that is all.'

'Goodness, if you harbor such emotion, be forewarned that hate sometimes turns to love,' Victoria teased her.

Elizabeth gave her a smug look. 'Not in this case.' Then she looked around again, and inquired of Julia, 'Who is that interesting man who keeps staring at our box? He is next to Victoria's gentleman of the chaise, Sir Edward.'

'That,' a disconcerted Julia observed, 'is the man whose eye I am to paint.'

Giggling, Elizabeth said, 'I wonder how you will feel to be so near to a stranger, and such a handsome one at that. For you must know that you cannot paint an eye from a great distance.' She peered closely at her sister from about a foot away, raising expressive brows. 'My, this could prove to be very intriguing.'

Further speculation was cut off when the door to their box opened, admitting none other than Lord Leighton.

Elizabeth had tilted her pretty nose in the air when the door opened again. Sir Edward appeared, followed by Mr Padbury. He was a plump man past his prime, but still most agreeable company.

Julia rose to greet the men, her knowledge of the *ton* coming to her aid. 'Lord Leighton, how nice to see you. And you, Sir Edward. And here is our good friend Mr Padbury. Won't you join us?' Since all three gentlemen were ones who got about Town, there was scarcely any need to make introductions.

Elizabeth glared at her sister, then edged away from them all, a polite smile freezing on her face. She knew better than to turn her back on their callers.

'How pleasant to see you ladies enjoying the pleasures of Town rather than being hard at your creating,' Mr Padbury exclaimed as he bowed—mostly to Julia.

'Does Miss Elizabeth create as well?' a languid Lord Leighton inquired. His gaze roamed over Elizabeth, making it evident she was the person of interest for him. It was also obvious he was most curious about precisely what the gorgeous Elizabeth spent her time crafting.

Victoria had been studying her younger sister and the man who hovered close to her, a gentleman she knew little about. The looks between those two were far too conscious. 'Elizabeth is quite skilled in engraving, sir. You must see her work sometime.' The glare from Elizabeth revealed little other than annoyance. Victoria politely turned to nod at Sir Edward. 'Good evening.'

'Little did I suspect we would meet again so soon.' He chatted on about nothing in particular, giving Victoria the sense she was secure from any speculation by others. A man so polite could hardly provide fodder for gossips. And with the other two men in the box, it diluted his impact considerably. The episode of the knife-throwing and the sequestered interlude in the windmill began to fade into obscurity. At least she told herself that was the case.

When the interval ended, the men left. Elizabeth let out an explosive sigh. 'I vow I was never so tempted to be rude to another in all my life. Victoria, if you love me, please say I need not see that man again.'

'You need not see that man again,' her sister obediently repeated with a gleam in her eyes. 'Although why you should cold-shoulder a perfectly good viscount is more than I can see. He is a highly eligible catch.'

'That is what *you* think,' Elizabeth declared, but was barred further discussion when the curtains parted and the drama raged on through to its final act.

Following the conclusion, and before the farce—a silly production called *Raising the Wind,* one of James Kenny's offerings— Elizabeth had a chance to explain what had occurred to anger her.

'I believe I ought to explain my remarks,' she began. When she finished, she darted glances from one sister to the other, waiting for their reactions.

'Ghastly,' Julia declared with firm control of her facial muscles. 'To insist you drive out with him.'

'I had thought better of Lord Leighton,' Victoria admitted. 'If he truly bothers you, my love, you have my permission to royally snub the man next time you see him.'

Elizabeth relaxed to enjoy the farce, declaring afterward, 'I do so like it when the hero bests his rival and the heroine's father. How lovely it would be to have someone so utterly devoted.'

'You did take note that this is a farce,' Victoria reminded. 'I doubt if you see such devotion in real life.'

On this note of skepticism the young women quickly rose and slipped away before any of the gentlemen who had called earlier could realize they had disappeared.

*   *   *

The next morning saw Victoria driving in an unsavory part of London that the members of the *ton* rarely, if ever, saw. She did not have to remind Sam to wait for her, for he wouldn't have left to save his hide.

A footman walked at her side, but she

actually felt perfectly safe with Sable joining her. She had been coming here for several years now, and had grown quite accustomed to the sounds and smells in the area. She entered the red-brick building, wrinkling her nose a trifle at the heat and odors stemming from the foundry. Her dog stayed close to her side, his watchful eyes noting everyone about.

'Mr Greene,' Victoria said, as a rotund man emerged from a small room, 'here I am with another head for you to cast.' She went over the details with him, then made an appointment to be present when the patina would be due for application. She always oversaw this important process, although she did not actually apply the acid herself. She usually preferred the end result for her sculpture to be a very dark brown, and wished to make certain that the color turned out precisely right.

From the foundry, she instructed Sam to take her to Bond Street. Settling back in her seat, she smiled to herself. What a vain creature she was becoming. First the new melon gown for the theater last evening and now a new hat to wear with the jade pelisse she had ordered.

At Madame Celeste's, Victoria tried on the pelisse, pronouncing it perfect. Indeed it was, for it didn't need another thing done to it. Then she walked two doors down and into the prettiest millinery shop in all of London.

Here, as she had expected, she found the precise hat for the pelisse, and she admitted to herself that it was ideal for the occasion. It was a neat little hat of straw, lined with jade satin, and had a small jade ostrich feather curled over the brim to one side in a most fetching manner.

How silly to let the teasing from Julia gnaw at her, but the fact of the matter was, it did. Nothing had happened during that isolation in the little windmill. Nothing at all. She ought to have been relieved, glad that she could hold up her head proudly. Instead, she almost felt like stamping her foot in annoyance. He had ignored her, save for that one sketchy kiss, and that was so brief it hardly counted. Now, while she had not wanted seduction, it irked her that she was so easy to dismiss. Hence the flattering pelisse and the utterly dashing new hat.

She might find the man detestable, while fascinating in a curious way, yet she perversely decided he was not going to ignore her.

At the appointed time, she dressed in a citron mull gown trimmed with cream lace, and donned her jade ensemble with a great deal of satisfaction. The reflection in her cheval glass was most reassuring, and when the maid came to let her know her caller had arrived, she went down the stairs well-pleased with herself. Yet, as she tugged on her gloves, she confessed to a tinge of nervousness. To

94

spy on a stranger while in his home was one thing, to snoop—for that is what it might be—on a man she was coming to know and somewhat respect was another.

Still, she had to admit to an insatiable curiosity about the man. All those many trips. Why were they made? Perhaps she might be able to lure some information from him, for her suspicions ran rampant. Not that she'd been asked to spy. No, her investigation was for herself.

'Good afternoon, Sir Edward. May I offer you refreshments? Or do you wish to depart directly?' Victoria paused after entering the drawing room. Sir Edward wore a corbeau tailcoat of impeccable cut and fit over pantaloons of palest dove gray. Polished Hessians, a cravat tied in a precise mathematical, and spotless gloves couldn't help but bring approval. She smiled cautiously at him.

'We have much to accomplish this afternoon. Although I would enjoy another chat, we had best be on our way.' They strolled down the stairs and out to the street. He negotiated the steps carefully, but well, she observed.

Victoria climbed up into his barouche, reveling in the lovely padded seats and neat finish of the carriage. She gave him an approving look. 'Very nice, sir.'

'A little easier for me than the phaeton I

normally drive.' He gestured to his cane, placed conveniently along his leg.

'Would it be terribly improper to inquire how you were injured? Please ignore my question if it troubles you to answer,' Victoria said lightly. It was the first of her many questions that she intended to have answered directly by him. There was nothing like going right to the source for information. Sometimes one even heard the truth.

The curving brim of her new hat allowed her to glance sideways at the man beside her. They jounced along over the cobbled streets for a short distance in silence. She was afraid she had offended him by her inquiry, when at last he spoke.

Smoothing the fine leather of his gloves, he began, 'Actually, it is rather amusing now, although perhaps embarrassing. You see, I had planned to go hunting. There was a great throng of my friends present and I was about to mount my horse when a sudden noise spooked him, throwing me quite violently to the ground at a very awkward angle. I broke my, er, leg.'

Victoria sensed he had been about to swear quite roundly at the abused leg. 'I am sorry. Did this happen last autumn?' His answering murmur of assent solved one mystery, but she felt there was still more to the episode. Still, she shied away from probing if there was a painful memory involved.

'Well, I think it tragic that you have been severely injured in such a bizarre accident. However, it prevented you from dashing madly into the war. I worry about my brother over there, and your family must be greatly relieved to have you at home. At least it served some purpose.'

'You do not sigh over the heroes from the Peninsula? I can assure you they do not consider themselves such. I supposed all women saw them as larger-than-life idols.'

'Not all of us.' Victoria heard the bitterness in his voice and decided she didn't want to dig into his past anymore. It was obviously vexatious to the man. But it didn't prevent her from wondering.

Their arrival at the carriage builder's ended all her speculation. As Higgens assisted her from the barouche, Victoria was well aware that a lady did not normally accompany a gentleman, particularly when he was not her husband, to such a place. It was a mark of her independence, she supposed, that she was permitted to come along. It was hard to say if she found this pleasing or not. Perhaps it made her appear unladylike, and this could not be liked at all. Yet she presumed by her very behavior that she invited such judgment. It was a lowering thought.

They walked along past bins of curled horsehair to be used for stuffing the seats, stacks of lumber to be used for various parts of the carriages: ash in great amounts, for it was the hardest and best. She identified elm, oak, Honduras mahogany, and deal by little signs above each pile. There were containers Victoria thought might contain glue, and some that obviously held paint. In one little room she glimpsed wet leather being stretched over a piece of wood.

'That will be japanned later, and end up a glossy black to do the new carriage owner proud,' Sir Edward said when he noticed her curiosity.

At last they located the owner of the establishment, a Mr Tilbury, who appeared overwhelmed at the mere notion that Sir Edward had taken a lady through the dust and noise of his premises.

'Sir Edward, how may I serve you?' he at last inquired when he had mastered his sense of propriety.

'I have shown this lady some of your enterprise so she might appreciate the quality of the carriages you produce. We have need to replace her chaise, and she fancies to add her comments to mine regarding the furbishing.'

At once Victoria could see the look of speculation that entered the carriage builder's eyes, and guessed his thoughts. She hastened to inform him otherwise. 'Sir Edward and I were involved in a bit of an accident. Although it really was not his fault—for circumstances were such that he could not help the crash—he insists upon replacing our family vehicle, a most handsome gesture, you must admit.' She noticed the subtle alteration of the man's expression, and was glad she had spoken.

'I doubt if Miss Dancy will concern herself regarding the basic construction of the carriage. After all'—Sir Edward smiled with teasing brilliance—'a woman can scarcely be expected to understand the finer points of the wheels, axles, or sway bars, can she?'

Victoria gave him a wry look. He was giving her and her family a highly expensive gift, one he need not offer. After all, it was not as though she was a ladybird and he was buying her a fancy carriage. No, it was to be a sensible traveling coach, a family vehicle. And she would get to see Sir Edward again.

'I would want excellent springs, sir,' she managed in a restrained voice. 'And comfortable, well-padded seats. Elizabeth wishes for an aquamarine interior. As well, I think the lamps ought to be large so as to give extraordinary light.'

'And I expect you would enjoy venetian blinds rather than silk curtains, as well?' Sir Edward inquired.

She glanced up to see a flirtatious light in his eyes.

'Pockets in the doors for my nieces' toys and books. The rumble ought to have adequate storage for luggage,' she declared with an emphatic nod of her head, quite ignoring that intriguing look.

'You observed the boot of my chaise, I take it. It's larger than the one you had on yours.' He turned to the carriage builder with a sigh. 'I presume you took note of Miss Dancy's desires?' At the man's confident nod, Sir Edward turned again to Victoria. 'Aquamarine?' Then he nodded slowly. 'Of course, your eyes have a touch of that color when you wear green, and I believe your younger sister even more so.'

Victoria found herself staring up into his eyes, utterly bemused. Those extremely dark brown eyes appeared warm, meltingly so. They reminded her of the sensual sweetness of chocolate, appealing to her tastes very much.

Mr Tilbury cleared his throat. Behind him, a workman dropped a length of iron, and it crashed against another with a great clang.

She blinked, then blushed in what Edward considered a rather charming manner, given her background. Again he wondered how much was veneer and how much was the real Victoria Dancy.

'May I see any samples of fabric you might have, sir?' she inquired of the carriage builder.

That gentleman admirably concealed any thoughts he might have entertained and ushered the pair of customers into a small, only slightly dusty room. On a deal table he found a pile of samples and offered them to Miss Dancy with a flourish.

It was a simple matter to select the fabrics for the interior, although she turned to Edward for confirmation of her choices. He watched as she pondered the choices for the interior of her new coach, and inwardly grimaced at the cost. Not that he was purse-pinched. But he would have to rearrange an investment or two to get his hands on the ready money, perhaps cash in a few consols? The government bonds were paying three and a half percent at the moment, and although they rarely varied, he was loath to lose the interest. However, after running his own establishment—discreetly from behind the scenes, naturally—he had acquired a better appreciation for the prompt payment of bills.

When she put down the piece of fabric she had shown to Mr Tilbury, following confirmation that it was suitable, Edward urged Victoria to the door and waiting carriage. 'Why not take a short drive through the park? It is a fine day and you said you had left your head at the foundry.'

'There are a good many days when I feel as though I have left my head elsewhere, sir. I vow a drive sounds lovely, to inhale the scents of spring while slowly pacing our way through the throng of carriages and horseflesh.'

'I suspect there is a hidden reproof in that remark. Do you not admire London in the spring, Miss Dancy?'

'I appreciate the smell of clean fresh country air a bit more, sir. Even the most devoted Town-lover would have to admit that London has unpleasant odors, once out of your door. Do not say that you find Kent unappealing.'

'Kent? Oh, yes, well, I do enjoy ruralizing from time to time.' He coughed into a hand. 'A man's estate cannot be neglected or it will cease to provide a decent income in no time.' He glanced at her face, admirably revealed for his inspection by that pretty hat she wore. 'You frown, dear lady. What can be amiss in that remark? You do not approve of a man working from time to time?'

'It is what you said about a man's estate. We try, we really do, but I fear that dear Geoffrey's estate has had little personal supervision, other than for his bailiff. I shall be vastly relieved when my brother is able to come home and tend to things on his own behalf.'

'What will you do if he marries? He probably will, sooner or later. Miss Elizabeth is quite young and most likely will be snapped up one of these days. You appear to shun matrimony. If I may have a turn at a personal question, why?' It was only fair he ask so pointed a query; hadn't she inquired about his wounded leg earlier? She stared straight ahead as they neared Hyde Park, her mouth

102

firm, hands clasped in her lap.

'I shan't tell you that no one has asked, for that would be a lie. Let us say that none has suited me to date. No doubt I shall end up on the shelf, living with dear Julia and the twins in a little cottage near my family home. We shouldn't wish to share the house with my brother and a bride, for I firmly believe that most relatives are troublemakers at best, even though they may mean well.'

'Indeed,' Edward murmured. 'You almost sound the romantic, expecting a husband and wife to live in each other's pockets.'

'I know it is not fashionable, but frankly, I think it sounds delightful.' Then she clamped her mouth shut again and turned her head as though to admire the approaching carriage and the couple who drove in it.

'Hm,' Edward replied to this bit of revealing news. In that beautifully rounded bosom Miss Dancy possessed a tender regard for the more personal side of marriage. He couldn't figure out where that view fitted in with the iris locket, however. They would seem at distinct odds. Most curious.

At a gasp from Victoria, he focused his attention on the approaching carriage. A casual friend, Lord Leighton, handled the ribbons, with Miss Elizabeth at his side.

'That little minx. I thought she intended not to favor him with her company. She knows that she ought to discuss such things with us before taking off,' Victoria said in an undertone.

'Leighton is a fine chap. You need have no worry on his score.' That was more than he could say for the Dancys. It seemed increasingly evident to him that they were not what they pretended to be.

The carriages drew to a halt, Elizabeth giving Victoria an uncomfortable look before dropping her gaze to her lap. Greetings were exchanged. Leighton said all that was admirable and Elizabeth remained oddly silent.

'We must be going,' Victoria prompted. 'I shall see you later, Elizabeth.' The words sounded more like a threat than a promise.

'Don't be too hard on the girl. I'm told Leighton is sufficient to turn any number of heads, being highly eligible.'

Victoria thought she detected a grim note in his voice and wondered if he felt that his limp would deter any woman from forming an attachment with him. 'I should think that you are equally eligible, Sir Edward. I have yet to hear anything to your detriment.' Although she certainly had kept her ears open wherever she went. Tidbits about mysterious trips—at least no one seemed to know precisely where he went—had reached her ears. And she had heard one rumor about his frequenting a gaming house that she intended to investigate further.

'I always wondered what damning with faint praise would be like, and now I believe I know. At least you do not have a disgust of me . . . I think?' His smile was wry, lopsided, and infinitely charming.

'I should.' She inspected the stitching on her gloves, then said. 'I dared not reveal all that occurred while in the windmill, lest my sisters make demands of you. Yet I would not have you believe that a woman might find anything objectionable about you.' She gave him an earnest look. 'I am certain that somewhere there is a fine woman who would be honored to be your wife, if you choose to ask her.'

'I am delighted, indeed, at your encomium, Miss Dancy. Perhaps one of these days I shall consider the matter at length.' His eyes looked amused, and held her captive for a moment.

When they stopped before the Dancy residence, Higgens handed her down with polite care, and she paused, turning to give Sir Edward one of the Dancy smiles. 'I thank you in advance for the carriage, Sir Edward. It is a most noble thing for you to do. I trust you will drive in it with me sometime?'

'Indeed,' he replied.

Victoria entered the house, her mind in a whirl. More than ever she had great curiosity about Sir Edward. He had traveled to Dover, only to be thwarted by their crash. Then he had declared he no longer needed to go there.

Curious. Odd behavior, unless. . . . Somehow she had to get into his house. But how?

6

'Elizabeth, why did you tell me that you wished never to see the man again, then go driving with him in the park?' Victoria said, trying not to sound like a scold. 'Can you truly have no notion of the sort of talk that brings? Driving out with Lord Leighton is perhaps acceptable, but not if you are intent upon depressing his interest. Please explain, for I fail to understand your reasoning.' Victoria had run her sister to ground in the breakfast room long after she had broken her own fast. Standing by the window that overlooked the street, she kept her own face in the shadows, while her sister bore the full brunt of the daylight through the blinds.

Seeing there was no escape, Elizabeth gave a dramatic sigh, then nodded. 'I suppose I do seem a mite contradictory at that. Truly, I intended and still intend to avoid that man. He likes to tease me, and I find that so vexing. The note he sent requesting I drive with him in the park was couched in such a way that I felt it quite necessary, you see.'

Elizabeth gave another sigh, then confessed in a rush, 'I'd the notion he suspected the sort of work we do by what he wrote in that note. Vicky, I had to go with him, if nothing more than to find out how much he knew, or guessed. I daresay it is the first time in that buckish life of his that he has had to use guile to persuade a woman to drive out with him.'

Victoria repressed the smile that longed to break forth. 'I had not considered Lord Leighton a buck. He is certainly a dashing fellow, and a bit of a dandy in his dress, but I truly could not say he is a fop or a *fast* man. I sense there is more to all this than you have told me, but, dearest, I would never pressure you to reveal something you wished to keep to yourself.' Pausing a moment, Victoria added, 'Unless it might be something that is compromising.' She recalled her own dark secret and fixed Elizabeth with a minatory eye.

Evading her sister's accusing gaze by means of buttering a slice of toast, Elizabeth shrugged her pretty shoulders and shook her head. 'Please do not worry about me. I shall come about eventually, once I can decide the best course to take.' The small crease on her forehead indicated that she had a way to go before she reached a decision, whatever it might be.

Not understanding the matter in the least, Victoria gave up the cause, fleeing the breakfast room to the haven of her workroom. Here she found Mr Padbury sitting quietly while Julia transferred her sketch of Viscount Temple's eye to the piece of ivory before her.

In Mr Padbury's lap reposed a tortoiseshell box. He was slowly ripping the gold thread from a sword knot, then pausing from time to time to wind it up on a spool that sat stuffed inside the box. Whenever he visited, which was often, he sat with his pastime.

'Drizzling again, Mr Padbury?' Drizzling was all the rage among the *ton*. It was a simple task, to unravel gold or silver thread from old brocades, the fancy epaulets no longer needed by ex-military gentlemen, and other passé adornments.

' 'Tis a soothing occupation for the hands.' Mr Padbury beamed a genial smile at her before returning to his task.

Victoria also knew that a great many women used the diversion as a means of making a tidy sum of pin money. All the gold and silver lace and the brocade gowns to be found in the various attics and stored in old trunks in lumber rooms were mines for the drizzler. And it seemed that everyone was doing it, even the Princess Charlotte. When the stylish Mr Padbury succumbed to the craze, it was indeed the *thing*.

Pausing by her sister's table, Victoria silently watched for a moment, then continued on to her own work area. Drat the others. Not that she didn't love Julia, and Mr Padbury was as harmless as a gnat, but she had hoped to be alone. Today she fully intended to begin work on the bust of Sir Edward, challenging her memory to a test such as it had never known before.

The wax beneath her hands rapidly warmed to a pliable state, and she began building up the basic form, figuring that neither of the others would be in the least interested in what she did at this point.

'Working at home, Victoria?' Julia inquired in an absent voice while intent upon her sketching.

'Umm,' murmured Victoria, hoping to discourage conversation.

The door opened and Elizabeth bounced into the room. 'Good morning, all. Lovely day, is it not?' She hummed a little tune, then stopped as she undoubtedly recalled there were those present who most definitely took a dim view of her lack of musical aptitude. 'I wish you to know that I have been commissioned to do a series of engravings for Mr Ackermann.' She darted a knowing look at Victoria, while waving a letter in her hand. 'A series of London scenes.'

'Excellent.' Any commission any one of them could manage in the 'regular' world was all to the good, for it served to cover up their more clandestine activities.

'I am so pleased, dear,' murmured Julia, still intent upon her sketch. She wore a frustrated look, causing Victoria to wonder if painting an eye was quite as simple a task as it sounded.

Since Elizabeth had not closed the door, Victoria was unaware that another had entered the room. With Mr Padbury present it was unlikely that anything out of line might be said; nevertheless, she was shaken to hear the voice of the very man she planned to execute in wax come from behind her shoulder. It was as though she had, by concentration, conjured him into the room.

'Good morning, Miss Dancy. Do you never take a rest? Your head went to the foundry yesterday, and already you begin another work. Who is it to be this time?'

Victoria hoped her start did not reveal how he disconcerted her.

'Ah, well, you see . . . that is, I haven't made up my mind. It is to be a surprise,' she concluded with what she just knew was a horrendous blush, not to mention blunder. One did not commence a project without anticipating the outcome. At least no artist she knew did such a thing.

Sir Edward smiled, patently amused at her flustered condition. 'Pity, that. I had hoped to entice you to do a bust of me. Vain creature that I am, I thought it might look well in my library, and be something to hand on to my children.'

'You are planning to be wed, Sir Edward?' Mr Padbury queried, wrapping another length of gold thread around his spool, then stuffing it back into his pretty box.

'Eventually,' Sir Edward replied in a drawl, with a dismissive wave of his hand. 'I expect to do my family duty, as all the other Hawkswood males have in the past. Cannot have the line die out.' He slid his gaze over to where a fascinated Victoria studied him.

'You wish me to do your head, sir?' She darted a glance to Julia and Elizabeth and caught their subtle nods. 'I should be most pleased to oblige you. As it happens, I am between commissions and can take you now, if that pleases.'

'Oh, that pleases very much,' he replied from her side, tilting his head at an angle to peruse the lump of wax on her stand.. 'What about your surprise? I should hate to disappoint someone.'

Victoria whirled about to draw him away from what she had begun to work on. ' 'Tis of no import and can wait.' She guided him a few steps toward the doorway. 'I should prefer to work at your home. I realize this is unorthodox for a young woman, but nobody seems to think it objectionable, for I always take Sable with me.' It was remarkable how Victoria had managed to scrape by with her daring behavior, but she was too grateful to question it. 'Sable usually depresses any tendency to familiarity,' she added for the benefit of Mr Padbury. As well as he knew them, she felt it wise to remind the gentleman of her desire for propriety.

She exchanged a look with Sir Edward, silently acknowledging between the two of them that her pet was an idiot when it came to this particular gentleman, and that Victoria would have to trust him to mind his manners. Besides, after all that had passed between them, she doubted Sir Edward was in the least interested in her anyway. He seemed to have had little difficulty in keeping his distance, something unheardof in the Minerva novels.

'Fine, fine,' he murmured, evidently wishing to seem all that was proper to the others, even Mr Padbury.

Only Victoria caught that devilish gleam in his eyes as he turned to face her once again. She fought the trembling that threatened to overcome her. Why now? She had gone to Admiral Chatham's house with not a quiver, although she knew he fancied himself a ladies' man. And a good many others had indicated they would be only too pleased to oblige her should she wish, which she never did, naturally. Sable had been her guardian. But now?

She ought to remain at home. Every sense in her body told her so. Yet she felt this need, this great curiosity. She was compelled to go. Perhaps she might learn something.

Edward watched as Miss Dancy appeared to struggle with some inward emotion. How neatly she had fallen into his trap. He had expected demure refusals. Yet, even her sisters supported her endeavors. Intriguing.

Last evening while at his club he had overheard the word 'iris' in a softly spoken conversation. Since it was not intended for his ears, he could scarcely ask for an explanation from the men who had tossed the clue into the midst of a discussion. But he was well-acquainted with the men—they frequented the war office and were involved with the efforts to snabble any who aided the French.

Was that the role Miss Dancy played? That of a spy for France? While her brother served in Portugal? Improbable. Unless there was something else involved, like blackmail. He ruefully confessed to himself that he really did not wish to see Miss Dancy as a spy, serving his country's enemy.

Yet, what else was he to think? The most damning evidence was the locket, studded with lapis and nestled against that exquisite bosom. That and her partiality for gentlemen associated with the war office as clients.

Well, he had set the snare out, and now would have the pleasure of watching Miss Dancy as she walked into the trap.

Victoria turned to smooth the surface of the wax, appearing deep in thought. 'Sir Edward, might I inspect the area in which I am to work? So that I shall know precisely what I ought to bring along? So often I find I take far more with me than I need. So trying, you know.'

Mr Padbury looked up, offering in his mild voice, 'You must not forget a footman to carry all your paraphernalia, Miss Dancy. 'Tis good your dog goes along with you. Of course, Sir Edward is a sterling fellow, but it will silence any wagging of tongues, you know. Ain't the usual sort of thing, for a respectable young woman to enter the home of a young gentleman. Best to observe the proprieties and take your maid.'

Including that gossipy tongue of yours, you old goat, thought Edward as he surveyed the other man. How Padbury could spend his hours occupied in that drizzling was more than Edward could imagine. It wasn't as though he was purse-pinched. Word had it he was very plump in the pocket, and on the lookout for a wife. Edward wondered if Padbury intended to offer for a quietly charming Mrs Winton. He entertained a momentary vision of the couple sitting through the years, Padbury drizzling in a chair, Mrs Winton bent over an oval of ivory.

Shaking himself from his abstraction, Edward gave Miss Dancy a bland look. 'I should be most pleased. I deem myself fortunate that you are free to do my likeness. I am at your service, dear lady.' He offered her his right arm, leaning on his cane while he waited for her to make up her mind.

'Lovely.' Victoria draped a damp cloth over the mound of wax, then wiped her hands on a towel. 'If it is agreeable with you, we could go immediately.' As far as she was concerned, the sooner she investigated Sir Edward's home, the better. How fortunate that he had presented himself so promptly after she had developed her suspicions about him.

'Your servant, Miss Dancy.'

She gave him a sharp glance before sweeping ahead of him as they left the room. Was he a trifle *too* eager? She had not dared to accept his arm just then. Passing through the doorway so close to his side was a trifle too intimate.

In the front hall she met the stately Evenson, who carried a slim white box, which he extended to her as she neared.

'This box, which I daresay is from a florist, just arrived for you, miss.' He proffered it with regal care.

Victoria accepted the slender white box with mild curiosity. Whatever the offering, and she received flowers from time to time, it was very dainty. Removing the cover, she drew in a sharp breath as she studied the contents.

'Something unusual, Miss Dancy?' Sir Edward said with mild concern in his voice. He took a step forward, and Victoria backed away.

' 'Tis nothing, sir. Nothing at all.' She hastily put the lid on the box, then managed a smile at Sir Edward. 'Let me just take this to my room while I fetch a pelisse and bonnet.'

Sir Edward nodded, but Victoria sensed he was intrigued with her reaction to the gift. She knew she must have paled, for her shock had been great.

She rushed up the stairs to her room, thanking what presence of mind she'd had that kept her from crying aloud or dropping the box in her horror. Inside that pretty white package had been a twisted and very dead blue iris. 'I have a message for you,' was the old meaning of the flower. Who had sent this, and what was the intended message?

It took but moments to shove the box under her bed, to be examined later, when she was in a calmer state of mind. After donning her pretty new pelisse and bonnet, she found her gloves. While drawing them on, she reflected over the meaning of the delivery of a dead, twisted iris. Absently picking up a reticule that matched her pelisse, she walked from her room and down the stairs.

Obviously it was someone who knew of her activities. But . . . was it a threat that she would end up the same way? Her neck twisted? Or was it a reminder that she had best cooperate with whatever came her way? Or might it merely be a prank? The last she dismissed immediately, for why would anyone do such a thing? She took great care to conceal the locket she always wore tucked inside her gowns, not that most people would know its meaning. In the event that she was captured, she could reveal that little iris, and hopefully save her life.

By the time she had returned to the ground floor, where Sir Edward awaited her, she was none the wiser as to who might have sent the warning. But she was quite sure it *was* a warning; there was no doubt whatsoever of that. She motioned for her maid, Letty, to join her on the foray to a gentleman's lodgings.

'You seem abstracted, Miss Dancy. I trust the gift was to your liking?' Sir Edward said as he ushered her from the house to where his barouche awaited.

'It was a unique gift, not at all in the ordinary,' was all Victoria could think of as a reply. Sir Edward was anything but stupid; he could guess that she had been shaken by the box's contents, even if he didn't see them.

'From someone you know well?' he inquired smoothly as he settled down in the carriage at her side. Letty sat, neat and quiet, across from them.

'Actually, it was anonymous. I have no idea who sent it,' she confessed.

'Ah,' he exclaimed softly, 'that explains why you looked so confused. I have found that it is never wise to do something like that. One may assume the recipient will jump to the correct conclusion, and that is not always the case. It is merely a matter of vanity, my dear Miss

Dancy. I have no fear that your sender will identify himself . . . soon.'

Words undoubtedly intended to comfort her made her all the more gloomy. When Sir Edward had said that the sender would identify himself soon, it had sounded too much like a death knell.

She managed the usual sort of social chitchat during the drive to his home. What a blessing he had not taken up residence at Albany, as so many bachelors did. Rather, he had a modest town house in a good location of Mayfair. After the carriage had come to a halt, she looked up to study his dwelling a moment before accepting the footman's hand to descend from the carriage.

Relatively new, the town house was of solid stone with an exquisite entry. To either side of the door were beautiful oil lamps to provide excellent light at night, rather than those smoky flambeaux that most homes possessed. Elegant leaded glass in a pretty design graced the fanlight above the door.

'You approve?' he prodded gently.

'You have a lovely home, Sir Edward.' Victoria accepted his arm, walking up the few steps to the door with no hint showing of the trepidations she felt. Letty followed them inside, sitting on a prim hall chair at Victoria's gesture.

Victoria retained her pelisse and bonnet, walking down the spacious hall until he

118

opened a door, then ushered her inside. She looked around with approval at what she saw.

'Very nice indeed, sir.' A good-sized window overlooked the rear of the property, which contained a modest patch of grass bordered by a neat row of shrubbery. To the rear she glimpsed what she surmised was a necessary house adjacent to an unpretentious stable. The town house was situated so that sunlight flooded the room in the morning, the best possible siting for her purposes.

Tearing her gaze from the pleasant scene, she began to absorb the contents of the room in which she would work, when she caught sight of it: a large framed botanical print of an iris. It hung on the wall directly behind an imposing desk.

She caught her breath. Two irises in one day? Without her realizing it, her hand wandered to her throat, to remain there while she considered the meaning of this. A coldness crept over her.

'You admire my latest purchase? I rather fancy it. Done by some French fellow, and a handsome frame, if I do say so.'

'Redouté, I believe,' Victoria murmured absently. 'You are partial to the iris, then?'

'I have found certain of the species interesting.'

His reply seemed odd, to say the least. She tried to ignore the incriminating picture on the wall, and strolled over to glance at his

119

collection of books, the volumes bound nicely in leather and looking as though he had dipped into them more than once.

'You enjoy reading as well as sculpturing, Miss Dancy?'

'Oh, yes . . . that is, when I have the time.'

'You travel often. Perhaps you have time to read then? If this is an indication of your preference for a workroom, I imagine you spend a good deal of time in one library or another.'

'Well,' she replied evasively, 'they often have excellent light, and few homes offer a room such as we have added to ours.'

'Would not a conservatory do as well?'

'Perhaps.'

Edward studied the woman who perused his selection of books with what he would wager were unseeing eyes. The trap he had set had sprung quite neatly. He had positioned himself to watch her face, and felt satisfied for his efforts. She had paled at the sight of the iris—more than paled. She had been shaken, much as she had reacted to that peculiar package that had been delivered just before they left her home. What had it been, to have unsettled her so? He would give a deal to know, and he suspected she'd not reveal those contents, no matter how skillfully he probed.

Just then his servant knocked, and, given permission, entered to inform Sir Edward that a gentleman had called to see him on a matter of urgency.

Edward gave Miss Dancy a look of frustration, wanting to remain where he could keep an eye on her. Yet he could hardly ask the man to come in here. It could compromise Miss Dancy, himself as well. He did not desire marriage to this luscious armful of suspicion.

'I shall be there directly.' Turning to Miss Dancy, he added, 'I am sorry that I must leave you for a few moments. I trust that you will be able to occupy yourself until I return?'

'Of course,' Victoria replied. 'I quite understand.' And, she admitted to herself, she was intensely curious about what else was contained in this room. Did the iris on his walls mean that he was a member of the iris ring? She longed to know more, and acknowledged that she hoped he was not.

Once he had departed for the front of the house, Victoria gingerly started her exploration. Heart beating unnaturally fast and mouth dry, she began with the desk. It seemed the most likely spot for documents of any sort, although she knew that any papers of a dangerous nature might be stashed away in a hiding place.

The desk was a smooth mahogany, designed most likely by Mr Sheridan. Elizabeth owned a drawing table from him, and found it excellent. Both bore his unmistakable stamp of design. There were papers scattered over the desk, but nothing

121

she could see that might point to any connection with the iris ring. Several drawers were locked, the open quite innocuous in regard to content.

Turning, she espied a tall gentleman's secretary. It was a massive article of furniture, with glass-fronted bookshelves for precious volumes to either side of the central portion. Curious, she let down the central door, just enough to see that the vertical slots were stuffed with papers and folders, the cubbyholes crammed with folded letters and various missives.

She crept to the door, opening it enough to hear if there were footsteps in the hall. She listened a moment. Only Letty could be seen, sitting patiently. Nothing else, but the drone of voices in the distance. Who had sought him out? No matter, it probably was a social thing.

She returned to the secretary and let the central door down, extending it until the hinges caught. She swiftly perused the contents of various compartments, then checked the drawers. In the bottom one she caught sight of a familiar piece of paper. It was identical to the one she had risked her life to bring to London, the very paper that had been in the packet she brought from Dover!

Hastily, after scanning the paper once again, she slammed the drawer shut, then restored the cover to the front of the secretary. Withdrawing to a far part of the room, she stared out of the window as she considered what she had just discovered. Her heart beat at double time and she knew a feeling of desolation.

Sir Edward *must* be a spy. Else how could he have a copy of the encoded letter? Had he untangled the cipher? Goodness knew that she had been confounded by the dratted thing. Never had she found a cipher so perplexing. The miserable handwriting had not helped in the least, and she suspected that it greatly contributed to her difficulty.

She felt ill. He couldn't be, yet he was. The man society adored was a spy for the French. She gave the botanical print that hung in pride of place behind the desk an angry glare. It was all of a piece—the print, the copy of the ciphered letter, his great curiosity about her. Oh, she was not so foolish as to think he was enamored of her. His behavior at the windmill had put paid to that notion.

The windmill. How wrong Sam had been to trust Sir Edward. While he had not ravished her, he had plundered something else. He must have searched her case and found the packet. Yet, all had been restored perfectly. How clever he must be!

She paced about the room, frowning at the library steps, skirting the elegant little chair that sat against the wall not far from the secretary and convenient for one who wished to sit there—most likely checking the contents of it.

Had she disturbed them? She believed she had replaced everything with her customary carefulness.

She had trained herself well in the past months. Never had anyone voiced the least suspicion of her investigations at the various homes where she had worked. Indeed, each lady commended Victoria for her neatness and the remarkable skill with which she recreated the husband's likeness.

Footsteps sounded in the hall, and within moments Sir Edward entered the room, gazing at her with a quizzical expression. 'You have been idle, staring out at nothing better than my poor landscape?'

'For a city house, it is quite acceptable, and you know it.' She pasted what she hoped to be an amiable look on her face, then sighed faintly.

'Ah, my neglect has made you long to be elsewhere. I cannot blame you, Miss Dancy. How utterly rude of me to leave you to your own devices for so long. The matter was pressing or I would have had my man send the fellow on his way.' His mouth tilted up at one corner in a regretful smile.

Victoria wondered just what that 'pressing' matter might have been. Sir Edward leaned on his cane a trifle, and she now wondered if it was a genuine injury or merely an affectation to gain him sympathy. Oh, how that foolish heart of hers wished to believe the man was innocent. Yet the evidence in the drawer of the secretary damned him beyond belief.

She scolded herself for the absurd softness in her silly heart. It must be those Minerva novels that she and her sisters liked to read. A tall dark man with a fascinating face usually turned out to be the hero in disguise. Sir Edward had evolved into the villain. She only wished she knew what his villainy might prove to be.

Would he plot against his country? He'd not served in the military. Although she had learned that he had been in Portugal. Not that she knew precisely when he'd been injured, so as to prevent his service, had he so wished.

'I had best return home now,' she said with a finality of tone that brooked no opposition.

Sir Edward, glancing about his library, could see nothing amiss. He would investigate more later. But he wondered at what made Miss Dancy look so down-pin. The notion that it had something to do with sculpturing the bust of him didn't set particularly well in the least. What could he do to encourage the woman to think more highly of him?

He'd send flowers. Perhaps irises? Blue ones.

7

'I declare, I have not the least notion as to who might have sent such a thing, but I can tell you that it frightened me excessively,' Victoria said in an unsteady little voice. She smoothed the soft chicken-skin gloves over her hands, staring out of the coach window while the young women jounced through the streets on their way to Lady Tichbourne's. The image of the wilted, twisted iris in the pristine coffin-like white box had haunted her sleep. The dead flower had nestled in the folds of white tissue like a crumpled body reposing upon its final satin.

'I feel certain you concealed it admirably,' Julia replied. She reached out to pat her sister's arm in a gesture of comfort. 'What shall we do?' she added, infinitely practical, and assuming that the problem confronting one of them affected them all equally.

'What about the box?' Elizabeth inquired, ever one to get to the heart of a matter. 'Any possibility of identifying the shop? Thus the sender?'

'No. It was merely a plain box, much like any other. And since there was no written message, there was no handwriting to study. I fear that is a futile quest.'

'Who knows us well enough to suspect what

Victoria does?' Julia demanded quietly. 'Someone who would stoop to threats of this nature? And for what reason? Do you suppose it has somehow seeped out that Victoria has been working on ciphers, and on that particular paper?'

Elizabeth glanced about as though to detect the unseen presence of another. 'Shh. We must be ever so careful.'

Victoria nodded her agreement, although thinking it unlikely that there would be anyone within hearing distance who would know incriminating information about the girls. One never took foolish chances. Even a footman was not to be trusted now.

She took a deep breath, then said, 'I shall be glad when this is all over and past us. It may seem exciting to be dashing about the countryside hunting for traitors while executing their heads in wax or clay. But,' she concluded, 'I think it will be wonderful to be able to relax. As it is, I search the area about me every step I take. Every word spoken must be chosen with care. It is an intolerable position to be in, to be sure.'

Elizabeth leaned over to peek around the corner at the footman so as to ascertain that he was beyond hearing. The folds of her cloak fell back to reveal her charming peach gown of Florence satin as she leaned farther out of the window to better see him.

'I doubt if he could make sense of this

conversation were he to hear it. The rumble of the wheels on the cobblestones ought to cover any words we utter,' Victoria said when she figured out what her sister was doing.

Elizabeth nodded in understanding, then smiled. 'You look so lovely, no one would suspect that you are a spy for the government. A *spy* in blue zephyr gingham, so sheer and silky as it swirls about a rather nice form? Never.'

Julia chuckled. 'Do not forget that clever little cap trimmed with blue feathers. I do believe you shall capture the evening, Vicky.' She uttered this compliment with the assurance of knowing she looked well enough in her gown of amaranthus gauze. The pinkish-purple shade became her remarkably well, and the style, although modest, was quite fashionable.

'Someone once told me that it is a wretched job to be a spy. I quite agree with her.' Victoria smiled her acceptance of their compliments, then shifted on the carriage seat as the vehicle drew to a halt before the imposing Tichbourne residence. Victoria resolved to put the iris from her mind and enjoy the evening.

A red carpet had been rolled out for the guests to tread when entering the house. Never would a lady have her slippers ruined while going into the Tichbournes' for one of their glittering evening affairs.

128

Elizabeth studied their footman as he handed each lady from the carriage. Her sharp gaze seemed to detect nothing out of the ordinary.

Victoria bit back a smile. Really, it was not amusing in the least, but she wondered if there was another woman in London who checked her servants to see if a spy might be lurking among them.

Julia slipped comforting arms around both sisters for a moment as they walked up the few steps to the front door.

'I wonder who is to attend this conversazione?' Victoria said softly. She found the gatherings for conversation with intellectuals from the arts, sciences, and literature vastly enjoyable. 'Lady Tichbourne usually has such fascinating people. I hope Mr Turner is here. I recently saw one of his paintings that intrigued me immensely,' Victoria added in an aside as they walked through the wide doorway into the house. She nodded to the butler before continuing. 'It depicted the Castle of Chillon in Switzerland, and 'twas such a romantic view.' She sighed, then grinned. 'I vow it would be an ideal spot for a honeymoon.'

'Are you planning upon marriage, Miss Dancy? The gentlemen of the *ton* will be desolate.' The women whirled about, Victoria nearly bumping into Sir Edward as he joined them in the entry.

She wondered just how much he had heard, and how he might interpret it. 'No, I fear not at this moment.' An imp possessed her to add, 'However, I should adore visiting Switzerland in the event I do wed. I should like to see how true-to-life that landscape painting might be. I could sit on the banks of Lake Geneva and while away the hours doing absolutely nothing but admiring the scenery.'

Sir Edward looked down at her, then said, 'I believe your husband would spend his hours admiring you, for you glow with radiant good health and beauty.'

'Why, Sir Edward, what a gallant you are.' Victoria smiled demurely, tapped his arm lightly with her fan, while resolving to stay as far from him as she could this evening. He might be a fascinating man, but she sensed danger when near him. What sort of danger, she didn't know. He knew things about her that he ought not know, of that she was almost positive. Whether the danger stemmed from this or the sensual attraction she felt for him was not clear to her. She took a step away, and was distinctly relieved when he made no effort to join her and her sisters.

Edward watched the three young women stroll across the room after they had greeted their hostess. Every male eye was fixed upon them. How vibrant they were, all of them, each in her own way. The lovely Julia radiated a serenity a man might long for, while the more dashing Elizabeth displayed the artless charm that he was coming to know was a part of her nature. However, it was Victoria Dancy who drew his gaze. It was more than the mystery of the blue-iris locket that intrigued him now, he admitted.

She possessed strength of character, but what else? Could she really be a spy? For whom? Countess Lieven he knew to be a spy for the Russians, and he had no doubt she knew all that went on in the Austrian court as well. Although in London but a brief time, she had managed to wiggle her restless self into the heart of the *ton.* Just as had Miss Dancy. In the course of his inquiries he had discovered that there were few doors closed to the Dancy women, for their brother was a baron, and apparently there was ample money. It mattered not that they were artistic, for they had no real need for the money they earned. Rather, this talent endeared them to their peers, and every man, certainly, fawned over them in a frightfully zealous manner.

One hand resting lightly on his cane, he leaned against a pillar while he observed those around him. His knee bothered him more than usual this evening. If he could rest a bit, his discomfort might ease up, yet he wished to study the men clustered around the Dancys. Could a clue to the mystery surrounding the Dancys be provided by the men in attendance?

'Watching the Three Graces, eh?' Mr Padbury said in an amiable way from close to Edward's side.

'Is that what they are called?' Edward concealed a start at the unexpected appearance of the little man. He found the genial gentleman a trifle irritating, and could not like him even if he did pay court to Mrs Winton and not the glorious Victoria.

'Naturally. Could there be a better title for them? Just look at how gracefully they move about, the elegance of their gestures, the refinement of their dress. No one else can touch them as individuals; as a trio, they are far beyond equal.'

Mr Padbury turned his head so as to study Edward, who found it disconcerting to have that direct gaze trained upon him.

'Indeed,' was Edward's only reply before he moved away from the pillar, leaning upon his cane to remind Mr Padbury that it was tedious to stand for long.

Once rid of the genial gentleman, as he thought of Padbury, Edward circulated about the room until he at last found himself on the edge of the group that surrounded the three Dancy women. He watched Victoria, dressed in a simple yet devastatingly ravishing gown of a blue that captured the color of her eyes. The creation dipped low over her bosom, yet not low enough to expose the iris locket he knew to be lurking just below the cut of the bodice.

Tiny sleeves puffed out above her graceful, slender arms. The skirt clung to her slim form, hinting at the luscious curves he knew existed.

'Have you heard from Geoffrey lately?' one buck inquired of Elizabeth.

Edward concentrated on her answer, as he thought it singular her brother should leave his sisters unprotected while he dashed about Portugal doing heaven-knew-what.

'No, Lord Leighton, I have not,' was her chilly reply.

Edward wondered why the lovely Miss Elizabeth edged away from Leighton, treating the man with a cool disdain. It was uncommon for any woman to shun a peer with pots of money and who was a handsome devil to boot. Edward resolved to get to know the younger man better. At present they were but casual friends at best. He walked to Leighton's side.

'Pleasant evening,' Edward commented, his gaze fixed on Victoria while she chatted with the artist, Turner. Evidently she was to have her desire, and he suddenly hoped she would not be disappointed in her quest.

'Some might think so.'

'I saw you chatting with Miss Elizabeth.'

'Dashed if I can imagine what ails the girl,' Leighton confided in an explosion of exasperation. He seemed to sense a kindred spirit in Sir Edward. 'I only intend an innocent flirtation; she gives me a freezing look and the coldest of shoulders. Blast it, makes a fellow feel a trifle reckless, but I reckon that would not do with the ever-so-proper Dancy women.'

'Proper, are they?' Edward said. His mind flashed back to the windmill and the image of the beautiful Victoria Dancy as she sprawled, unconscious, on the cot, all but naked. The vivid blue lapis iris had peeped from beneath her shift, exposed along with a vast amount of creamy skin. He had remained the gentleman, but it had not been easy. Yet he knew the peril of an illness, the danger possible from a seemingly slight chill. His care had been necessary.

He shifted weight from his bad leg, leaning more heavily upon his cane for support. That memory of her in the flickering firelight, with that enticing, alluring, and incredibly provoking body, caused him internal discomfort.

'Exceedingly,' replied the younger Lord Leighton with feeling. 'Although, do you know that I suspect Miss Elizabeth is up to something? I found her coming out of the war office last week. Dashed odd place for a female to be. Seems to me her brother ought to be home looking after his sisters instead of off serving in Portugal or wherever he is now'

'Perhaps that is precisely why he is over there; he does not relish riding herd on three headstrong young women,' Edward replied in an undertone, although he quite agreed with Leighton on the matter.

'You may have the right of it,' Leighton replied with a considering look. 'Miss Elizabeth is a handful, if what I have seen is true of her nature. Mind you, she stays within the boundaries of propriety, but . . . . However, I do enjoy teasing the chit.' He flashed a grin at Edward.

'Enough of this,' Edward said, nudging Leighton with his free hand. 'Why do we not join the men over there? I confess I would like to ask Davy about that discovery of his, and if it is really true that this gas will alleviate pain.'

Suddenly realizing that the man at his side looked pale with the effort of standing so long, Leighton quickly agreed. The two men strolled across the room, where Sir Edward found a comfortable chair and began to quiz the famous scientist about his findings.

From her vantage point Victoria kept a surreptitious watch on Sir Edward. She knew when he had joined the group that hovered about the sisters, and when he began to chat with Lord Leighton. She immediately noticed when Sir Edward limped over to join Sir Humphry Davy, who was seated with several men of science.

It was, she reflected, a stimulating company this evening. There was not only the intriguing Mr Turner, a man most modest about his talents, but the eminent Sir Humphry. She wondered what Sir Edward found to quiz him about with such intensity. Without managing to appear obvious, she edged and sidled her way to a place where she might catch the drift of their conversation. It assuredly was not a private one, for several others had joined in with questions of their own regarding the topic.

'Indeed, quite painless,' insisted Sir Humphry when Victoria drew close enough to overhear what was said. 'I had wanted to test the gas myself, you see, and it worked well on me. I frequently do tests, not always with happy results,' the scientist admitted a bit ruefully amid light laughter from the others.

'But it only stops the pain while inhaling the gas?' Edward persisted.

'It has been demonstrated that after inhaling the nitrous oxide the person cannot feel pain, thus compelling one to accept that it possesses anesthetic properties. I believe it to have a similar effect to ether, although ether has not been sufficiently tested, to my way of thinking.'

'But it is only for a limited duration? Could it be breathed only enough for a knee surgery, for example?' Sir Edward said with an intense curiosity.

'Probably. You would still have the problem of infection to deal with, I suspect. We don't understand why this happens, even with the best of care.' It was clear this disturbed Sir Humphry.

'Basilicum powder notwithstanding?' Sir

Edward queried.

'I fear so. I have heard tell of some success with a kind of mold, but that is most likely fanciful talk by the country folk.' There was an appreciative chuckle from several who held dim views of folk medicine. 'Some doctors insist upon covering a wound, others claim air is better,' Davy continued. 'Most want to bleed the patient, yet a few say that the loss of blood, particularly if there is surgery involved, makes that a dangerous practice. The high loss of life is not encouraging to a surgeon, in spite of his skill with the knife.'

'Indeed.' Sir Edward appeared to give the discussion deep thought while the others in the group veered off to debate the merits of leeches as opposed to bleeding.

Victoria found the conversation depressing, and she drifted across to another part of the room. Her thoughts returned to the exchange she overheard between Sir Humphry and Sir Edward. From his strong curiosity about the painkilling nature of the nitrous oxide, she suspected Sir Edward truly suffered more than a little from his injury. Did he contemplate surgery? A dangerous undertaking at best, surgery. Few she had heard of who dared such a course survived for long. Infection, as Sir Humphry said, took its toll. Some doctors insisted it was bad humors of the blood, others, vapors in the air. But how to prevent it, or control such a thing, when you knew not what caused it?

'Dear Victoria,' gushed one of the newer writers, a Miss Courtenay, who had inveigled an invitation to this select gathering, 'what is your next project? Some prominent statesman, no doubt?'

'Miss Dancy has a rare opportunity, one given to few women,' Mr Padbury inserted with good humor. Lucius Padbury might not be a man of letters, nor inclined to the arts or science, but he was an excellent conversationalist and thus had earned a permanent place on Lady Tichbourne's guest list.

Miss Courtenay smiled, then, unable to resist, asked, 'Do tell me all.

Victoria, knowing full well that Miss Courtenay was a gabster, sighed, then said with gracious charm, 'I have been requested to create a likeness of Sir Edward Hawkswood.'

'Oh,' breathed the young writer, 'I should be terrified of such a project. And do you go to his home?' she inquired with an avid expression on her pink-cheeked face.

'I trust that if she does, it is not early in the day. Sir Edward tends to spend his evenings at the clubs, one in particular,' Mr Padbury declared with a smile.

'He is a gamester, Mr Padbury?' Victoria said with dismay.

'As to that,' Mr Padbury said with commendable hesitancy, 'I am not certain. I have seen him thereabouts often, but if he plays at cards, it is not deeply. He seems to have the admirable notion that a man gambles only if he can afford to lose, and only with money not actually needed.'

'Praiseworthy, indeed,' Victoria murmured, casting a glance at the gentleman in question. She was startled to catch his gaze upon her, and found to her further dismay that she blushed. How deeply, she couldn't say, but the heat in her face was evident. It was to be hoped the candlelight would diffuse her high color.

As if drawn by her look, Sir Edward rose and approached. As he drew near, Miss Courtenay vanished in the opposite direction, a flutter of pink draperies and white feathers.

'I trust I did not drive the lady away from a pleasant conversation?' Sir Edward said with a hint of laughter in his deep voice.

When he smiled at Victoria, she wondered for a moment what he referred to, before swiftly recalling the tiresome and garrulous young writer.

'Miss Courtenay has a tongue that flaps like a flag in a stiff breeze,' Mr Padbury interjected, reminding Victoria that he remained at her side.

'Oh, perhaps not,' Victoria said kindly, not wishing to sound like a prattlebox herself. Miss Courtenay might be a gossip, but it was not gracious to say so. Victoria had no love for gossips, and certainly did not wish to emulate one.

'Nonsense,' Mr Padbury asserted. 'You are too generous, but then, you Dancy women are ever considerate to those less fortunate in their character.' He gave the pair a curious look, then strolled off to join Mr Turner and several other gentlemen.

'Tell me,' Sir Edward said in an abstracted voice, 'is he dangling after Mrs Winton?'

'Julia and Mr Padbury?' Victoria considered the matter a few moments, then replied, 'I could not say. He is ever around the house, and seems content to merely be where he can admire Julia and visit with her. I cannot think him the least loverlike.'

'Genial, he might be. Loverlike, no, I must agree.'

Mindful of Sir Edward's earlier conversation with Sir Humphry, Victoria unobtrusively guided him toward an arrangement of exceedingly comfortable chairs, gesturing with one hand. 'What do you say to sitting here? I become a bit tired of standing about forever, although I hate to confess it. A young woman is not supposed to admit such, I know.' She watched with approval as he settled onto a chair that had an extra pillow at the back, with an ottoman upon which to recline his foot if he so chose.

He placed both feet upon the ottoman after her encouraging nod, keeping his cane to hand. His sigh contained a hint of frustration.

'You need have a care for your injury, Sir Edward,' Victoria chided. 'Tell me, do you plan to risk surgery? I feel guilty, thinking that your rescue of me from the carriage may have made your injury worse. Please do not contemplate such an action without deep consideration of the peril involved.'

'Do you always insert yourself into others' lives, Miss Dancy?' Edward said testily. 'I am tired of people poking and prodding into the matter of my accident and resultant injury.'

Victoria repressed a hasty answer. Given the background of his accident and the comments she'd overheard, not to mention the pain he must suffer as well, it was understandable that he be irritable at times. 'Sometimes,' she finally admitted, 'I if I find my concern is unwelcome, I usually withdraw it.'

'Forgive me. I do not mean to be an old wigsby. Most of the time my knee is tolerable. Today is worse, for some odd reason, and I snap at your kindness like an old crab.'

'My Aunt Bel would say 'tis the damp weather. Perhaps it would be better if you went to bed earlier and kept your knee warm. Gallivanting about in the evening till late hours cannot be beneficial to one's health,' Victoria said in what she hoped was a reasonable manner.

He gave her a narrow look. 'You would

have me act like a man in his dotage?' His affront was almost amusing.

'You enjoy the evening? Sir Humphry is interesting.' He nodded, then added, 'Did Mr Turner satisfy your curiosity about his landscape?'

'Indeed, yes. He claims the scene is as he depicted it. I should like to see it, I believe.'

'On your honeymoon, you said.' Sir Edward looked amused again.

Victoria decided to change the subject. In spite of her earlier sensation of danger emanating from this man, she now felt him to be relatively harmless at the moment—as long as he avoided the subject of marriage. Perhaps it was the thought that he suffered pain that made him appear less daunting.

'What time do you wish me to be at your home to begin work on your sculpture?' This ought to be a safe subject.

Then the image of that paper she had seen in his desk returned to mind, and she watched him with a wary eye. If she were to investigate his library, especially his desk, she wanted to begin as soon as possible. The solving of the cipher was proving an impossible task, one that was giving her severe headaches. If there might be a clue to be found, she desperately needed to find it.

Sir Edward reflected a moment, then replied, 'Anytime after noon tomorrow should be fine.' He appeared to look forward to the sitting, yet she'd not missed the fleeting expression of speculation in his eyes.

Impulsively, without giving her words careful thought, Victoria said, 'Quite as Mr Padbury predicted. Do you intend to go gambling this evening, then? Even though you remain here until a late hour?'

Sir Edward stiffened slightly, and slid his good leg to the floor. 'I do not believe that doing my portrait in wax permits you such liberty, Miss Dancy. And Leighton claimed you to be such a proper miss. What I do during my hours is not your affair.'

The not-so-gentle reproof brought another blush to her cheeks. Really, Victoria chided herself, never had she been so guilty of social misconduct. 'I beg your pardon, Sir Edward. Mark it to a desire to have my patron in the best possible condition for his sitting.' She forced herself to meet that steady gaze of his, refusing to flinch at what she thought she saw there.

'Apology accepted,' Edward replied handsomely. 'I tend to be a bit edgy regarding my injury, if you must know.' Then in a rare flash of revelation he added, 'I have the irrational feeling that Society knows the circumstances and is amused by them. It is not pleasant to think yourself the object of entertainment,' he concluded with a wry twist of his mouth.

Startled by this more intimate view of

his thoughts, Victoria nodded with understanding. 'I have at times felt censure due to my unorthodox behavior—going to various homes and staring at a gentleman's face for hours. Julia has endured such as well. One must do what one feels necessary, however.'

The pensive look on his face made her uneasy. Whatever evaluation he did of her motives seemed severe in its conclusions.

That feeling of disquiet increased, and she rose to her feet, gesturing to Sir Edward to remain seated. 'I must find my sisters, for no doubt it is time for us to depart. Please do not disturb yourself, sir.'

She whirled about and left before he had time to react.

Edward felt like a bloody fool, sitting there like an old hen that was too tired to get off the nest. She was right. He ought to go home, have hot compresses on his knee—or was it cold ones that felt better? However, self-indulgence was not permitted yet. Later, perhaps. He needed to get to his club and listen to the talk that flowed over the cards with the lubrication of liquor to loosen the tongues.

He watched as the Dancy women drifted toward the door like a sunset cloud of peach, lavender, and blue. They paused to bid their hostess a fond farewell, from the look of it, then left the room.

'Still here?' Mr Padbury exclaimed in surprise as he bustled up to Edward. 'I thought sure you'd be off to the clubs by now But then,' he said with a genial chuckle, 'the Dancy girls *are* charming. Hard for a man to ignore such grace and beauty, what?'

'Indeed,' was Edward's only response. It was difficult for him to understand how the Dancy women could tolerate this man underfoot all the time. Unable to put his finger on the cause for his dislike, he chalked it up to the silly business of that genial smile. While in Italy he had seen a painting of a woman with a smile that resembled Padbury's. Unsettling.

He eased himself up from the comfort of the chair, resolving to inquire of his hostess its manufactory source. Pausing to chat with Leighton again, making a date to meet soon, he then approached Lady Tichbourne to take his leave.

As he entered his carriage after paying handsome compliments and jotting the name of the chairmaker in his notebook, he returned to the matter of Victoria Dancy.

How long would he have to observe her in close quarters? While it lasted, he would make the most of his time. In the meanwhile, he would listen, see what he might hear, and only hope that someone would drop more than a mere phrase about the blue-iris group. He was determined to uncover all he could about

Victoria Dancy, right down to the blue-iris locket she always wore . . . and kept concealed.

8

'I should like to know what Sir Edward does while at these gaming establishments, if he isn't an out-and-out gamester,' Victoria mused aloud to Julia over breakfast the following morning. 'This is a man who is frequently in pain, yet he spends his nights lounging about in gaming hells, from what Mr Padbury says. Be an angel and find out if he knows which club Sir Edward patronizes the most, will you?'

'What do you have in mind, love?' Julia replied with caution. She gave her dear sister a shrewd look before dropping her gaze to the plate before her.

'It is but vague at the moment. Something urges me to investigate, and you know how my hunches are.' She shot a look at Julia, then became silent as Elizabeth bounced into the room.

'Really, Lizzie,' Julia remonstrated, 'must you be quite so exuberant? I declare, we ought to persuade Aunt Bel to join us for a time. *She* would have you behaving the lady in no time.'

Elizabeth frowned at the use of the hated

'Lizzie,' then gathered what she wished from the sideboard before joining her sisters at the polished mahogany table. 'You know full well she loathes London living, and besides, she has Cousin Hyacinthe in her care. I should not wish that young lady under our feet.' Elizabeth made a horrid face that quite adequately expressed her feelings about her cousin.

'She is very beautiful,' agreed Victoria with a smile, 'and exceedingly proper.'

'Hah!' Elizabeth exclaimed. 'That is only because no one knows what goes on in her head and the scheming that is so carefully executed when no one is looking. Proper, bah.'

Julia and Victoria exchanged amused glances, fully aware that Hyacinthe was indeed a pretty schemer, but probably no more so than any other lovely young miss trying to capture a respectable husband.

'Lord Leighton sent you a lovely bouquet of flowers. Did you see them as you came down for breakfast?' Victoria inquired of her younger sister.

Elizabeth gave them a startled look and shook her head. 'That man. What a nosy creature, asking where Geoffrey is and when he is coming home. As if I should know!' She nibbled on her toast before adding, 'I do wish our dear brother *would* come home. Things might be a little easier were we to have a man

147

about the house.'

Julia nodded as her eyes met Victoria's wary gaze. 'None of us knows a thing, and I suspect everyone believes we make up our ignorance out of whole cloth.'

'Have you suffered unwanted advances from Lord Leighton, Elizabeth?' Victoria demanded quietly.

'Well,' Elizabeth admitted reluctantly, 'just the kisses at Lady Fenwick's ball. I was most annoyed,' she added for good measure. At least she had persuaded herself she was annoyed. At the time it had seemed romantic and the kisses quite heavenly, until she realized the impropriety of it all. 'Dastardly man,' she declared, but without her usual fervency. 'Now he teases me like Geoffrey used to do. I find him most disagreeable.'

'I can see why you have shunned him,' Julia said in her most soothing manner. 'Say no more and we shall see to it he is kept from your side.'

Elizabeth nodded, but somehow looked rather unconvinced that having Lord Leighton at a distance would solve her confusion.

Victoria turned to matters more important than the harassment of her younger sister. 'I had a message from the war office this morning. They beg that I double my efforts at deciphering the message. It seems their best man has not been able to accomplish it either. What a pity we cannot put our heads together.

Perhaps we might just solve it with a combined effort.'

'You well know Lord Bathurst decided that the fewer who knew about your efforts, the better,' Julia reminded her. 'It is a dangerous business, Vicky. I shudder to think what might happen to you if more people knew.'

'Like another box with a dead iris?'

'Victoria! Please do not say such. We know nothing about that sender either,' Julia reminded.

'I detest unknown quantities,' Victoria declared. 'They are so unsettling.'

Evenson entered the room just then to announce the arrival of Mr Padbury. 'I put him in the study, Mrs Winton. He seemed to think that the place to wait for you.'

Victoria recalled that she had left the missive from the war office on her desk, and chided herself for her rare carelessness. She shook her head at Julia.

'Why not invite him to join us in the morning room?' Elizabeth suggested, aware of undercurrents, even though she did not know what caused them. The three sisters had grown far closer than the usual sibling relationship, partly owing to the loss of their parents and partly owing to the danger they shared.

'Excellent idea,' Julia agreed. 'Be so good as to show Mr Padbury in there.' Once Evenson had left the room, she whispered,

149

'Why, Vicky?'

'I forgot that letter on the desk. Although we know Mr Padbury to be harmless as a gnat, we cannot take any chances, can we?' Victoria whispered back, then joined her sisters in a hasty flit to the morning room as Mr Padbury was ushered in by Evenson. The morning light revealed the young ladies in impeccable day dress, all perched on chairs, wearing expectant looks.

'Good day, dear ladies. I can see you rested well after your late evening at Lady Tichbourne's. Mrs Winton, lovely as ever,' he avowed, bowing toward Julia.

Victoria bit back a smile at the 'genial gentleman' as she recollected Sir Edward calling him. He was so much the well-mannered, civil London man-about-the-town. Julia said nothing in regard to her feelings about him. Victoria hoped that her elder sister did not feel constrained to marry merely to remove herself from the Dancy household.

It would seem that subject was also on Mr Padbury's mind as well this morning, for he said, following the usual chitchat about the weather, 'I note that Lord Simpson has wed. What will you charming ladies do when your brother marries? Or what if he should return with a wife? I hear there are a great number of Englishwomen, not to mention those dark-eyed ladies of Spain and Portugal, who cast out lures to the soldiers over there.'

Victoria exchanged looks with Elizabeth and Julia. They all knew the possibility existed, naturally. However, they had pushed aside the actuality of the matter.

'I doubt my brother would order us out of our family home, Mr Padbury,' Julia exclaimed softly.

'The gentleman has a point, Julia. We ought to form plans. It is only sensible. What bride would want to enter a household where three sisters have reigned for years? Perhaps we shall hunt about for a suitable house of our own. Would that appeal to you? At least until Elizabeth marries, at any rate.'

'You have no intention of being wed? I understood you planned to take a wedding trip to Switzerland.'

Victoria gave Mr Padbury a curious look. That exchange, however nonsensical, had been between Sir Edward and herself. Somehow, she doubted that Sir Edward was the sort to confide in the man he oddly seemed to dislike. Perhaps her voice had carried farther than she believed.

'A jest, Mr Padbury, nothing more. Coffee, sir?' She signaled to Evenson, who had remained near the door. 'Coffee for Mr Padbury.' With that, she rose from her chair and escaped from the room, intent upon placing that paper from the war office in a locked drawer.

Once that was accomplished, she headed to

the workroom to assemble her materials. All her tools went into the neat case made just for that purpose. The incipient wax sculpture, carefully kept clean and wrapped, was placed in a dampened cloth bag. By the end of the morning she was satisfied that she was as ready as she might be—at least for her work. Dealing with Sir Edward was another matter entirely.

*   *   *

It was nearing two of the clock when Victoria, accompanied by Sable and a footman, left the house. Admonitions from Julia, Elizabeth, and Mr Padbury—who had lingered for lunch—still rang in her ears as she entered her town carriage.

'Honestly,' Victoria declared in mild affront, 'one would think I've not done this sort of thing before.'

But inwardly she knew this time was different. Never before had she felt such an attraction to her patron, nor had she to cope with a protector who adored the one to be guarded against. 'Sable, what shall I do with you? You are to make the man stay away from me. Do you understand, I wonder.'

Sighing with frustration—for she knew once her silly dog got a sniff of Sir Edward it would be pointless to command the animal to stand guard—she absently stroked his silken head.

Her thoughts returned to the matter Mr Padbury had raised that morning. What *would* they do if Geoffrey returned with a bride? Or when he married, as he must, to preserve the line? How foolish of the sisters not to have a plan for that event. However, it was not too late. Elizabeth must marry, of course. And Julia? Would she become Mrs Padbury? Somehow Victoria doubted it, but one never knew, and she would not probe. Perhaps obliquely inquire, nevertheless. If she had to be alone, she might as well prepare for it. Not one suitor who had approached was welcomed by Victoria. She wanted someone strong, capable, and she wanted a love match such as her parents seemed to have had.

They had refused to be parted from each other, which was why the girls were left orphans. Granted permission from the French government—indeed, Napoleon himself—to travel to Paris to study a Sanskrit manuscript kept at the Bibliothèque, they had been subsequently accused of treasonous activities. Before help could arrive, they were dead. Murdered! Victoria tried not to dwell on the manner of that death. Small wonder that she and her sisters did anything they might to fight the French.

She welcomed her arrival at Sir Edward's handsome establishment, for it forced her to think of the approaching afternoon and what she might learn. She would make certain the gentleman kept his distance.

After her footman's rap on the door, she was ushered inside. The footman carried her paraphernalia to the study, where she found a very nice stand placed in just about the precise location she would have wished it.

'Thank you, James. That will be all for now,' She waved a dismissal to the footman, then removed her pelisse, absently handing the lovely jade garment to the butler.

'Perhaps to the left a trifle.' She squinted at the window, her prime source of lighting, then placed the wax form on the stand, pleased with her decision. It was a pity she couldn't tell a soul that this rudimentary head had been intended for the very man she now prepared to sculpture. What a delicious joke to have to keep to herself. She chuckled while removing a tool from her case.

'You find this amusing, Miss Dancy?'

Startled out of her wits, Victoria clutched the fine tool used for modeling delicate features to her breast as she whirled about to face Sir Edward. How long had he been standing there observing her?

He held her jade pelisse in his hands, which meant that he had come into the room directly behind her. Victoria's cheeks flamed at the realization that she had treated him like his own servant.

Just then the butler entered, accepted the pelisse from Sir Edward, then nodded at the request for tea to be brought.

'I trust you become thirsty while in the creative mood?'

At the forgiving twinkle in his eyes, she relaxed sufficiently to add, 'Hungry, too.'

'My excellent housekeeper has anticipated this, I feel sure. Lemon wafers and ratafia biscuits, I believe she promised.'

Since lemon wafers were a favorite with Victoria, she smiled, then turned to business again. She simply could not allow herself to be enticed by the fascinating intensity of this man. Capable and strong, he also intimidated her, and she was too spirited to permit some man to rule her. It didn't seem to occur to her that the present description she had assigned to Sir Edward came remarkably close to matching her own requirements for a mate.

Sir Edward watched her efficiently go about the arrangements for her work with an intent gaze, missing not a thing she did. When she at last instructed him as to where he was to sit, he obliged quietly.

Victoria felt a quiver run through her as she touched his face to position it just so. Like so many, he tried to comply with her orders, but it took a touch of her hand to get the matter right. His skin felt warm and surprisingly smooth, firm. He was freshly shaved, and the scent of his lotion was pleasantly spicy. Not having her brother around for ages, she didn't know what the fragrance might be, but she suspected it was costly.

'Can you maintain that pose, Sir Edward? Or shall I find something for you to lean upon?'

'Proceed,' came his reply as the butler entered with the tray of tea and biscuits.

Hoping that her consumption of tea would not offend Sir Edward, Victoria poured a small amount, sipped, then began. In moments she was totally lost to the world. This was what she had longed to do. The transfer of his features, the clean line of his profile and that magnificent, aristocratic nose, to the fluidity of the wax had drawn her since she had met the man. Never had she been so fascinated with a profile. The hollows and planes, the faint crinkles about his eyes, everything about him enthralled her. The man behind the face was another enigma she desired to uncover. That, she knew full well, would take time, and might never be accomplished.

At the faintest droop of a shoulder, she stopped, checked her timepiece, and exclaimed in horror, 'Sir Edward, I do apologize! I did not intend to weary you to this degree, believe me.'

Sable looked up at the sound of her voice from where he had curled up at Sir Edward's feet. Victoria gave the traitorous dog a frown. 'I had best leave now. You deserve a rest after that long a sitting. But then, if you remain home this evening, you can relish your repose.'

'Are you probing into my activities, Miss Dancy?' he inquired in dulcet tones. 'I assure you that I intend to make my usual rounds of an evening.' He flexed his muscles while she covered the bust with a dampened cloth.

'I shall return on the morrow if it pleases you.'

Sir Edward nodded. 'I shall be ready for you.'

Victoria was very much aware of his brooding gaze as she fled the room with Sable reluctantly at her heels.

*　　　*　　　*

Once home, and still shaken by the intensity in Sir Edward's voice before she had left his home, Victoria found Julia waiting for her.

'I have some news for you, Vicky. Mr Padbury said that, while he often goes to other places, Sir Edward can most frequently be found at the Golden Bird. Is that what you wished to know?'

Victoria undid the last of the fastenings of her pelisse, then paused as the import of the words sank in. 'Indeed,' she breathed. 'That is precisely what I wished to know. Thank you, Julia.' She absently strolled up to her room, intent upon the plans forming in her mind.

At the foot of the stairs Julia stared after

her, and hoped her little sister was not getting
into trouble.

*   *   *

Sir Edward glanced about the Golden Bird,
noting with care who was here this evening,
who was absent. He drifted from group to
group, pausing to chat now and again,
always moving on, ever circulating, always
listening.

He felt unusually restless this evening. Oh,
his knee did not particularly ache, nor had he
observed any gaming irregularities among the
patrons. Not one of the *ton* who frequented
this place guessed he had a proprietary
interest in the gaming establishment. His part-
ownership was more to permit him to rove at
will whenever he pleased, rather than for the
monetary gain, though to be sure, that had
proved to be more than adequate.

It was Victoria Dancy. She lingered in his
mind, as she had since he had first caught
sight of her. When she had taken his chin in
her slender, capable hand to position his head,
he had been tempted to move just so she
would be forced to touch him again. Her gown
had rustled softly about her form, and she'd
smelled like lilacs in the spring, fresh and
sweet. How did that poem go? The one by
Marlowe?

Come live with me, and be my love,
And we will all the pleasures prove

Why that came to mind, he didn't know.
Yes, he did. He hated to admit it, but he
wanted to prove all the pleasures of the world
with Victoria Dancy. He wanted to take her in
his arms and make love to her until they were
both utterly exhausted. And then repeat it.
Annoying, but there it was. Would he ever get
her out of his mind? He very much doubted
he would have the opportunity to do as he
pleased. His esteemed butler had hovered
near the open door to the library like a
confounded Spanish duenna. That blasted dog
draped itself across his feet, effectively
reminding Edward what was his due to a lady.
And Victoria Dancy was no doxy. She was not
the kind of woman a man could trifle with in
the least, more's the pity.

The gaming room was not brightly lit, no
distracting pictures hung on the wall. Over
each table hung a shaded Argand lamp that lit
up the table below, nothing else. The faces of
the players remained shadowy, obscure, just
the way they preferred. There were still a few
old beaux who wore the floppy straw hats
decorated with flowers that effectively
concealed expressions. The younger men
relied on a passive countenance, rigid control.
There was a stir near the door and he turned
to discover the cause.

A woman entered the main room. Her black silk cloak whispered as she moved toward him, her half-mask concealing most of her face from view. He wondered if he had conjured her into being. It was the redoubtable Miss Dancy . . . in the flesh. He'd know her anywhere, even with a mask. She glanced about the large room, and he wondered what she thought of the place. What had she expected when she came incognito? He ought to be shocked at her presence, but somehow wasn't. Miss Dancy seemed to dare anything.

'It is an honor to see you so soon, my dear,' he said in a soft voice.

'You recognize me?' she replied faintly, the alarm clear in her voice. Quite obviously Miss Dancy had not expected to be recognized so quickly. What had she hoped to do? Perhaps watch the play, or did she have something more sinister in mind? He'd take care of that.

Edward glanced about them, taking note of the gamesters, who concentrated on their game. As far as he knew, no one had paid the least attention to the woman in black. Her shadowed figure had not proved of interest to those intent upon winning money.

'Come, let us find a more private place, so we can . . . talk.' He wondered for one wild moment if his desires were by some chance to be granted. Then, quickly ushering Miss Dancy into a small room removed from the

160

eyes of the others, he knew he could not take advantage of her. Not unless she permitted. That last thought proved interesting, and he savored the notion for a bit.

She covered her nervousness by whipping off her taffeta cloak, draping it across the chair closest to the door. Removing her no-longer-needed mask, she toyed with it as she turned to face Sir Edward. 'What a pity you recognized me so soon.'

Edward stared at the woman before him, feeling as though he had been punched in the stomach. Hard. Victoria wore a gown that defied belief. Made of a nearly transparent fabric that he knew to be called aerophane crepe, it was a rich cream, so delicate that it appeared to blend with her skin. It was almost as though she wore nothing at all. He supposed she had a petticoat of fine silk underneath, for naturally the gown was not really transparent. But the illusion was there. He swallowed with difficulty and wondered how he was to survive this meeting in one piece. He was no green youth, but then, Victoria Dancy was no ordinary woman either.

Victoria returned his gaze. 'Is something wrong, Sir Edward?' she inquired sweetly.

'You ought not to be here, and you know it.' He held her eyes with his, feeling a blazing warmth stealing over him.

'Could we play a game of cards?' she inquired at length, her words falling into the silence of the room with startling clarity.

She had shrugged as she spoke. Edward wondered if the dainty straps that held up her bodice would tolerate such motion. Intrigued by her possible motive in coming to the gaming hell, he nodded, then removed a fresh deck of cards from a drawer in the table.

He dealt after she cut the cards, and the game proceeded silently. She was good, he reflected as she made an excellent play. Had her absent brother taught her? Or had one of the men who hovered at her shoulder been permitted that privilege? He firmed his mouth in a grim smile, then played his next card.

It took more concentration than he knew he had to *not* watch the dipping neckline of her gown. Perhaps that was why she wore it? She intended to fleece him through distraction. It might just work, he thought as he observed the bodice slip lower when she leaned forward to discard. Just another inch and he would see the blue-iris locket. The delicate gold chain slipped inside her bodice, leading the eye, tantalizing the imagination.

'Why are you here?' he demanded quietly.

'Curious.'

'About what? Gaming hells?'

'Is that what this is? I thought they were wretched places. This one seems fairly respectable.'

'It is. However, it is not Brooks's or White's. I repeat, why did you come here

162

tonight?'

'It seemed like a good idea when I first thought of it,' she confessed, but not to his enlightenment.

'Now, that's a taradiddle if ever I heard one.'

'Well, you might have accepted it.'

'But for your gown, perhaps.'

'What has this gown to do with anything? I chose it because I felt it to be unobtrusive. A plain color that no one would remember.'

Sir Edward raised his gaze to the ceiling, wondering how anyone had let this child out of the house without a keeper.

'Did you check yourself in your looking glass before you left the house?' he inquired in what he hoped to be a mild tone.

She shrugged again, and Sir Edward thought he just might lose what sanity he had remaining. Tossing his cards on the table, he abruptly rose and walked around to confront her. 'Get up.'

Clearly puzzled, she obeyed, standing to face him with an inquisitive defiance. 'Well?'

'Miss Dancy, whoever designed that gown did not have a simple, unobtrusive impression in mind. Not in the least. Would you like to know the effect it gives?' he inquired politely.

'Indeed.' She trembled, yet did not yield an inch at his searching gaze. He'd wager she was frightened right down to the soles of her satin slippers.

163

He slowly reached out to grasp her shoulders, drawing her to him with an exquisitely unhurried movement. She ought to *look* afraid, yet she remained motionless, controlling her fears admirably.

And then Victoria Dancy found herself kissed with a thoroughness Edward suspected she'd not known before. His hands played over her back with a delicate caress, so light it was but a burning whisper on her satin skin. He felt her resist, then slowly yield to his practiced enticement. The delicate silk slid beneath his fingers as he pleasured himself.

She melted against him, seeming to surrender.

Edward deepened the kiss, a shudder racking his frame as he fought for control even as he enfolded her more tightly in his arms. He had wanted this, her, since he tended her that night at the windmill.

Then she tore herself from his arms, backing away a few steps. Her superb bosom heaving, she merely stared at him for a moment, speechless. Her mouth was a bruised pink bud, her cheeks wildly flushed. Those eyes flashed with a blue flame. One of the straps of her gown slipped down her left shoulder and she ignored it. 'That was most unfair, Sir Edward,' she said in a breathy wisp of a voice.

Edward met her gaze evenly, glad he had dared to take this chance, yet in agony that she had stopped him. Hands clenched at his sides, he bowed his head in acknowledgment for her denunciation. 'I did warn you that your gown was not meant for you to be ignored.' He paused, flicking a warm look over her. 'May I suggest that you find your nanny and go home, young lady? When you are able and willing to play a woman's game, wear that gown again, and we shall resume this enchanting interlude.' He hoped his words would sting, alert her to the danger of treading where she ought not.

Victoria closed her eyes a moment, as though to gather her strength, then flashed him a look of anger. 'When I see you on the morrow we shall forget this happened, sirrah.' Head high, she swept her taffeta cloak about her, replaced her mask, then stalked from the room in silent fury, closing the door behind her with a vehement snap.

Edward watched her depart, rubbing his chin with an absent gesture, willing his desire to subside. He had seen that blue-iris locket again, and it intrigued him more than ever. Why had she appeared here tonight? Could the elegantly beautiful Miss Dancy be spying upon *him*?

'I was never so humiliated in my entire life,' Victoria declared the following morning. She paced back and forth before the fireplace in the morning room while Julia and Elizabeth watched with round, horrified eyes.

'You were foolish beyond permission even to contemplate such action, Vicky,' Julia chided her gently.

'That is a useless reflection at this point in time,' Victoria countered. She contemplated the rug at her feet, where Sable had curled up, yet kept a close watch on his mistress.

'Positively rag-mannered behavior,' Elizabeth added with a lofty pose. 'And I thought *I* was the totty-headed one in the family. Time out of mind I have been lectured. I must say, it is a comfort to know you can be foolish as well. At least no one there knew who you were,' she finished, with the air of the very righteous, for once not being censured herself.

'Do you suspect that Mr Padbury believes I went to the Golden Bird? What, exactly, did he say?' Victoria paused in her perambulations to stare at Julia.

'Merely replied to an oblique question I posed about the haunts of London gentlemen. I asked where one might go if he did not attend to White's or Brooks's. Then I queried about someone like Sir Edward, for example. If Lucius thought anything about it, he may have felt we were curious about the gentleman because of your being at his home.'

'I do hope so,' Victoria replied slowly.

'Well, do not put yourself into a stew over it,' Elizabeth advised airily. 'I daresay that Sir Edward will have forgotten all about it by this afternoon.'

Victoria and Julia exchanged glances, then both looked at their younger sister with dismay in their eyes.

'Dearest,' Julia explained calmly, 'I somehow doubt if Sir Edward has that short a memory, nor do I believe he will forget the scene so easily. That really is a wicked gown that Vicky wore. We can but hope that he is a true gentleman about the entire thing, and allows her to complete his head with no further difficulties.' Julia looked at Victoria, wondering just how far that little scene had progressed. Victoria had been a bit evasive when it came to the actual confrontation. He had kissed her, but Julia knew full well that there were kisses and there were . . . kisses.

'Well,' Elizabeth declared, 'you ought to have had more sense than to do anything so addlepated. If I were you, I should put that gown to the back of my closet or . . . you might give it to me?' she concluded with a lopsided grin.

'Have you windmills in your head, Lizzie? Unless you are trying to seduce Lord Leighton,' Victoria said with faint irritation.

At that Elizabeth jumped to her feet. 'Never. The man merely teases me to death.'

'I thought him to be very well-mannered the other evening,' Julia said with a frown. 'I do hope you have not misjudged him, love.'

'I very much doubt that,' Elizabeth replied crisply. 'He is a flirt and a rake, never forget.' Then she turned to Victoria, hands folded and quite businesslike. 'I believe you are to bring several of your works to that display of women artists that is to be held this coming week. Was it this morning?'

'Heavens, yes!' Victoria started, then began to move to the door. 'The affair with Sir Edward quite drove it from my mind. It is to be madly wonderful, is it not? Paintings by Angelica Kauffmann and that fabulous Marie-Louise Vigée-Lebrun will be displayed. Now, *that* is something to consider, becoming as wealthy as Vigée-Lebrun. I hear she has amassed a fortune.'

'I cannot quite approve of her, leaving her husband and jauntering all over the Continent to paint portraits, dragging her daughter with her. I understand the paintings in the exhibit come from Russia. Fancy working in Russia.'

'Julia,' replied Victoria as the three women hurried down the hall to their workroom, 'I feel certain the country cannot be quite as

168

barbaric as you think. That is, if there is much left of it after the war. It will take years to rebuild Moscow, I am sure.' They entered the workroom in a flurry, pleased to see the twins waiting for them.

Rosemary and Tansy had been brought down to Julia to play on the floor while she painted. The girls settled down with a few dolls and wooden toys, chattering in their incomprehensible way to one another.

'I do hope I can understand them, eventually,' Julia murmured to Victoria, mixing a lovely shade of brown with more-than-necessary vigor.

'I am certain you will in time, love,' Victoria answered in a soothing way. But she was absorbed in selecting her sculptures for the exhibit, placing each in one of the special boxes brought up for this event. 'Do you know, they are even going to include several sculptures by that former American, Patience Lovell Wright?' Victoria gave Julia a meaningful look, adding, 'I believe she was a spy, was she not?'

'Interesting,' Julia commented while applying a light touch of the brown paint to the hair in the small portrait she worked on. Several of her miniatures were already boxed and awaited transport to the exhibit. Each sister had been asked to join the select group of women artists.

Across the room, Elizabeth frowned at the

stack of engravings on her table. 'The man who stopped by to select my entries picked these, and I cannot fathom why. Oh, well, it seems to make little difference. They are all of a muchness, anyway.' She placed tissue between each matted picture, then inserted the lot into a portfolio.

'Shall we go?' Elizabeth said to Victoria.

'By all means. Activity is much to be preferred to dwelling on last evening.' Victoria paused to smile at Julia. 'We shall give you a full report later. I shan't forget that I am to be at Sir Edward's this afternoon. Although,' she added as she drifted through the doorway, 'I cannot but wonder how I shall go on.'

A footman was dispatched to fetch the various boxes and parcels while the two girls hurried to their rooms to don pelisses, hats, and gloves.

Elizabeth wore her favorite aquamarine, while Victoria selected a lovely shade of rose. They met in the entry to inspect the packages due to accompany them on their brief errand. Then they entered the carriage and were off to the exhibit hall.

Later, on their way back home, Victoria compressed her lips, while Elizabeth expressed her indignation at what they had encountered. 'I could quite easily fall into a green melancholy at the very thought of those men. Imagine saying your work was too good for the exhibit. I am glad you insisted upon leaving it there. That one fellow had the nerve to tell you that a man ought to put his name to your sculpture, it wasn't fitting for a mere woman to know so much about a male!'

'When I pointed out to that benighted gentleman that Angelica Kauffmann or Vigée-Lebrun might take exception to such actions, he shut his mouth. He didn't even know that Angelica died in 1807.' Victoria sighed with disdain.

'It passes the bounds of all belief! Such effrontery,' Elizabeth snapped as they left the carriage to enter the house. 'Just wait until our dearest Julia hears what was said about her miniatures.'

'Lizzie,' Victoria said in an overly casual manner, 'did you notice that she called Mr Padbury "Lucius" this morning? I wonder if that means she has serious intentions regarding him. One simply does not refer to a gentleman by his first name.'

'Well, I should never call Lord Leighton "David," if that is what you mean,' Elizabeth replied thoughtfully.

'Nor would I omit the "Sir" with regards to Sir Edward Hawkswood. How singularly appropriate his name is,' Victoria added softly.

'I could never wish that Julia marry Mr Padbury, even if it might be good for Rosemary and Tansy to have a father and a home of their own. We are happy here and make a nice family without a man in residence.' Elizabeth paused at the bottom of the stairs to give her sister a deeply concerned look. 'He is pleasant enough, but I should not like him for Julia.'

'But,' Victoria reminded her, worry reflected in her voice, 'things may not remain the way they are now. If Julia feels forced to accept Mr Padbury's suit, I shan't forgive myself. I believe I am the one who mentioned the possibility that Geoffrey would marry.'

'We can find a dear little house of our own somewhere in the country. The girls can grow plump on clotted cream, and eggs, and fresh air, and we can do just as we please,' Elizabeth decided with a happy bounce.

'Without commissions?'

'Must we work? I thought we were sufficiently well-off so that it was not a necessity.' Elizabeth paused in her upward climb to stare at Victoria.

'Once Geoffrey weds, he will have his own household to tend. We shall have the portions Father set up for us, but with the rising cost of everything, it could be nip and tuck. Perhaps you could marry?' Victoria guided her sister on up the stairs, glancing at her obliquely at this suggestion. 'The gentlemen cluster about you wherever we go.'

'Why me?' Elizabeth demanded rather inelegantly. 'You are the most fetching of the three of us and you know it. I should think that all you have to do is snap your fingers and a dozen men would fall at your feet.'

Victoria chuckled, shaking her head. 'What utter rubbish, my love. Come, we had best change. But consider it, please. Try to find someone you could care for.'

Leaving Elizabeth frowning fiercely, Victoria entered her room. It was all well and good to tell her younger sister to find a man with whom she might be content, but when Elizabeth had suggested that Victoria marry, something deep inside her had rebelled. Marry? Be tied to another for the rest of her life?

'Who could fit that consideration?' she murmured to her looking glass, which had the discretion not to reply. It certainly would *not* be Sir Edward Hawkswood! The man was utterly heartless and as rude as could stare. Yet, as she had pointed out to Elizabeth, single women had a dreadful inclination to poverty. For it was men who controlled the wealth of the nation, not to mention families. Which brought her back to the matter of their brother and his necessarily approaching marriage.

Elizabeth was correct. The three women would have to leave, find a neat home off in a village such as Knightsbridge or some such place. They should be close enough to occasionally come to London, yet able to live more cheaply. One did what one must.

Victoria was spoiled with their life in London; pretty gowns, nice parties, handsome, agreeable company . . . for the most part. Why, oh, why did her mind continually return to Sir Edward? He was the very worst sort of ghost, one you couldn't shoo away.

She changed into the prim lilac gown she intended to wear this afternoon, then gathered her lilac pelisse, gloves, and a most demure bonnet—she had to try to dispel the image he must surely retain after last night—and went downstairs.

The noon meal was light, Julia prying details of the morning's expedition from her sisters. She was not terribly surprised at their discovery.

'You know the attitude that gentlemen hold regarding women. They see us as being weaker, and somewhat helpless. Never mind that we run our households, bear the children, and in general cope with the difficulties of life, smoothing their days and pampering them dreadfully. I firmly believe that men are spoiled rotten.'

'How fascinating,' Elizabeth exclaimed. 'I daresay if I must pick a husband, I had best find out what he believes.'

Victoria cast a relieved glance at her younger sister. At least the girl was considering marriage. There were a number of pleasant young men of quite respectable birth and fortune who would pick up any handkerchief she chose to drop—if only she could make up her mind to do so. Why Lizzie had to take such an aversion to Lord Leighton, Victoria couldn't guess. Lizzie had mentioned stolen kisses, but gracious, at least that proved the man was interested. And what was a bit of teasing?

'Take care, dear,' Julia admonished while Tansy tugged at her skirts. 'Sable does guard you?' She had joined Victoria, watching anxiously as her younger sister prepared to leave.

Victoria, quite unable to disabuse her sister of the illusion, merely nodded, urging the large poodle into the carriage, then checked to see that she had her case in there as well before they left.

'Now, see here, Sable,' Victoria solemnly lectured him when the carriage moved away, 'there will be none of this adoration of the man. Do you hear me? Today I want you to sit at my side and look positively ferocious.'

The poodle simply gave his mistress a knowing look, then turned to eye the passing scene from the window.

'Wretch,' Victoria muttered.

At Sir Edward's she found herself ushered into the library, where a small fire burned in the grate to remove the chill from the spring air. Her unfinished sculpture sat precisely where it had the day before.

'Your tea, miss. Sir Edward begs your forgiveness. He is detained, but shall be with you directly.' The butler placed a rather nice tea tray on a small table, then retreated to the door.

'Quite all right,' Victoria replied graciously. 'I shan't need you in that case.'

The butler nodded with understanding, and marched off down the hall to the rear of the house.

Here was her chance. Pausing to listen, she heard only the faint sounds of traffic outside the house, and the normal noise one hears within a domicile. Drawing off her gloves, she then removed her bonnet, placing all of them near the edge of the desk. It gave her an excuse for being in that location should anyone appear suddenly.

She skimmed around the desk to look over the papers rather than attempt the secretary. A hunch told her he would have moved the cipher. The neatly stacked papers atop the desk were intriguing stuff, having to do with some enterprise Sir Edward appeared to share with others. She caught sight of the words 'Golden Bird' and nodded. That was it, he must be a partner in the place. It was all of a piece, that ease he possessed while there, the fact that no one had questioned his expropriating the private card room.

Quickly dismissing those papers, she

checked the drawers that yielded to her tug. She caught her breath as the contents of one revealed the paper she sought. The cipher copy *had* been transferred to this desk, and notations indicated he had worked at breaking it. However, it appeared he had not found the solution.

She hastily shut the drawer, then scanned the desk to make certain all was as it had been when she arrived. She dashed to the tea table, poured out a cup of still-warm brew, and took a deep swallow. She nibbled a lemon wafer while contemplating what this meant. There were any number of answers to her question. He might be affiliated with the war office. Yet she had never seen him there on her occasional visits. He seemed too much the dilettante, hardly a professional in the field. Curiosity was not enough in this job. The document had not been passed along, which meant he worked at it under direction. But for whom did he work? And why?

Her tea grew cold, and she took the liberty of dumping the contents on a potted fern that struggled for life in a corner of the room not far from the window.

'How kind of you to remember that plant. I fear it gets quite neglected. My mother fondly believes that if she keeps it there I shall become homesick and visit her in the country.'

Victoria felt the blush creep over her face, down her neck, and goodness knew where else. 'I am dreadfully sorry. The tea grew cold, you see.'

'Don't apologize. I wouldn't.' He took her teacup and poured her another, then tested it, holding the cup to his lips to see how warm the liquid might be.

She watched the cup that she had held to her mouth now touch his lips and quivered at the image it provoked. Last night, with all the tumult of emotions that had battled inside her, returned full force.

'Unorthodox method, but efficient.' He handed her the cup of tea. 'And I believe we are quite past all the customary formalities, are we not, Victoria?'

His voice mocked her gently and she longed to tweak his beak of a nose. Forced to accept the cup, she defiantly drank deeply of her tea. If he thought he was going to put her out of countenance, he was mistaken.

'You look lovely today. *Most* proper.' He bowed faintly, that sensuous mouth curving into a half-smile as he stared deeply into her eyes.

Victoria felt secure, swathed from the double frill at her neck to the flounce at the hem of the most delicate yet unrevealing gown imaginable. The scent of lilacs, which was most appropriate for the pretty lilac ensemble she wore, surrounded her. She hoped the message she sought to convey did not fail to reach him.

178

'Shall I begin work, Sir Edward?' she said in a frosty, impersonal tone.

He nodded, seating himself as yesterday, then waited.

'Gracious,' she murmured, 'you are not even close.'

Stretching out a slender hand, she moved his face, tilting it slightly to achieve the pose she wanted. Her hand hesitated before touching his chin. Memories of last evening lingered too vividly yet for her to feel at ease so close to him. Again his skin felt warm to her touch, and she found it difficult to release it. Then she returned to her stand, completely ignoring Sable. The dog had once again assumed a position at Sir Edward's feet, draping itself across the man's boots. It would be ruinous to the shine. Victoria smiled, a devious little grin.

After slipping an enveloping apron over her gown, she tried to concentrate on her task. She must think of line and form, texture, not necessarily the man inside the body. You couldn't totally divorce the two, however, or one would fail to capture the essence of spirit imperative to achieve a true likeness. He moved.

'You are drooping like a new-planted periwinkle, Sir Edward,' she admonished. Returning to his side, she swiftly positioned his head, taking note of the little gleam that quickly vanished when he appeared to see her look at his eyes. 'Perhaps I could shift around?' she suggested. 'I need to get a different perspective of you anyway.'

Turning her back on her patron, she dragged the stand to the left, closer to the desk and farther from the door, and quite out of his line of vision. 'Just keep your eyes fixed on the same point. I am still here, even if you can't see me.' She chuckled softly, pleased to be free of that penetrating gaze. There were moments when she felt certain that he could read her mind, and that was most disconcerting for a young woman. Especially one who entertained such scandalous thoughts at times.

Things were proceeding well. He had said nothing of last night, unless you considered his comment about her appearance to be an oblique reference to that rather shocking creation she'd worn then. Why had she not noticed how daring it was? She had seen nothing improper in the neckline when she had checked herself before her looking glass. Perhaps it happened when she moved. Or bent over. She frowned at that thought. While most would not bat an eyelash at her unusual locket with the lapis-lazuli iris, a spy might know the significance of it and wonder.

Her sigh was monumental at the very idea. She always wore the necklace. Although it was for her protection should she be uncovered as an agent, it had the secret purpose of reminding her why she had chosen this life. The miniatures of her parents served as inspiration when she was tempted to cease her spy activity.

There were men who gave their lives for their country, and seemed to do so willingly. She would sacrifice her interest in the one man who intrigued her, for she would not marry one who could betray his country. If Julia accepted Mr Padbury, Victoria would see to it that Elizabeth made a good marriage. Then Victoria could retire to the country, perhaps in the Cotswolds, far from civilization.

'That sigh sounded extremely woeful, Victoria.'

His voice startled her, and she dropped the tiny tool she held in her hand. It clattered to the floor, sounding like a shot in the quiet of the room.

'Sorry, sir.' She stopped to pick up the tool, promptly returning to her work.

'May I inquire what brought it on?'

There was no reason why he couldn't speak. She had managed before when her subject became tired of sitting in silence.

'What a pity we cannot have a musician here to play for you. Music is so soothing. Do you not think so?'

'So you will not discuss what is bothering you?'

Before she paused to realize that she was

confiding in the dratted man, Victoria popped back, 'I worry about my sister.'

'Mr Padbury?'

She gasped. 'Did he say something to you about offering for Julia's hand?'

'No,' Edward admitted, 'but it seemed a likely course. What about Miss Elizabeth? I doubt Leighton is serious, but perhaps there is someone else?'

Relieved to have someone with whom to discuss what concerned her, Victoria said, 'She has taken Lord Leighton in the oddest dislike. I vow that I cannot for the life of me see why. But perhaps it is good she does not sigh over him. As to another, there are several who trail after her.'

'Perhaps she is afraid of marriage. There are women who fear intimacy.' His voice was impersonal, no coloring of his thoughts revealed.

'Sir Edward, I suspect you ought not say such things to me,' Victoria admonished. 'I doubt that of Elizabeth, at any rate,' Victoria declared. 'We shall see. She has promised me to consider marriage, however.'

'Do you mean you worry about the future of your sisters? They call you the Three Graces. Surely such accredited beauties need merely select the husbands they wish from the throng at their feet?'

'You sound like Elizabeth,' she muttered, while squinting at him to check her

182

perspective.

'Does Miss Elizabeth think you ought to marry as well?' Concentrating on the precise curve of his cheek, Victoria absently replied, 'No. For it would be pointless.'

'Then you do not intend to marry?' His words were smooth, soft, and evenly said.

'Umm,' she murmured, quite satisfied that she had achieved his straight nose and the faintly arrogant jut of his chin.

'I believe that was a negative reply you gave me. What a pity.'

'Pity?' Her attention captured, Victoria glanced up, startled, to find he was looking at her with amused eyes.

'I am aware you do not wish to talk about last evening, but I feel it incumbent upon me to apologize for my actions. Not that I didn't enjoy the kiss. I believe we both did, even if Colosseum lions couldn't drag that snippet from you.'

'Indeed,' she murmured repressively, dropping her gaze down to the bust on the stand.

'Indeed,' he agreed, much to her annoyance. 'Do you mean to tell me that you have some maggoty notion that you will not marry?'

'No.'

'Well, I am relieved to hear that.' He crossed his arms before him, looking—when she chanced a peek—like the lord of the world.

Victoria wiped her hands on a cloth, then went over to reposition his head. 'What I meant was, I am not going to satisfy your curiosity about what I intend to do with my life.'

'I shall find out, nonetheless. I intend to know all about you, Victoria. You have quite piqued my curiosity. And if I do say so, I am rather good at solving mysteries.'

Victoria returned to bend her head over her work, praying she might leave the house without revealing anything else. The man was skilled at persuasion. He could probably convince a clam to talk. If she applied herself with great dedication, she might finish the sculpture in record time. And that, she fervently decided, was absolutely necessary.

*   *   *

When Victoria at last escaped from Sir Edward's tantalizing and oddly frustrating company, she returned to her home in an unsettled mood. She strolled down the hall to the workroom, where she found Julia in what could only be described as a case of the dismals.

'Something has happened. What?' Victoria quietly demanded. Had Padbury offered for Julia and that widgeon accepted, thinking it the best, when her heart was not engaged?

184

Victoria prayed that was not the explanation.

'Mr Padbury was here,' Julia replied, gesturing to the now-vacant chair. 'He drizzled, picking apart a perfectly lovely piece of gold fabric. It seems a shame that because 'tis all the rage, those magnificent fabrics must be lost forever.'

'And?' Victoria prompted, sensing there was more to come.

'He commented on the girls, said it was a pity I had not produced a boy, so as to remain Lady Winton and in control of the future heir to the Winton fortune. He pressed to know why I refuse to use my rightful style of "Lady Winton." I told him.'

'They treated you shabbily, dearest. I cannot blame you for not liking the connection.'

'He also reminded me that when Geoffrey marries I shall need a home.' Julia pleated her skirt with nervous hands.

'You shall never lack such, and you must know that,' Victoria inserted, anxious to smooth the frown from her sister's brow.

'He asked if I had given thought to another marriage.' Julia raised her lovely eyes to meet Victoria's gaze. 'I have, you know. For I am often lonely and miss the love I knew. Mr Padbury had also been thinking of marriage.'

Victoria watched as Julia jumped up from her chair and began to restlessly pace about the room, fingering the various tools, turning

185

to gaze at her twins where they played not far from the fire.

'I suppose he offered for me, but it was a most peculiar proposal. He announced that the girls would be given over to a nanny, then sent off to school. He doesn't hold with their being underfoot, you see,' she concluded with a bitter twist of her mouth.

'Horrid man,' Victoria said in disgust.

'I would have to cease my painting, for it is not fitting, you see. And he intended to move in with us for the time being. He claimed his house too small.'

'Never say so. And you replied?'

'I most primly declared we should not suit.'

'I must say you showed your usual good sense. What did he do?' Victoria asked, curious about the genial gentleman's reaction to rejection.

'He snatched up his drizzling box and fabric, then marched to the door, declaring me to be a shameless flirt. I had thought I might do it, you see. But when he said he would take the twins from me, I knew I could not. If I accept a man, he must take me complete with the girls.'

'There will be someone, love,' Victoria said softly.

'And pigs might fly,' Julia retorted. Yet there lurked a hopeful gleam in her eyes that Victoria did not miss.

10

'I do believe I shall go out of my mind if I cannot solve this cipher soon,' Victoria declared. She ran her fingers through her disordered hair in total frustration. The end of her pen looked worse for wear where she had nibbled on it; blots of ink dotted the paper she used for scribbling possible solutions. The untidy mess littered her desk, her sculpture of the fascinating Sir Edward set aside for the moment.

However, Victoria spared the man a consideration. Why had she not informed her superiors of his possession of the cipher? It was most unlike her. She ought to have dashed to the war office with her knowledge. Yet she had seen that incriminating bit of paper once, then a second time, with notations that indicated he found it as hard to break as she did. Yet she knew she could not turn him in, even trained as she was in espionage. Could it be that she hoped he would prove to be other than she suspected. He had most likely saved her life with his care while in the windmill. She owed him something, did she not?

Across from her Elizabeth sat working with concentrated effort on a sheet of engravings, giving them their final touch of color. To one side the copper plates from which she had printed the sheet of bills lay neatly stacked, for once. A smudge of ink daubed her cheek, and a frown marred her lovely forehead while she carefully executed fine details with the help of a magnifying glass.

Only Julia sat quietly, her hands idle, even though she had a small painting half-finished in front of her on her slanted table. The morning sun highlighted the still figure, giving her the look of a painted statue.

When Victoria glanced up, she observed this uncharacteristic behavior. 'What is it, Julia? You are unusually silent this morning. Come to think on it, you have said remarkably little since our visit after I came home from Sir Edward's house yesterday. Does the scene with Mr Padbury still bother you?' she added with a shrewd guess.

'Actually, yes.' When Elizabeth looked up in startled alarm, Julia went on to say, 'He asked for my hand, but as sorely as I am tempted to secure a future for the twins, I simply could not accept the man. Assure me that what I did was right.' Delicate violet shadows emphasized Julia's lovely eyes and gave indication of her lost sleep.

Victoria exchanged a look with Elizabeth, then nodded her head. 'Of course you did. The man is an insufferable snob, wanting you to resume your style of "Lady Winton," then insisting the four of you would live here with us. As though residing in the house of a baron would elevate his status.'

Julia peered first at one sister, then the other. 'Mr Padbury did not actually propose, you know, he rather informed me that if I had been thinking about marriage again, so had he.'

Victoria gave a disgusted sniff. 'I cannot countenance that he wanted to remove the twins from your care. How utterly heartless of the man.'

Elizabeth cried, 'But that is infamous! Send those precious darlings away from you?'

Julia gave her sisters a wan smile. 'I wonder if he paused to consider that when I marry, I should not have the right to style myself as 'Lady Padbury.' He had best search out the daughter of an earl, if all he desires is a secondhand title.'

'Horrid man,' Victoria declared with vehemence.

'It is well I did not accept his odd proposal, then, for he declared that the four of us would have to live here until such time as he could find a larger house to suit him and hold us all, and who knows how long that might take? I fail to see why his present abode would prove too small.'

'Unless,' Elizabeth said, with her eyes narrowed and thoughtful, 'he actually is under the hatches and no one has heard about it. You know how these sorts of things may be hidden and buried.'

'He did drizzle all the time,' Victoria

reminded her sisters. 'I always thought that only those who needed the small sums of money they made drizzled—especially as much as he does.'

'Indeed,' Julia murmured in agreement. 'He sat and drizzled all the time he discussed our proposed coming arrangement.'

'No!' Victoria and Elizabeth exclaimed in unison, Elizabeth falling into a fit of giggles at the image provoked by Julia's words.

'That is the outside of enough,' Victoria declared. 'And I had thought him such a genial man, so proper in his feelings.'

Turning to Elizabeth, Julia said, 'I hope this prosaic proposal I received does not put you off the thought of marriage. Not all men are like Mr Padbury.'

Victoria nodded. 'That is true. Julia is far better off with Mr Padbury out of the picture. One never knows when the right man will present himself That goes for you as well, Elizabeth.'

'That remains to be seen,' Elizabeth muttered. Her face clearly reflected her skepticism regarding the likelihood of this event.

'Yet I wonder if I did the right thing. I confess there are few gentlemen I find appealing. If Geoffrey comes home with a wife who will not tolerate us, will the girls and I be any better off?'

'We shall be together, never fear,' Victoria

assured Julia. 'I have no plans to wed, although Elizabeth has promised me that she intends to at least look for a husband.' Victoria fixed a minatory eye on her younger sister, defying her to deny her agreement.

'I trust you do not remain single to help me,' Julia scolded. But the sisters knew that Victoria had become more reserved this past year, and while she lightly flirted, she encouraged no man to get close to her. But then, as she was so often away from Society, it might be that she simply had not met the right man. Julia exchanged a hopeful look with Elizabeth and they both smiled.

'I await my prince,' Victoria stated dramatically, then chuckled at the face Elizabeth made. 'No one could ever suffer any pretensions in this house for long.'

'Then it is well that Mr Padbury will look elsewhere for a wife,' Julia commented before picking up her brush. Do you know, there were times when I believe we became a trifle too complacent when he was about. I should hate to think I look for a spy everywhere, but I confess that I now wonder about him. He seemed to listen so intently to all that was said while he sat with us. Is it possible we inadvertently revealed something we ought not have said?'

'Oh, pooh,' Elizabeth scoffed. 'That little man? Do you know that had you married him, you would have been taller than your husband? I cannot think *him* a spy. Yet I know we must be careful. I should suspect a new footman, more likely.'

'Except we do not have one about.' Victoria sighed, resuming her frustrating work on the cipher.

'Well, I have completed the last of these banknotes. We shan't have to spend good English pounds and thus finance the French, when our spies can use these instead.' She blew on the paper to dry the last of the special paint she used for this task, then turned to face Victoria. 'You do not fear whoever it was that sent the dead iris to you? There has been nothing more in the few days since then?'

Nibbling at the end of her pen, Victoria shook her pretty head. 'I try not to dwell on the matter. We can but take our usual precautions. Do you send for a messenger to pick up those banknotes?'

'I shall be very daring and deliver them myself. You see,' she added with a twinkle in her eyes, 'there is the most handsome gentleman I meet when I go to the war office. He admires what I do, and that is rather nice.'

Victoria repressed a grin, then scolded, 'See that you are careful.'

'Oh, pooh, what can happen to me in the middle of the day in the heart of London?' Elizabeth first placed the copper plates in a cupboard, then gathered her stack of beautifully colored notes, ready to be cut and 'weathered.' She slowly walked to the door. 'Nevertheless, I will do as you say. Sam will drive me in our old carriage, and I shall not attract attention when dressed simply. Should I wear a veil, do you think?'

Julia chuckled at this bit of nonsense. 'Now, that would cause people to stare. You might as well wear Victoria's half-mask. There is nothing so intriguing as seeing someone who doesn't wish to be seen, if you follow my meaning.'

Elizabeth agreed and left the room.

Victoria and Julia sat in resumed silence, broken only from time to time by baffled sighs from Victoria.

*   *   *

It was shortly before Victoria was to leave for Sir Edward's home that Elizabeth returned from her errand. She looked furious, her pelisse was badly soiled, and that lovely bonnet with the cherries on the brim looked a trifle the worse for wear. She paused on the threshold, looking from one sister to the other.

'Whatever happened, love?' Victoria inquired with concern. She'd had reservations about permitting Elizabeth to dash off to the war office on her own, and this proved that the trip could be hazardous.

'You will never guess what happened,'

Elizabeth declared, marching into the room with a dramatic flair.

'Nothing seriously bad, I trust?' Julia said, a tremor in her voice. 'For I must tell you that you look an utter fright, my dear.'

'I shall tell you all about it, if I may.' Not waiting for their assent, for she knew they perished from curiosity, Elizabeth continued.

'Sam brought the carriage to a halt just before the office, and the groom let down the steps for me as usual. I took my folio under my arm, and had scarcely begun to walk to the building when a scruffy lad came tearing through the crowd directly at me.' Here Elizabeth paused and sank down to rest upon her high stool.

'Mercy!' Julia exclaimed, her hand fluttering to her throat at the image provoked.

'Well, down I went with a whoosh, landing rather hard on my, er, posterior. I managed to hold tightly to the folio, for do you know, I am convinced that lad wanted it.'

'Whatever for?' Victoria wondered. 'Unless. . . .'

'Precisely,' Elizabeth said, then continued. 'I believe that someone was out to get those notes, which means that someone knows what I do! And that is not all. Who should be witness to this calamity but Lord Leighton. Oh, it does not bear thinking how embarrassed I was that he should see me tumbled on the ground, my skirt above my ankles, I'm sure, and my poor bonnet down over my eyes.' Elizabeth sighed, then said, 'He helped me up, though I wished him to the ends of the earth. You can guess how he will tease me about this.'

'He does seem to keep turning up like a bad penny,' Victoria observed with a twinkle in her eyes.

'He claimed he was just passing when he recognized my pelisse. That smooth tongue of his said that it is a color uniquely mine. Rubbish.' Elizabeth brushed a speck of dust from her rumpled pelisse.

'It does become you, love,' Julia reminded her.

'Well, he also claims that he dashed after the lad, but the young one got away. Most likely Lord Leighton is out of condition. No one usually runs *from* him—except me, that is.' She grinned at her sisters, then settled more comfortably on her stool, prepared to continue.

'He brushed me off. Mind you, I did not ask him to, but I thought it a scandalous thing of him to do—so very familiar. But rakes do things like that, I expect.'

'Scandalous, indeed,' Victoria murmured, trying hard not to laugh.

Julia was more serious. 'He ought not take liberties with a young woman of quality. Do you see now why I wish you to have a maid with you at all times?'

Elizabeth nodded, then went on. 'I put him in his place, reminded him that he had been on his way out of the building, and that I'd not wish to detain him. He had to leave then, you see, not escort me inside.' Her lovely face clouded. 'But little good it did me. I found that the handsome blond I so admired is married, for he inquired who my mantua maker is in order to have a pelisse made up for his wife. What a disappointment that was.'

'I am so sorry, love,' Victoria said softly, this time with true regret. She had hoped there would be someone to take Elizabeth's mind off Lord Leighton, and now it seemed the replacement had yet to appear.

'As if that were not enough, that old wigsby I report to patted me on the head and told me not to worry about a thing. He feels it was merely a lad trying to snatch something of value. No instinct at all. *I* knew in my bones that something was havey-cavey about the incident.'

'You most likely have the right of it,' Victoria agreed, glancing at Julia to see her reaction.

'I am not finished,' Elizabeth said after her pause. At the alarmed look from her sisters, she said in a dramatic manner, 'He was waiting for me in the carriage!'

'Who?' Victoria and Julia demanded to know.

'Why, Lord Leighton,' Elizabeth said with

surprise in her voice. 'Whom else have I been talking about? He said I needed extra escort after such a nasty attack. As though Sam and the groom would not be sufficient. I waited for Leighton to tease me, but he didn't. He will, though, I suspect. I depend upon you girls to help me think of some way to depress that man. Oh, he is insufferable.' With these words she jumped down from the stool and marched to the door. 'I intend to forget the man ever lived. And I shall take great pleasure in giving him a royal setdown whenever I see him.'

Once she had left the room, Victoria and Julia stared at each other, then burst into gentle laughter.

'Do you suppose she can forget such a man?' Victoria said when she could speak.

'Rakes make excellent husbands, or so I am told,' Julia said in reply, frowning as she considered Elizabeth and her evident infatuation with a man who merely liked to tease. It was to be devoutly hoped that another young man would supplant Lord Leighton in Elizabeth's thoughts.

'But I worry about what else Elizabeth revealed in her chatter. There is someone who knows far more than he ought about our activities. If he tried to get those notes from her, what will he attempt next?'

'Mercy,' Julia whispered, and looked very much as though she wished her sisters did not partake in such daring activities, although she knew and agreed with their reasons for doing so. Revenge proved a strong motive.

Victoria sighed and put aside her papers, resolving to return to them later that evening.

*   *   *

At Sir Edward's elegant town house, Victoria worked in silence, intending to say as little as possible. She had the headache today, no doubt owing to hours spent poring over that dratted cipher.

'Did you leave Mr Padbury entertaining Mrs Winton today as usual?' Sir Edward's voice fell into the stillness of the room like a pebble in a pond.

Victoria jumped, for her mind had been far from the subject of her sister and her erstwhile swain. 'No.'

'I thought the man was quite devoted to the lady?'

'Well, he isn't anymore.' Victoria shifted around to squint at the bust of Sir Edward, wondering if she had begun to capture the true essence of his powerful personality.

'How interesting. What happened?'

'She decided they would not suit. Really, Sir Edward, do you encourage me to gossip? Vastly improper of you.' Her head was throbbing; how could she continue with her work? Placing the dampened cover over the head, regardless that she had accomplished very

198

little on it today, she then wiped her hands. 'I am sorry, Sir Edward. I fear I have a fierce headache. It is best if I leave immediately.'

At once he moved to her side, solicitous as she might wish. He studied her wan face, then said, 'Hm, I have just the thing for a headache of that proportion.' Leaving her to droop against the desk, he walked to the hall, calling to his butler. After several minutes of blessed silence he returned carrying a glass holding a ghastly-looking liquid.

Victoria eyed the contents of the glass with disfavor. 'You cannot expect me to drink that.'

'Every last drop.'

Actually, the taste was not quite what she feared. Victoria swallowed the lot, placed the empty glass on the table, then crossed to get her pelisse and bonnet.

'I insist upon seeing you home.'

He would not accept her assurances that she felt better and could manage nicely by herself. Actually, it was rather gratifying to have someone fuss over her. At home it seemed that she was always the one to organize, to plan, to forge ahead with whatever scheme needed to be accomplished. It would be, she thought as he shortly helped her into his carriage, lovely to have a firm shoulder to lean upon.

Then she recalled the iris locket and what it meant. Could any gentleman wish to ally himself with a woman who was a spy? She didn't regret what she'd agreed to do. But any man who would marry her must be someone who'd not cavil at her serving her country. It would take someone with strength of character, and they seemed thin on the ground.

'You still frown. I thought you said your headache was better?'

'But it is,' she said, then realized that whatever he'd given her had worked extremely well. 'I must get the recipe from you, for it is surprisingly fast. I just happened to remember something I needed to do.'

'Unpleasant, from the looks of it.'

'The looks?' Did he read her mind again? She darted a startled glance at him, then prepared to get out when they arrived at the Dancy house.

He remained at her side, entering the house as though he had every right to do so, no matter that she would have been quite pleased to bid him farewell. She smiled sweetly at her escort.

'I had best see how Julia does. Thank you for your help, sir.'

'I should also like to see how she does.'

Annoyed, yet too polite to show it, Victoria led the way to the rear of the house. Once there, she consulted Julia as to how the afternoon had gone.

After a dutiful and exceedingly correct greeting, Edward sauntered about the room. He had hoped to do precisely this. He wondered what Miss Dancy had been doing to get such a fierce headache. The remedy he'd poured down her throat was one he used for the most violent of aches.

He paused. Miss Elizabeth had left her desk neat and tidy, compared to the last time he had seen it. That probably meant a completed project. He strolled on.

Atop the small desk in the corner of the room he espied a familiar-looking paper. Without seeming to do so, he edged closer for a better look. Obviously Miss Dancy was deep into espionage, if what he saw was any indication. He knew that paper! Disillusionment washed over him, for he had hoped to be wrong about her. She most definitely was a spy, and not only that, but an inferior one, to leave a document like that out on her desk where anyone might see it.

Late yesterday he had paused at the exhibit hall where the collection of art from various women was scheduled to take place next week. As a patron, he wished to see how it looked. As anticipated, every one of her heads was a parliamentarian, each representing a man who figured prominently in politics and the controversy over the war. Someone else might not notice the connection, but he had hunted for it.

And now? What was he to do? Report her? He stared blindly at a head on one of the shelves. He knew his duty, but for once he was loath to perform it.

'I fear my collection is rather slim, Sir Edward. I took nearly all of what I retained to the exhibit hall.'

'I see.' Edward turned to study her, then moved suddenly toward the door. 'Forgive me, ladies, I just remembered an engagement. I shall see you later.'

Victoria watched with puzzled eyes as Sir Edward bowed, then left in a tearing hurry. Turning to Julia, she said, 'I would give a sizable amount to know what that was all about.'

'Do you think the day will ever come when we shall *not* speculate over the actions and words of the people we know?'

'Come, Julia. I want to know where he dashed off to in such a hurry.' She grabbed her sister's hand, then ran to the front of the hall.

'Which way did he go, Evenson?' she demanded of the correct family retainer.

Being quite accustomed to the eccentric behavior of his young ladies by this time, he informed her, then turned to order the carriage be brought round.

Since Sam had been ready to leave in order to pick her up at Sir Edward's, the carriage was in front of the house within moments. Victoria gave the orders, then hauled her sister into the carriage after her and they were off.

'I do not see quite how you expect to find him in all this traffic,' Julia complained. She straightened her hastily donned hat, pulled on her gloves—thankful no one had seen her leave the house without them on—and leaned back to take a deep breath.

'You heard me tell Sam to follow that man,' Victoria replied over her shoulder. She leaned out of the window to search the street ahead.

'Well,' Julia said with a practical turn of mind, 'that does not mean you will find him.'

'Pay attention. Stick your head out of the window to see if you can spot him. I should very much like to know what it was that sent him off in a pelter, and just where he went. Not necessarily in that order, mind you.'

Considering that two elegant young ladies hung out either window of the carriage, and that they rattled down one of the more important streets of the capital at top speed, it was curious that they attracted only mild notice.

'Sam must think us utterly mad,' Julia called across the interior of the carriage.

'Well, he does know us pretty well,' Victoria countered.

Julia stiffened, then withdrew to the interior. Tugging on her sister's arm, she explained, 'I just saw Mr Padbury. He was dressed in the oddest clothes, very plain and rather dun-colored, not his usual hues at all. Just as though he didn't wish to be noticed. And, Victoria, I believe he was searching for someone. He sat in his phaeton, but I should wager he paid not the least attention to anything but the road ahead, much like we do. I wonder who it is that he searches for. Not a lady, I'd say.'

Victoria absorbed this while she stuck her head out of the window once again. They neared the vicinity of the war office, but saw no sign of Sir Edward. He had vanished.

'We might as well return to our house, Sam,' she announced to the coachman, distinctly disgruntled. 'We lost him.' She slumped back against the squabs with a sigh and a wry look at Julia.

'I thought it a harebrained thing from the first,' Julia said. 'Once a man gets his lead, there is no following him, is there?'

Victoria folded her hands, contemplating them while she considered the evidence. 'I cannot begin to make any sense of this. I think we had better have a cup of steaming hot tea and some biscuits before I acquire another headache. I do not have the recipe for that excellent restorative Sir Edward gave me . . . yet. But I fully intend to get it, among other things.' Her voice had trailed off into a whisper toward the end of her words.

*   *   *

At the war department the gentleman Elizabeth had dismissed as an incompetent and overly paternal old wigsby raised a surprised face as the door opened to admit one of his more useful and productive agents.

'I say, Hawkswood, you were not due in today. Something special?' Bushy gray brows rose as his visitor advanced upon the desk with what seemed like menacing steps.

'What do you know of Victoria Dancy?'

A cautious façade slipped over the esteemed gentleman's face. 'Why?'

'You just may recall that particular document you gave me to decipher, the one that has proved to be such an enigma?'

'Indeed. And?' The gentleman in black looked from beneath his gray brows, frowning slightly at a man he considered his friend.

'I just saw a duplicate of that paper on a desk in Miss Dancy's house.' Edward placed his fists upon the desk to confront his superior.

'Um. Most remiss of her. I shall have to scold her next I see her.' The mild tone was at odds with the seriousness of the case. Leaving papers about was not the done thing, even if they seemed to be innocent lists from all appearances.

Edward leaned across the desk, pinning the gentleman with a fierce gaze. 'You mean she is a spy for *our* side?'

'Quite. I usually try to keep my agents apart. The less you know about each other, the less danger you are in.'

'But a woman? A frail, delicate woman?'

'Anyone less frail and delicate than Miss Dancy I have yet to meet. She's as tough as old boots, in spite of her appearance. Used her for a couple of years now. A pity Napoleon murdered her parents, but it brought us valuable help, what with Miss Elizabeth so skilled in counterfeiting.'

Edward stared slack-jawed at his superior. He groped for a chair, then eased himself down. 'I think you had better tell me everything, and start at the beginning, if you please.'

*　　　*　　　*

Victoria poured out the steaming tea into delicate porcelain cups with a steady hand. She offered a cup to Julia, then looked up as Elizabeth flounced into the drawing room. 'Trouble?'

'I am still annoyed with that old wigsby at the war office who patted me on the head, assuring me that the attack was nothing at all. I suspect quite differently.'

'You reminded him of the dead iris?'

'Indeed I did.' Elizabeth dropped down upon a fragile chair covered with needlepoint and accepted a cup of tea. The sisters chatted for a time, discussing the matter that most involved them at the moment.

The door opened again, and Sir Edward strode into the room. He stopped before the trio, looking at first one, then another, fixing his gaze upon Victoria last of all.

'I trust there is an explanation for your unusual behavior,' Victoria said in a quiet little voice. In this mood, Sir Edward was more than a bit intimidating.

'I should like a cup of tea, if you please,' he said as calm as he could be, seating himself on the sofa tolerably close to where Victoria perched in wide-eyed amazement. 'And then, Miss Dancy, I believe you and I ought to put our heads together. Perhaps, just perhaps, we might solve that cipher!'

The fragile china cup fell from Victoria's hand to crash on the carpet.

*   *   *

That night Victoria went upstairs, completely forgetting her candle, with a most confused head. Sir Edward working along with her in the same cause? What a relief he was not a spy for the enemy. That the news offered all sorts of opportunities escaped her for the moment.

She slipped inside her room, then softly closed her door behind her, leaning against it as she contemplated the altered circumstances in her life. She welcomed the dark, wanting to be alone with her thoughts, and Letty would be in here the minute she saw a light.

A faint scraping noise alerted Victoria, and

she froze. Someone was in the room with her. It was *not* Letty, who feared the dark and would have candles blazing. Victoria thought the noise was the sound of a drawer.

She clamped her mouth shut, inching along the wall, hoping to see something, anything. How fortunate she wore thin leather slippers and a gown that didn't whisper.

Suddenly she espied a figure, faintly silhouetted against the dim light that came in through the window. He was all in black, with a mask, and a black cap on his head. He was soundlessly plowing through a drawer of her bureau, tossing things left and right.

Her foot struck the leg of a chair he must have moved, and he paused, glancing up directly at her. He started toward her.

Victoria screamed.

The figure in black panicked, dashing pell-mell toward the window, and went over the ledge. How he managed the two-story drop to the ground, she didn't know, and dared not run to the window to find out. He might have a gun.

Julia threw open the door, bringing candlelight on the scene. 'Goodness, what happened?' She surveyed the mess of clothing tossed about the room with concern.

'Tomorrow we are taking our guns out for a bit of practice,' Victoria said in a voice that shook just a mite. 'Someone is a trifle too inquisitive.'

11

The sun had barely risen when Victoria slipped from her bed, relieved to be able to get up at last. She'd slept poorly, tossing and turning while she puzzled over who might be the masked intruder. There had been a familiarity about that shape, had there not? But it had been so dark, how could she be sure? Yet, had she come marching in with a candle, she might have been harmed, or worse.

Once she slipped a pretty blue muslin day dress over her head, she began to organize and sort her belongings into piles, thinking all the while. She confessed that the sneak thief had not been the only man on her mind during the long hours of the night. Sir Edward had loomed there as well.

He was not her enemy. He had a right to all those papers she had seen in his library. If she had revealed what she'd discovered, she would have known sooner! Now she could finish sculpturing his head, then go on to her next real assignment without a backward look—but certainly with regrets. Her mistrust of him had colored her words, her thoughts. How he must feel about a young woman who did the sort of things she did was not something to dwell upon.

Pausing in her work, she considered her position. Perhaps—if she had not ventured into such a daring, unladylike pursuit—he might possibly. . . . No, she shook her head at the very nonsensical notion. Besides, she possessed a strong desire for revenge. The Dancys owed Napoleon and his minions their due.

Letty entered the room, gasping in dismay at the chaos. 'A fine mess this is!' Victoria declared as she placed a neat stack of shifts back into a drawer.

Timid little Letty glanced up with enormous gray eyes and silently nodded while folding one of the sheer cambric nightgowns to be returned to the bureau. She worked quickly, efficiently, and said nothing.

Sable poked his nose around the door, then trotted in to sit at Victoria's feet. He looked about with curiosity.

'And well you might wonder, Sable,' she said to the dog.

The last of the neatly folded garments was plopped in a drawer. Victoria pushed it shut, then dismissed Letty with a pleasant word. She did not *feel* pleasant, however. Now that she was alone, her room returned to more normal state, she was able to hunt out her gun, prudently tucked in a tiny drawer in her bedside nightstand. Would she use it? Could she, in defense of herself or her country? Men had to face that decision, why shouldn't she?

210

'Mercy, Victoria, do put that nasty thing down. I never suffer an attack of nerves, but I shall if you continue to wave that gun about in the air like that.' Julia paused in the doorway before entering the room.

'It is not loaded.' Victoria lowered the pistol so the end aimed at the floor, then studied her sister's face. 'What have you done, love? You have the oddest expression. I should say you look guilty of something.'

Julia fidgeted with the handkerchief she carried. Avoiding her sister's eyes, she inquired, 'Did you truly mean that you want us to go out to the edge of town to practice our shooting?'

'We can scarcely go to Manton's to test our aim.' The noted gunsmith kept a gallery where gentlemen practiced daily to improve their skill. Victoria had never heard of any lady who went there.

'Very well. Only, you must know I am not happy about this in the least.' Julia turned to meet her sister's curious gaze with obvious reluctance.

'What have you done?' Victoria knew her elder sister all too well. The handkerchief turned into a tight little ball as Julia took a deep breath. 'I sent a note to Sir Edward, requesting his help.' At the look on Victoria's face, she continued. 'This is serious, not a prank. We need a sharp-witted head to assist us. If he believes we are wise to practice with the guns, I shall go with you and not complain.'

Victoria stood silently a moment, considering Julia's words. Her natural desire to run from the man who fascinated her to the point of idiocy warred with the very practical necessity of obtaining support in the threat against her and her family. Her sigh was neither deep nor angry, more like one of regret.

'Of course, my dear. You are using that great common sense you possess in such abundance. It is foolish beyond permission for us to go haring off without advice.' She gave Julia a rather vulnerable grin. 'Perhaps we can persuade him to set up the targets for us?'

'Targets? What targets?'

The rich male voice brought Victoria around to the door in a whirl. 'Sir Edward? What are you doing up here?'

'Mrs Winton urged me to come over to investigate the scene where the intruder had been at work. Pity you restored order so quickly. I should have liked to observe the room just as he left it.' He limped into the bedroom, poking his cane about, inspecting the four corners, the bureau—where one dainty lace snippet peeked from a drawer — and the bed.

'Next time I shan't touch a thing until you have surveyed all, sirrah.' He was merely being helpful, she reminded herself. But she had caught him eyeing her bed.

Had he kept from touching her at the windmill because he was a gentleman, as Sam seemed to believe so strongly, defending Sir Edward with vigor? This was a new perception, one she had not truly considered before. Rather than believing her uninteresting and unworthy of his attention, had he considered her beyond intimacy? She glanced at him, wondering which motive had prompted his behavior.

Of course, she had never wished him to make love to her. She was not so stupid as all that. But his kiss was another matter. It had been thrilling. And, she readily admitted, she would have enjoyed more than the one she had received before that hateful taunting.

'Your sister said you intend to practice with your guns. When? And where do you plan to go?'

Giving Julia a pleased glance, Victoria explained about the vast meadow beyond London where they had drilled in the past. 'I propose that we go directly we are ready. Shall you wish to act the referee, sir?' she inquired. It was well-known that gentlemen usually did not approve of women shooting guns, believing it to be a male province.

'I think I shall, actually.'

The speculative look on his face forced Victoria to turn aside with concealed delight. Then she quickly sobered. This was not a game they played. The practice could mean saving a life, one's own life, and that raised it far above a mere game. She pulled a jade jockey hat from her wardrobe, then turned to Julia. 'The sooner done, the better. I know you do not relish it, but think of the girls. Would you not defend their lives the best you could if necessary?'

That suggestion galvanized Julia into action as nothing else might. She swiftly marched from Victoria's bedroom with a purposeful stride.

'A mother protecting her own is a fearsome thing,' Sir Edward commented.

'A natural instinct, I am told,' replied Victoria with spirit. 'Had I been blessed with children, I should feel quite the same. As it is, I wish to defend myself and my family.'

'Ever the tigress, I suspect.' He paused at her side, looking down at her, his dark eyes with a totally unreadable expression. Victoria wondered what went on in his mind.

The group that clattered down the stairs to the entry did not appear in high spirits. Rather, they were silent, serious, and properly worried.

The front door opened, and Lord Leighton stepped inside. At the sight of Sir Edward surrounded by the Dancy girls, he stopped in his tracks. 'Egad, Hawkswood, starting a harem?'

Edward ventured a faint smile. 'We are

going out to Burton's meadow for a bit of shooting practice. Care to join us?' He held up the gun case, opening it to reveal three small, if deadly, pistols.

The jaunty smile immediately left Leighton's face. 'This is serious. What has happened?'

'I can explain with Miss Dancy's help on the way out. We do not wish to delay the trip.'

Leighton immediately fell in with their plans, offering his phaeton for the trip, so they all need not be crowded into Sir Edward's carriage.

'Julia and I could go in the phaeton,' Elizabeth offered. 'I am accredited to be a fair whip, and will drive with utmost care.'

Clearly that was not what Leighton had in mind, but he merely nodded at her suggestion. If he were to know the gist of the affair, he would have to travel with Miss Dancy and Hawkswood. By all means, ladies.'

Elizabeth beamed, bustling up to the phaeton with a proud tilt of her head. Since all knew the way, and Victoria doubted if the intruder of last night wished to do them physical harm, Elizabeth and Julia went ahead. The others followed.

By the time they reached Burton's meadow, Leighton had been apprised of all that had transpired. In the inquiries Edward had performed regarding Leighton, he had become impressed with the younger man's excellent reputation and sound head. Why Miss Elizabeth had taken such a smashing young man, and a highly eligible one at that, into such strong dislike was indeed puzzling. Of course, Leighton was a bit of a tease, 'twas true.

Once the target was set up by Sir Edward's groom, with a bit of help from Sir Edward and Leighton, the girls were ready to begin.

Julia went first, her aim less than perfect. Yet she persisted with admirable determination until she improved.

Victoria followed in turn. She aimed with care, squeezing the trigger just so, yet with the speed that would be required in an emergency such as she might face. How gratifying to see her bullet go to the center more often than not.

When Elizabeth stepped forward, her gun ready and primed to go, she hit dead center every time. No matter where or how she stood, her bullet went true to the dead middle of the target that sat in the midst of a mass of wildflowers. That it was an incongruous sight mattered to no one.

The two men exchanged guarded looks, then joined the women once the last shot had been fired. 'From where we stood, it seems that Miss Elizabeth is the best shot.'

The young woman in question gave Leighton a defiant glance, then turned on her heel to replace her gun in the case.

'I suppose if we are practical, Elizabeth is the logical one to stay in my room in the event that the intruder will return to hunt for whatever it was he sought and failed to find.' Victoria placed her gun in the case as well, thus missing the look of horror that crossed the men's faces.

'Quite so,' replied Elizabeth in a doubtful voice.

'We shall see,' Sir Edward said, after placing a cautioning hand on Leighton's arm when the younger man looked about to explode in protest.

Somehow Leighton and Elizabeth ended up in the phaeton, while Julia, Victoria, and Sir Edward drove in his carriage on the return trip to London.

Elizabeth gave the man who now drove the elegant phaeton an offended look. 'I thought you trusted me to drive, sir.'

'I wished to talk with you.' He didn't excuse the change of drivers. 'I cannot like the notion of you hiding in Victoria's bedroom with the intent of shooting at the thief.'

Elizabeth nodded her agreement. 'I suppose I ought to be willing, but I fear I mislike the idea of truly shooting at a man. I am not a bloodthirsty person, in spite of what he has done or the threat he offers.'

'You prefer the game of shooting at a target.'

'Precisely,' Elizabeth replied, pleased that

someone understood the matter. 'A bit like archery.'

They jogged along in silence for a time, and Elizabeth felt almost in charity with Lord Leighton. While she did not forget for a moment that he was a frightful rake and a provoking tease, she found the day too lovely for argument. Forgetting herself, she began to hum a gay little tune.

Only when she became aware of the pained expression of the man at her side did she abruptly cease. 'Oh, I am sorry. Victoria insists I have a tin ear, and I daresay she is right. Julia sings tolerably well, and Victoria warbles like an angel. I guess when the voices were handed out, they ran out of musical ones for me.'

'It is well to know one's strengths and weaknesses, Miss Elizabeth,' he replied with admirable restraint, rather than his customary gibe.

She tilted her pretty nose in the air and remained quiet the rest of the trip, in spite of his efforts to charm her out of her silence.

In the rear carriage that held back to avoid excessive dust, Sir Edward studied Victoria. 'You do not actually intend to allow your little sister to remain in your bedroom waiting for the villain to return. What if he is able to avoid the bullet she fires at him? Can she reload in the dark? Could she fight him off were he to tackle her, engage her in a contest of strength? What if he has a knife?'

Victoria stared at Sir Edward with a pale, worried face. 'Well. . .'

'Of course she cannot permit such a thing,' Julia interposed.

'Julia is right. I could never permit her to place herself in such danger. I shall be there. With all three guns at hand, I shan't worry about missing.'

Sir Edward shook his head. 'I suggest a different plan. Not but what you could not handle the task,' he added with diplomacy. 'I would never rest if I thought that for one moment your life was in peril.'

'What do you propose?' Victoria queried. 'I confess I do not relish facing the intruder again. Anticipation is worse than the actuality, I suspect.'

'I intend to take over your bedroom—with your permission, of course.' He leaned forward in his seat, giving what he hoped was an earnest and convincing look at Victoria. 'I have greater strength, even if I am plagued with a bad knee.' He tightened the grip on his blackthorn cane. His knee had been much improved these past days, but it was far from back to normal. 'I am reckoned to be a good shot. And I should present a more menacing shape than a woman would.'

'True,' Victoria admitted readily.

'It is kind of you to take such a risk,' Julia added. 'But perhaps we ought to consult a

219

Bow Street runner, sir? Would such a person not be the logical one to do such work?' She clenched her hands in her lap and looked more worried than ever, if possible.

'Possibly. Yet I am loath to bring in an outsider. Each night I shall conceal myself in your room. We should not tell the servants, other than Evenson—I shall require someone to let me in once it is dark. But you can see that the fewer who know about it, the better.'

'I could sleep in the guest room, or perhaps with the children, for there is a cot in there that is not in use, and it would create less talk,' Victoria said, her growing acceptance for the scheme evident.

'The very ticket,' Sir Edward exclaimed with approval.

By the time they reached the Dancy house, matters had been settled to the last detail. Sir Edward would spend an evening with the family, to get to know the layout of the house better, and the habits of the servants, and such. Then later he would return for the night.

Victoria drew a sharp breath as she considered the threat to him. 'I trust you will not be injured, sir,' she said as they were about to enter the house.

'I find it touching that you are concerned, Victoria.'

Her frown at his use of her Christian name made him smile. With all her unconventional behavior, at heart she observed Society's dictates.

He appealed to Julia. 'Do you not think it would be acceptable if we resort to Christian names during this time, at least? The servants will take note of it, and I will be far less suspect as I roam about.'

She nodded her head. 'I believe that would be agreeable. I, for one, have no objection.'

'Since you are the proper one of the family, who am I to disagree?' murmured Victoria with good grace.

Elizabeth and Lord Leighton sat in the drawing room. Teacup in hand, she kept a discreet distance from Lord Leighton. A freshly brought tea tray waited for the others.

Immediately Victoria plunged into an explanation of what they planned to do.

All agreed. Sir Edward hastily swallowed his tea, then rose to depart. 'There are a number of things I must take care of before this evening. It will be feasible at that time?'

The girls exchanged looks. Julia admitted, 'We had intended to visit the opera this evening, Sir Edward.'

'Edward,' he corrected automatically. He frowned in thought for a few moments, then looked at Leighton. 'What do you say to an evening at the opera, David? By the bye, we had decided that for the nonce we shall all be on a Christian-name basis. There are good reasons.'

Obviously delighted to be included in the

venture, Lord Leighton nodded, his eyes sparkling as when he ribbed Elizabeth.

'We had best meet here for dinner first, then. Sir Edward will have that time to prowl about beforehand, and still accomplish what he hoped.'

'Excellent thinking, Victoria.' He smiled at her, the sort of smile that melted her insides.

She gave him a tentative smile as he departed, reflecting that he was a most engaging, compelling man. How she was to rid herself of her fascination for him, when he persisted in being underfoot, she didn't know. Perhaps with familiarity would come disillusionment. On both sides.

The cook raised her hands in horror when Victoria informed her of the change in dinner plans. A dash of soothing and a dollop of flattery, with an ounce of coaxing, worked the trick. That and a promise of an extra half-day off.

Thus it was that when the guests assembled for the evening meal, an excellent array was presented for their enjoyment. All ate with pleasure, yet with an awareness that this was no ordinary dinner party with ordinary intent.

Following the meal, Sir Edward wandered down the hall, Victoria at his side, to explore the morning room, the neat library, and cast a glance into the area behind the green baize door.

Satisfied for the moment, he joined her in a

walk up the stairs, with a look about the first floor, then up to investigate the second. He peered out windows, checked wardrobes, and in general did not miss much.

When they came to Victoria's room he stopped, studying the layout with keen eyes. His glance skittered over the bed. 'Shall I have Sable with me? Do you usually sleep with the dog in here?'

'Sometimes. Julia thinks it terrible of me, claims he will bring in fleas or something. But we bathe him from time to time, and indeed the dog is not allowed to run free any old place.'

Edward opened the wardrobe, checked the contents with an experienced eye, then poked about in the back. He glanced at her. 'Just in the event I must conceal myself, you know.'

Thinking of the aerophane crepe dress that lingered in the back of the wardrobe, she gave him a strained smile, then nodded. 'What if he decides to try another room next time?'

'I thought of that. Leighton could bed down in the library if you have no objection.'

'None in the least. However, Elizabeth might take exception to the plan.'

'Then I suggest you don't tell her. She can't argue if she knows nothing about it.'

'Wise man. Tell me, how did you become so knowledgeable about women?' she said with amusement. Then she immediately realized the impropriety of her question, and blushed as she stammered, 'Do not answer that, I beg you.'

He chuckled as he drew her into his arms, placing a chaste kiss on her forehead. 'Sisters and cousins and a mother about the house.'

'I feel foolish, sir.' At his look of rebuke, she amended that to 'Edward. My brother was easy to tease, and I suppose I became used to it.'

'You miss him a great deal, I suspect.'

'I do,' she admitted freely. 'He is between Julia and me in age, and a bigger torment one could not find, as far as a brother is concerned, I am sure. But he was always good to us, and looked after us when things went bad. One of these days. . . .' She turned to leave the room after catching a glimpse of her clock and the time.

'Do you want to take your night things out now, or wait until later?'

For some peculiar reason, the query about her nightclothes affected her more than that chaste kiss had done. She colored a fiery red, and murmured something about later. Surely she had blushed more in the past few weeks than in the past year.

They walked down to the first floor together, side by side.

Edward leaned on his cane more than usual, and Victoria fretted about his knee and his health all the way.

'Are you certain you feel up to all of this?'

Victoria chided him before they entered the drawing room.

'Hush, I shall be fine.' Edward covered her hand with his own, and she became oddly still, searching his face with worried eyes.

'If you say so.' Victoria moved away from that tense encounter to join the others. She urged them all to the waiting carriage. At the opera house she fussed over Elizabeth.

'Victoria,' her dear sister cautioned at last, 'I am quite fine. Please?'

'I wish Julia were with us.'

'She felt it incumbent upon her to remain with the children. I doubt she would have enjoyed one note, what with worry over the girls.'

With those words Victoria settled down to enjoy the evening as much as she might. Elizabeth sat next to her, wearing a wary expression that Victoria would have questioned at any other time. Assuming that it had to do with the villain, she said nothing.

Behind the young women, Hawkswood and Leighton stood for a time, watching the people in the opposite boxes. Hawkswood shifted when his knee began to ache, while wondering who out there might be the one they sought.

How he guessed it might be someone of the upper class, he didn't know, except that he suspected a true felon would have knocked Victoria over the head and continued with his hunt.

'Dreary, isn't it?' Leighton whispered at the singing which was coming forth from the stage. Catalani was smiling for all she was worth while caroling something utterly tragic in content.

'Quite,' Edward replied.

Elizabeth sniffed into her handkerchief, giving the men a baleful glance afterward. 'The story is exceeding sad.'

'I see Padbury is attending. He no longer comes around?' Leighton mused, ignoring the stiff back presented to him.

'Mrs Winton turned down his offer,' Edward explained.

'No!' Leighton was shushed again, and paid as much attention to it as he had before. 'But he was there all the time. Someone joked they thought the chap had taken up residence.'

'That so? Know anything about his finances?'

'Not a thing. You question his hobby of drizzling?'

'Perhaps.'

The two men fell silent as Catalani again burst forth with an impressive aria.

When the opera concluded, the men welcomed the chance to leave. 'Set for the night?' Leighton asked, watching as his companion firmed his lips.

'I will be. Would you consent to spend a night or two in the Dancy library? I daresay it will not be very comfortable, but I doubt I shall get much sleep either.'

Leighton readily agreed.

'You two did not hear a note that was sung. I declare,' Victoria scolded them with a smile, 'I was most put out, or at least the woman in the next box was.'

'We had a lot on our minds, Victoria, you know that.'

'Yes, I do.' She instantly sobered, and the drive to the Dancy house was accomplished by going over once again what the plans were, and who was to be where.

'I saw Mr Padbury at the opera. He was with Miss Flowerday,' Elizabeth said before they got out of the carriage. 'You know, the heiress.'

'I noticed a rather plump woman with purple plumes waving about in the air,' Edward replied, holding Victoria's hand longer than strictly necessary as he helped her from the carriage. He smiled at her pinkened cheeks.

'Indeed,' Victoria added, 'there is a good deal of speculation around, from what someone poured in my ears this morning.'

'With good intentions, I fancy,' Lord Leighton said, his mouth twisting in a grimace.

'Of course. All gossips intend their news for the very best of reasons. I feel sure they wanted to know if Julia was wearing the willow for Padbury.'

'How did she do?' Edward queried as they sauntered into the entry. 'She sweetly told them how pleased she was that dear Mr Padbury had found someone worthy of him.'

There was general laughter at this. The women walked up the stairs, the men hung back. Julia stood at the top of the stairs, waiting for a full report. The three women drifted out of sight toward the drawing room.

Below, Edward gestured toward the rear of the house. 'The library is back there. Evenson,' he said, turning to the dignified butler, 'Lord Leighton will take up position in the library for the night. You will let him in, and quietly show him where he can sleep?'

'Naturally, Sir Edward,' Evenson intoned with obvious approval of the scheme.

'I shall be here later, as well. Miss Dancy will sleep in another room, while the dog and I will take over hers.'

'May I say, sir, that I think that an admirable plan.'

'You may, and let us hope that all goes well.'

When the men went up to join the others, Victoria raised her head to study the two who entered, but said nothing. Worry lit her eyes for a time; then she tried to mask her fears, and sipped the tea offered her by Julia.

*   *   *

All went as planned for the night. Leighton found a surprisingly comfortable sofa in the library that now boasted a down pillow and soft wool blankets.

Upstairs, Edward tiptoed down the hall, easing the well-oiled hinges of Victoria's door open, then slipped inside.

'You are early, sir,' said a low voice by the wardrobe. The room was softly lit by two candles. Victoria faced him from across the bedroom, still in the lovely blue-and-gold gown she had worn to the opera. She carried a robe, along with a lacy froth of a nightgown. The cambric gown had inserts of delicate lace and embroidery, and must have required yards to make. From her fingers dangled a confection of lace that passed for a nightcap. Edward repressed a smile. It seemed the dauntless Miss Dancy preferred feminine frippery at night.

'Sorry.'

'Let us hope that you will not feel that way in the morning. Good night, sir.' She made a formal curtsy, then whisked herself from the room in a rush.

Edward stared at the door, then prepared himself for the night to come. At his side, Sable growled, then settled by the bed. Everyone was on edge.

12

'If we put our heads together, we might be able to solve this cipher,' came a deep voice from the doorway.

Victoria turned from where she stood by the morning-room window to survey her early-morning guest. He was scarcely a newcomer, having spent the previous two nights in her bedroom after creeping into the house late at night, leaving before dawn, and therefore need not be accorded the civilities due a conventional caller. She dropped the drapery cord she had been toying with and crossed the room to join Sir Edward.

Sable trotted along, obviously happy to see him. The dog sat at Edward's feet bestowing his usual adoring look at his gentleman friend. Victoria glanced at her large pet, then away. That animal could at least remain at the side of his loving mistress, rather than turn to another. She felt slightly betrayed.

'You most likely are right. Come, let us go to the library, where we can be private.' She ushered Sir Edward to the small but neat room to the rear of the house. 'Just a moment, and I'll fetch my scribblings from the desk in the workroom.'

Edward watched as Victoria whirled about and swiftly walked back to the room where he had seen that incriminating bit of paper.

In moments she returned, a sheaf of papers in hand, closing the door behind her with a decisive click. She'd no need to worry about being caught in a compromising position in *this* household. Her sisters well understood the dilemma that faced the two cipher solvers.

'I quite believed that the Vigenère table would be the most logical system to use,' she said, referring to the simple but effective cipher system developed back in 1585 by the Frenchman Blaise de Vigenère. 'It is a fairly simple cipher, and even though the French are familiar with it, I think it superior to the more complex Porta system. While I can have the Porta cipher table here, it is doubtful that the person the message was being sent to would dare to carry such upon his person, if using it. And *that* system defies solution without the tables.'

Edward nodded, then countered, 'I see what you mean, but consider—the French have set up a series of poles with attached arms across the countryside. Anyone with a bit of intelligence can figure out what the position of those arms means. They are placed close enough together so one might be seen from another, and it is evident that the purpose is military. I doubt it takes long before it becomes obvious whether the arms tell victory or defeat. Would the French be that careful?'

'I had not thought of that, truly.' Victoria

crossed to spread her papers on the desk. 'Still, most people consider the Vigenère system to be unbreakable. Only if you go about it in reverse can you hope to figure out the message. And yet the solution to this eludes me.' She pointed out the various combinations she had tried, while he shook his head in dismay.

'We have been duplicating efforts, for I have worked in the same direction. I understand why our esteemed superior preferred to have us separate, but it does seem foolish to have this sort of duplication of effort.'

Before Victoria could agree with him, there was a rap on the door. 'Enter.' She stared impatiently, wondering who dared to disturb her, while she placed a sheet of blank paper over the work.

Evenson presented himself with an apologetic mien, yet there was a twinkle in his eyes that told Victoria she would forgive him readily. 'This letter was delivered by a young soldier, miss. He said he was in a bit of a hurry and could not stay, but he had promised to bring it as soon as he might. Judging by the scrawl on the cover, I deemed it sufficiently important to interrupt you.'

Victoria rushed to take the letter from the silver salver, where the stained and crumpled missive looked sadly out-of-place.

'A letter from Geoffrey! What a relief.' Her

smile was radiant, yet there was a hint of reserve in her blue eyes that revealed she was not totally without worry. It had been far too long since they last heard from the young head of the family.

Begging Sir Edward's pardon, she slit the seal of the cover, then unfolded the letter contained within. As she read, her face grew grave, and she sank down upon the side chair with suddenly weak knees.

'What is it?' Edward stood by the desk, watching her.

'He is with the Marquess of Wellington,' she replied, quite absorbed. 'He writes of their battles in the north of Spain. It sounds utterly ghastly. The date tells me it was written recently, and this is not the kind of news to put one's mind at ease.' She continued to consume the letter, a worried frown pleating her forehead.

'What else?' Edward wandered around the desk, coming closer to where Victoria perched.

'He wonders if the rumors flying about could be true, that Mary Anne Clark has been delving into selling military commissions and promotions, and that the Princess of Wales is causing a flap.' She gave Edward an amused glance before continuing to read. 'Fancy, that they are curious about what goes on at home, even in the midst of all they do.'

Then she gave Edward a puzzled look. 'He

233

writes something in code here.'

'What is it?' He took a step closer, peering at the letter, although not actually reading it, for she had not offered it to him.

'A simple thing, let me see . . . I believe this is a code we have used before when we wished privacy, unsure as to whether our words might be seen by others.' She studied the page for a few minutes, then slowly translated, "Wellington has succeeded in fooling the French by transporting his bridging-train from the Tagus to the Douro. The French apparently haven't a clue of his action or intent."'

Sir Edward smiled back her. When it was possible to put one over on the enemy, it was time to rejoice. 'Your brother seems in good spirits.'

'He does not mention a woman, at any rate,' she declared with relief. 'Although the conditions over there are scarcely the sort to encourage a relationship of the proper sort.'

'My dear innocent, that does not mean that he might not get tripped into an unwanted marriage.'

'Have you ever met Kitty Pakenham? Wellington's Irish wife?' Victoria demanded.

'I cannot say I have the pleasure of knowing her well. She squints,' he added in a reflective voice.

'Maria Edgeworth praises her as having dignified and graceful simplicity, in spite of the fact that Kitty can scarcely see beyond the end of her nose. But according to the gossip, Kitty is not the same woman Wellington fell in love with years ago. She changed. I strongly suspect that he would not favor a marriage where the groom was imperiled with a bad union. I believe Geoffrey may avoid any unpleasant connection.'

'Indeed.' Edward rubbed his chin as he spoke. 'This is the sort of information that a woman proves useful in gathering. True, there are some gossips who spread their news to anyone convenient. Others prefer the tea table to scatter their blossoms of social destruction abroad. A wise one knows how to sort out one from the other.' He shared a knowing look with her, dropping his hand to his side while he waited for her to conclude her news.

'Geoffrey also says that Wellington is very secretive. He talks about spending next winter in Portugal, yet Geoffrey suspects he has a trick or two up his sleeve. He doubts Wellington is about to yield to the French, especially now that Jourdan has replaced Soult.'

'That was a stupid thing for Joseph Bonaparte to do, but it is to our advantage, I believe.'

'So I have been told.'

The door crashed open and Elizabeth marched into the room, hands on hips.

Victoria jumped to her feet, standing close to Sir Edward as though for protection. 'Elizabeth, what is the meaning of this?'

'Why did no one deem it necessary to inform me that Lord Leighton has been spending his nights on the sofa in this room?' Sparks danced in Elizabeth's eyes as she surveyed the pair before her. 'I did not think it important,' Victoria replied blandly.

'The man is a worse tease than Geoffrey, and a beau, to boot. He gives such particular attention to his dress that I cannot see what use he can be. What good does it do to have him sleeping in here? He'd likely take forever to arrange his apparel before chasing a villain.' Elizabeth stamped a softly slippered foot with annoyance.

'Sir Edward feels him helpful, and you, dear goose, are being silly,' Victoria pointed out in what she hoped was a reasonable fashion.

Elizabeth bestowed an abashed grin on her sister, then gave the letter in Victoria's hand a curious look.

Victoria flashed a look of gratitude at Elizabeth for dropping the entire matter at once. It proved too close to the subject Victoria wished to avoid. Sir Edward slept in *her* room, perhaps an improper arrangement to some. She still feared exposure of the windmill episode, but for different reasons. Were she to wed, she'd wish for another basis than compulsion.

236

Wellington's marriage was a case in point. Victoria suspected that before long, if not at this stage, the man would supplant his wife with another woman. Oblique references to his visiting Harriette Wilson, that queen of the courtesans, had reached Victoria's ears. She supposed that was to be expected of a man who no longer could tolerate his wife.

Wives were supposed to expect that sort of thing, even welcome it, if they feared excessive births and the declining health that went with that state. It seemed to Victoria that the most important thing a wife did was to produce one child after another for her husband. While a wife went about in that fruitful condition, he waltzed off to enjoy the favors of other women. Being in the family way apparently involved the husband only at the beginning.

That was not what Victoria wanted in the least. And since it was unlikely she might find true love and faithfulness, she would rather go without, thank you very much. She repressed the ironic twist of her mouth at this thought, while offering the letter to Elizabeth in hopes of distracting her.

'I believe you judge Leighton too harshly, Miss Elizabeth,' Sir Edward scolded her gently as he watched the sisters.

'This is from Geoffrey! What does he say?' Elizabeth demanded as she unfolded the missive. She completely ignored Sir Edward's defense of Lord Leighton.

237

'I suggest you take it along to share with Julia. It arrived not long ago by special messenger, some young soldier who had returned from the Continent.' Turning to Edward, she added, 'I wish I knew his name. He may be injured and in need of a helping hand.'

'Perhaps Evenson made a record of it. I shall check.'

She watched him depart, then gave a sigh. While they were no closer to solving the curious and difficult cipher, she felt better with having another simply to discuss the matter with, and one to whom she might turn.

'Some of this must be in code, for it makes no sense whatsoever,' Elizabeth murmured, scanning the letter.

Victoria quickly explained; then Elizabeth took the letter along down the hall to give to Julia. None of the sisters would be inclined to repeat anything contained in the letter, especially the portion in code.

Sir Edward found Victoria standing by the desk, another frown on her face, as again she struggled with the cipher. She rubbed her forehead, sighing with exasperation. 'If only the dratted man who wrote this muddle had a better hand. It is dreadful.'

'Why do we not take a drive out in the fresh air? It would do us both good. Perhaps you would like to visit the carriage builder to inspect the progress on your coach?'

238

Victoria was torn, and her indecision clearly sat on her brow. 'We need to know the names contained in this list. From what little we have gleaned otherwise, there is a group of men who seek to thwart Wellington at every turn. How can such traitors be permitted to continue their evil work? I feel guilty every time I put down this page.'

'It will not help if you become ill. I have seen a man driven to the point of madness trying to solve a difficult code. Every year the enemy, whoever it might be, tries to improve and perfect a more difficult means of concealing secrets and military information. We do the same. We shall break it in due time. Come'—he held out his hand—'we shall go for a drive in the park, and stop by the carriage builder. Evenson gave me the name and direction of the young fellow who brought the letter. If you like, we can stop by there as well.'

'Very well. My head aches dreadfully and I fear it will only become worse if I remain at the desk.' She carefully locked their papers away, meeting his approving gaze with a nod.

She crossed to pass him on her way to her room, and Edward placed a detaining hand on her arm. Victoria paused, looking up at him with her question plain in her eyes.

'I admire your devotion to the cause. It is as rare as you are gifted. Now, don a pretty bonnet. I shall send for my carriage immediately.'

Her face relaxed in a smile, and she floated up the stairs with a lighter heart. They had heard from her brother, and he was well, if impatient. Why did young men want things to 'happen'? Whether it be war, or life in general, they sought action, diversion.

After she had tidied her hair and put on her favorite jade pelisse with the pretty bonnet that looked so well with it, she returned to the entry. Evenson was in conversation with Sir Edward. Victoria pulled on her gloves as she observed the fine deference the butler gave to Sir Edward. It certainly spoke highly for him. Evenson was as discriminating as the most pompous of London majordomos.

They entered the carriage, Victoria taking note that Sir Edward did not seem as dependent upon his cane today.

'Your knee feels a bit better?'

He gave the signal to proceed, then replied, 'A trifle.'

'Good.' She lapsed into silence, not sure what to say to him.

'We shall succeed in our efforts.' He reached over to place a comforting pat on her hand. 'Someone must be quite certain of it, to be trying to plow through your belongings.'

Victoria glanced at the coachman, then decided that any words she spoke would be drowned by the sound of the wheels on the cobbled streets, not to mention the considerable traffic and hawking of the vendors.

'What has me puzzled is his entering my bedroom. Would he not be more likely to find what he wants in the library?'

'Too obvious. The man believes a woman would conceal an important paper among her personal things—and so he tears apart your drawers, hunts among your things.'

Victoria nodded, knowing her conversation was unseemly but practical. She could not be missish in her work. 'I suppose so.'

They entered Hyde Park and drove along the green expanse dotted with magnificent trees. Inconsequential people occasioned the park at this hour of the day, which suited Victoria quite well.

'I see a familiar face,' she pointed out to Edward. 'Our genial gentleman is out driving with Miss Flowerday. How odd he chooses this hour.'

'We do as well, Victoria. Perhaps Padbury wishes to avoid the sort of speculation you fear.'

'How did you know that?'

He merely smiled and refused to reply.

'There are times I believe I should have taken advantage of you while at the windmill—after you fell asleep—to give you a good thump on the head,' Victoria said with asperity.

'I suffered somewhat similar feelings, only

mine did not extend to a thump on the head, but something more interesting.' Edward half-turned to study his companion.

Victoria felt a blush creep over her cheeks, and dared not meet his gaze. However, it did not suit her plans to flirt with the man she found so fascinating. She repressed a smile, and chided him, her eyes sparkling, 'That was most improper, even if you *did* merely think it.'

'Most likely,' he agreed. 'Victoria, what if someone digs around, discovers what happened in the windmill? Were a suspicious man to hunt, he might find that farmer who gave you a ride, put together the information regarding your damaged post chaise.'

'Nothing happened in the windmill,' she whispered, but her eyes grew wary.

'That is what we say. Yet who would believe a healthy man, or even an injured man like myself, would carry a beautiful young woman into a deserted windmill and then claim nothing occurred in the next two days?' His voice reflected more than polite concern.

'Has someone said something that you have heard and not told me about?' She swiftly turned to him, placing her free hand tightly over his in her concern. 'I shall not compel any man into marriage. I think it utterly unconscionable.' She searched his face for a clue to the truth. Would he conceal such a story from her, with a futile attempt to keep her from hearing of it?

'I admire you for your position. But you must consider mine as well, Victoria. I do not relish being considered a seducer of a lady of quality. An unmarried lady, at that.' He gave her a wry look. 'I doubt if our friendship has gone totally unnoticed. While I am not living in your pocket, someone may learn I have ordered a traveling coach for you, and refuse to believe the truth—that it is to repay your family for the one ruined in the crash. What then? Gossip can destroy you totally. You will be out of polite society in that event. As would your sisters.'

Her sisters! She raised horrified eyes to his. 'Julia insists she has no desire to wed, but Elizabeth must make a good marriage. She is young and pretty, and possessed of a most devoted nature.'

Sir Edward nodded. 'I have asked you before, I believe, yet you avoided an answer. Do you not plan to wed?'

She waved a dismissing hand. 'I live a pleasant life with my dog and sisters. If Elizabeth marries, Julia and I shall find a little place of our own, for as you pointed out, Geoffrey must have an heir.'

'Unnatural girl,' Edward murmured not far from her ear.

The conversation drew to a halt when the vehicle pulled up before the carriage builder. Edward assisted Victoria down with a possessive touch, then tucked her hand close to his side as they walked inside to inspect the progress on her coach. Their arrival was noted by Lord Leighton, who happened to be on the way to an appointment with a friend in the area.

When they finished their inspection of the chaise in progress, and Victoria was satisfied that all was being properly done as to the furbishment of the interior, they left the carriage maker's and continued on along through the streets to an area alien to Victoria.

'Your young soldier.' Sir Edward gave Victoria an approving look as she nodded her appreciation of his thoughtfulness. He followed her into the modest dwelling, where they spent some time chatting with the soldier and his young wife, sipping tea, and talking of the war.

'That was nice,' Victoria concluded as they left the simple lodgings sometime later. 'I so wished to thank him. It had been quite long since we heard from Geoffrey, and it was excessively kind of this man to take such trouble.'

'The mails are slow, not to mention costly, coming from Spain,' Edward agreed. 'He seems a good chap, and I shall be happy to put in a good word for him.'

Victoria sat back in the carriage, content with her day. If the evening presented a threat, that was something she would consider later.

At the dinner table Julia, Elizabeth, and Victoria were all oddly silent. Each seemed to be preoccupied and murmured only vague general comments, if anything.

'I say we ought to share what is on our minds,' Elizabeth burst out after some time.

Startled, Victoria nodded hesitant agreement.

'Lord Leighton came here again today. Said something about having seen you with Sir Edward and implied that it was acceptable that he come to visit. Did you give him leave?' Elizabeth demanded of Victoria.

'I fear I did not see him.'

'I suspected as much,' Elizabeth said with an annoyed air. 'I complained about his sleeping here the past two nights. All he did was adjust his cream leather gloves and talk about the dangers from some villain. Still, he did me a favor.'

'That's nice, dear,' Julia murmured.

Casting a dark look at Julia, Elizabeth turned to Victoria and continued, 'I wanted to go along the Thames to sketch a scene, and he accompanied me. I suspect he had nothing better to do and found me amusing. Yet I felt safer with him at my side. He is intimidating, you know. Those burly-looking fellows took one look at him and turned away from us.' It was clear that Elizabeth was impressed, if she did not precisely say so.

'Indeed,' Victoria said in a subdued voice.

'He insisted that I am in danger and came along to discourage any trouble. Although he calls me infant and teases me like Geoffrey.' She sighed, then added, 'I expect I need to stay with Aunt Bel to acquire some polish from her.'

'That might be nice,' Julia said, her mind clearly elsewhere.

'Well, he carried a pistol in his pocket and said he had a handy pair of fives. Even if he does not care a jot about me, it is rather interesting to be protected by a rake.'

Victoria shared a commiserating look with her younger sister, then turned her attention to Julia. 'What has happened today to give you such an abstracted air?'

'Oh, does it show to such a degree? If you must know, I was at Lord Temple's house today, painting, you know. His sister, Lady Chatterton, was also there. She talked, or I should say gossiped, until I nearly got the headache.'

'Did she say anything to upset you?'

'She mentioned the Princess Charlotte flirting with the Duke of Devonshire, and how furious her father will be when he hears about it. It seems Lady Chatterton feels his daughter must marry higher than a mere duke.'

'And what else transpired?' Victoria queried, knowing there was something else, since Julia had been in the dismals again, which was unlike her.

'She treated me as though I did not exist, like I was transparent.'

Elizabeth nodded sagely. 'You mean like a servant. I seem to recall hearing she is a dreadful snob.'

'I have experienced all I care to of her snobbery, I can tell you that.' Julia gave a distressed sigh.

'How did Lord Temple react to her behavior?' Victoria inquired, wondering if Julia was succumbing to his charms.

Julia chuckled. 'It seemed as though he was most annoyed with his sister, for I suspect he invented the appointment he suddenly recalled. She was very put out when he bustled her from the house moments after I left. He asked me to return tomorrow, and I shall. But he took care his sister did not overhear our talk.'

'Well, then, it seems to me that his lordship has a proper sense of what is right and you need not worry.' But Victoria was concerned, for this was the first time, other than Mr Padbury, that Julia had evinced an interest in a gentleman. And Lord Temple was a far cry from Mr Padbury in every way. She joined her sisters in leaving the table, strolling along to the drawing room with a restless heart.

To Victoria the evening dragged past, minute by minute. Would the intruder return

247

tonight? Could she sleep, knowing that each night made it more likely he would return if he truly intended to hunt for papers—the special papers she had used when trying to decipher the message and list? Papers now locked in her safe.

'Victoria,' Elizabeth declared in a huff, 'please sit down or I shall go quietly mad with your ramblings about the room.'

'Now, Elizabeth,' Julia rebuked her, with an impatient glance at both sisters, 'she has a great deal on her mind.' And it seemed, from her frequently absent stare into the distance, that Julia Winton also had a great deal on her mind. But whatever it was, she hugged it to herself.

At last it came time to retire for the night.

Elizabeth drifted up the stairs and down the hall, looking rather bemused.

Julia took her night candle, pausing at the top of the stairs to speak to Victoria. 'I fancy I shall complete the miniature tomorrow. Lord Temple seems anxious to be done with the work on it.'

'I expect you will be relieved as well,' Victoria replied, wondering at the sad expression in Julia's eyes.

'Try not to worry overmuch, dear,' Julia said before walking along to her room.

Victoria went along to the little room she had taken over from the twins. She sat on the edge of the cot, wondering about the night to come. Then she exclaimed softly with exasperation when she observed the maid must have put her nightgown back in her drawer after laundering it. Why had she not thought of that earlier?

Not bothering with a candle, for she knew her home well enough to go about blindfolded, Victoria resolved to fetch what she wished. Slipping from the children's room, she tiptoed down the hall until she reached her room, depressing the door lever with care. The room was in darkness and total silence. She hurried to her bureau, pulling open one of the drawers to remove a fine cambric nightgown.

And then she found herself pinioned against a hard body, strong arms quickly wrapping about her.

Her call for help was naught but a rasp. However, she was released immediately, and a candle was lit within moments.

'Why the devil do you walk about in the dark? Next time you venture out at night, take a candle with you,' Sir Edward scolded, his voice harsh with a strange intensity.

Victoria felt blinded by the sudden light. Clutching her gown to her chest, she licked nervous lips, nodding. 'I shall,' she replied, wondering at her breathless, shaken voice. She ought to edge toward the door, yet she froze.

Edward shook his head at her, a half-smile

playing over his lips. The dim light brought that aristocratic nose into high relief, and Victoria thought he resembled a painting she had seen of a prince. He looked born to command.

'Do not look at me like that. Do you not know you ought to flee this room?' His voice was but a thread of sound, yet she heard every syllable clearly.

Victoria nodded, then shook her head. Oddly enough, she did not fear him, although she knew she ought to run away.

'Oh, Victoria,' Edward whispered, then gathered her unprotesting self into his arms to bestow a tender kiss on a highly bemused girl.

The gown forgotten, she wound her arms about him, taking all she might of that kiss. A wisp of thought wove through her mind that she had missed a great deal in life, having had so few of his kisses. Resolved to make up for that deficiency, she was startled when he removed her arms and put her away from him, stuffing the nightgown into her hands.

'Good night, my dear.' He held her with a gentle insistence. 'You had best seek your temporary bed before I forget what I should do and take you to your own bed, here.'

Victoria gasped, appalled at her foolishness, dashing from her room and down the hall as though he might pursue her. He didn't, and for that she could almost be sorry.

13

'I fear the gentleman is far too fascinating. This will never do at all.'

Victoria stared morosely into her coffee cup, sighing with regret that she must forget his wondrous kiss of last night, never know such again.

'So true.' Across the table Elizabeth idly stirred a cooling cup of tea, equally sunk in a fit of dismals. At her sister's softly spoken words she had nodded, thinking of the brotherly attentions of Lord Leighton. Yes, Lord Leighton, the society rake, must be banished. He clearly bedeviled her to amuse himself.

'I quite agree.' At the head of the table the normally practical Julia also daydreamed over her tea, dropping several spoons of sugar into the cup, when she normally would have used no more than one. She stirred with bemused refinement, her mind quite obviously far away on something—or someone—else.

'Indeed. Sad, but true,' Victoria murmured. 'I could never have any peace of mind.'

The other two nodded with dream-filled eyes. The trio sank further into their green melancholy as Victoria continued, 'It is not as though one could not do well enough under other circumstances, mind you. But there are obstacles in the path, too great to overcome, I fear.'

Victoria regretted the dashing sort of life she led, spending her time staring at men to create their likenesses. Most likely Sir Edward might be attracted to her—as long as they worked to solve the cipher—but would she be the sort of woman he might marry? She doubted it, although they shared a number of interests. She realized with a plummeting heart that they could not unravel ciphers forever, for the war must come to an end sooner or later. And then what? Even his particular attentions were nothing more than government-inspired! She sighed.

Elizabeth creased her napkin into little pleats, remembering how Lord Leighton had patiently sat at her side while she sketched along the Thames. Scruffy men in the area had taken one look at the powerfully built young lord and hurried away. But as Victoria pointed out, there were definitely obstacles. Elizabeth did not know how her sister had learned so much of the matter, but she certainly knew how hopeless the situation was.

In the Minerva novels the heroine was always saved by a fine, noble hero who was as virtuous as the driven snow, or a dashing rake who was totally reformed by the pure, unselfish love of the heroine. Scarcely true in this case, what with the reputation Lord Leighton held, according to all the gossip she had heard. She clenched her hands together as she contemplated the aggravating man. Mercy, but her future looked dull, even if he did drive her mad with his teasing. A little sigh escaped from her sweet lips.

Julia wondered what had given her away to Victoria. She thought she concealed her growing attraction to Lord Temple in a clever manner. She might have known that her astute sister would see to her heart. Well, Victoria was correct. There were obstacles far too great to overcome. The widowed Lord Temple was considerably above her. Although she was the daughter of a baron, that alone did not make her the proper wife for a viscount. He admired her ability to paint, nothing more. He was courteous, kind, handsome, and might as well be on the moon, as far as she was concerned.

She recalled how his sister had totally ignored her, as though Julia were nothing more than a speck on the wall or a servant of the lowest order. How galling that had been. Oh, she knew how hopeless her attraction was, yet. . . . She sighed with regret at what could never be.

'But life flows on, does it not?' Victoria stared out the window, catching a glimpse of scudding clouds above the chimney pots. 'Elizabeth,' she said suddenly, 'no suitable gentleman looms on the horizon?'

'Suitable? But you yourself said he would

not do,' Elizabeth replied, her confusion obvious.

'I did?' Victoria wondered if she might be losing her mind, along with her heart.

'Elizabeth, she was talking about my foolish attraction, not yours,' Julia confessed.

'I was?' Victoria mistrusted her ears. Had she heard right? Julia felt an attraction that she thought Victoria knew about? She went over the words she realized she had uttered aloud rather than thought. Good grief, both of her sisters had tumbled into a fascination for the wrong man! It appeared all three of them were doomed to disappointment.

Her compassion deeply stirred, Victoria gave them a wobbly smile. 'Never you mind. We shall deal famously together. We will find that perfect little cottage in the country—Knightsbridge, perhaps—and have a wonderful time together.'

Elizabeth listened to this pronouncement of their future, then burst into tears and fled from the room.

Julia and Victoria stared at each other in dismay.

'Lord Leighton, I suppose,' Victoria offered.

'No doubt,' Julia replied, hoping that Victoria would not probe. 'A girlish infatuation.'

'And since Mr Padbury is as stale as last week's bread, I gather you must have developed a *tendre* for Lord Temple. But that certainly is not hopeless, Julia.'

'Oh, no? May I remind you that his sister, Lady Chatterton, was present yesterday, and I might have been a lesser servant for all she acknowledged me.'

'True, she is the highest stickler in society, outdoing Mrs Drummond-Burrell. As Lizzie said, a snob of the first water. I fear that if he matches her in pretensions, you are quite defeated before you begin. What a pity, for he sounds like a lovely man, otherwise.'

'He seems kind and good, with a charming twinkle in his eyes. I noticed that when I was painting, you see,' Julia said, her voice sounding tight.

'That and a good deal more, most likely. Do not worry, we shall find that cottage if necessary, Julia. Never fear about the future for you and the girls, our combined allowances should do things nicely. Unless Elizabeth can overcome her infatuation for Lord Leighton, it will be the three of us forever. I can see it now, three lace caps over tea in the afternoon, doddering old women talking about our lost loves. Shall we potter about a garden as well?' She managed a giggle.

'There is no hope with Sir Edward? I thought he seemed most particular in his attentions.'

'Government-ordained attentions,' Victoria

bit out. 'He has joined with me to solve the cipher, no more. Nothing personal has been said.' While nothing had been said, Victoria omitted the kisses exchanged, for they could be the result of mere proximity, or compelling temptation. 'I fancy that once the cipher solution is found, he will take himself back to wherever he was before, and that will be the end of it.'

'Oh, dear heaven,' Julia murmured. 'But what about the chaise? Surely he'd not bestow that upon just anyone.'

'Guilt, I suppose. Although he could not actually help colliding with us, because of the wretched weather. He has made a point of the chaise being for the family. Most proper, you see, and nothing at all to do with me.'

'Well,' Julia mused, 'you could always claim that you desire his company to test the chaise.'

'I have already thought of that. He promised to drive in the park with me. But one need test a carriage only once, drat it.' Victoria rested her chin on her hand as she considered possibilities, of which there appeared to be very few.

'There will be the three of us in lace caps over tea, then,' Julia confirmed. 'I see no other recourse. Unless Elizabeth recovers from her ailment of the heart to love another. Poor honey, infatuation can seem quite real.'

'She complains he treats her like a sister,' Victoria said, rising from the table. 'You know what a tease Geoffrey was when he was a lad. Utterly impossible. But our brother grew out of that silly behavior. Pity Lord Leighton sees Elizabeth as fair game.' The toast lay reduced to crumbs, the coffee was cold, the rest of the morning repast had been totally ignored by the blue-deviled young women.

Victoria walked around the table to put a comforting arm about her sister. 'What do you do today? Finish the painting?'

Nodding, Julia replied, 'What a shame I cannot be like Penelope, undoing my weaving every night to prolong the waiting period. I suppose I can scarcely do something that reprehensible.' She met Victoria's amazed gaze, then smiled. 'What a touching trio we are, indeed.'

'A lovelorn lot, 'tis true.' Victoria chuckled with determination. 'There is more to life than men, you know.'

'As long as we have money, we shall manage. Being poor would be dreadful.'

'Perhaps I should call on our man of business to see how things stand.'

'Excellent notion,' Julia declared.

With those optimistic words the sisters went to the workroom to collect what materials they required that day.

Julia left the house first, for Victoria must wait as usual until later in the afternoon.

Julia was not gone very long, for indeed, as she had said, the painting was actually finished. Victoria glanced up when her dear sister entered the workroom sometime later, her eyes dreamy and filled with hope.

'I trust things went well?' Victoria inquired cautiously.

'Quite. Today the servant who showed me in was most deferential, unlike yesterday. It eased the memory of that dreadful Lady Chatterton considerably.' Julia grimaced, then raised her brows in imitation of a very snooty lady. 'She was so condescending.'

'Did he like the painting? Do you think he will recommend you to others?' Many of Julia's commissions came from such praise.

'He seemed most pleased.' Julia bit her lip, then gave Victoria an embarrassed look. 'I told him I am entitled to be styled "Lady Winton," and he called me that the rest of the morning. I think perhaps. . . .' She cast an optimistic look at her sister. 'Do you?'

'Well, did he want to know more about you? That is a promising sign, or so I am told.'

'As a matter of fact, he did.' Julia wrapped her arms about her, hugging herself as she continued. 'I told him about the twins, and he thought their names pretty. He has a daughter as well. But no heir, so he really ought to marry again, especially since he admitted there is a profligate cousin waiting in the wings to inherit should Lord Temple fail to do just that.'

'Good!' Victoria said with a nod of her

head.

'That does not mean he has an interest in a widow with twins, however. I showed him the finished miniature and he approved it as complete. Now I shall coat it with varnish, then have it delivered to his residence.'

'I suppose it would not be proper for you to take it there; it might seem a bit coming.' Victoria considered the possibility of such conduct, rejecting it before Julia replied.

'It would do no good, he leaves for the country to see his mother and daughter. Some problem seems to have cropped up. He sounded more than a bit distracted as he spoke. Perhaps had he a wife, he would find his domestic situation running more smoothly.' Julia gave Victoria a knowing look.

'Of course.' Victoria chuckled. 'I believe a little bird ought to tell Lord Temple he needs a widow experienced in household management to take over his problems.'

Julia smiled; then her expression altered to become serious. 'I shan't marry to be some man's housekeeper, or whatever you call it. I should like to feel a stronger emotion than gratitude or even a mere liking.'

'Shall you see him again?'

Julia's face cleared and she smiled. 'As a matter of fact, I shall. When he returns in a month or so he has some business he wishes to discuss with me.' Her sudden look of dismay was almost comical. 'Gracious, you do not suppose he actually intends to ask me to be his household manager, do you?'

'Never,' Victoria replied, but wondered if his lordship might not have such notions. For Julia's sake, she hoped he was inclined in a more interesting direction.

A glance at the clock reminded Victoria it was time for her to be on her way before long. She joined Julia in a light repast in the breakfast room, debating the merits of other men they had met, discarding every one of them for the most absurd reasons—like bushy eyebrows, or narrow shoulders, or that dreadful man with the squeaky voice who talked incessantly about turtles.

She still smiled as she left the house, thankful that both she and her sister were still able to laugh at their problems.

Victoria paused before Sir Edward's elegant town house, then entered, with Sable and her footman beside her, once the butler had answered the brisk rap of the brass knocker.

'Sir Edward will be down directly, miss. Everything is ready for you. Shall I bring a pot of tea, as usual?'

'Thank you.'

She directed the footman to place her things where she wished, then dismissed him. Sable sat down near the chair Sir Edward usually occupied while Victoria worked.

'You are early. Did you sleep well last

night?' Sir Edward entered the room with a brisk step. He looked fresh and rested; nothing appeared to have kept him awake for long. He was dressed in a smart blue coat over a white waistcoat and gray pantaloons. His highly polished boots and that quizzing glass he carried declared him to be most fashionable.

Victoria didn't know where to look when he mentioned last night. 'Yes, eventually.' Drat, she had not intended he know that she had been so shaken by that kiss that she had curled into a huddle beneath her covers, thinking, dreaming for a long time before sleep crept over her.

'You are a tantalizing creature, you know.' These provoking words were spoken in an amazingly prosaic manner.

And I suppose that excuses your actions?' She could not refrain from frowning at the man. Oh, he seemed so sure of himself, so blasted confident.

'Naturally.'

'Odious man,' she scolded, reluctantly displaying a half-smile. 'You do not know the half of it,' she muttered to herself, forgetting what acute hearing he possessed.

'Are you about finished? The head looks remarkably complete to me.' He sat properly as she had arranged all these days, falling into the chosen pose quite easily.

She examined the sculpture. Like Julia, she

wished there was some way she might have undone each night all that had been accomplished during the day. Foolish thought.

'A few minor touches and I can take your head to the foundry.'

'Sounds disagreeable.'

'Yes, I suppose it does.' She fiddled with the slender chain that held her iris pendant. What had it brought her to? Sir Edward now knew she was not a member of the iris group, yet he had never said a word about it. Had he noticed the pendant? She usually concealed it from view, not wishing probing questions. Not in all her travels had there been occasion to need it. She had been too clever for that. Or perhaps not under sufficient suspicion?

She allowed the pendant to fall free, turning to face him. Would he observe it now and comment?

'Pity there was no luck last night.'

'How like you to think it bad luck that the intruder failed to show. You men, so eager for a fight or a war.'

'I gather you think of your brother. I daresay that were my knee to permit, I should be off to serve my country.' He fingered his cane as he spoke. 'When I visited Portugal, I could see they need all the good men they can get.'

'To defeat the French? What you do is just as important,' Victoria reminded him. 'Do you believe the villain will come?'

'I shall be in your room tonight in the event he does. May I have Sable again? He is a great comfort during the waiting hours.'

Victoria looked at her pet, cozily snuggled up to his hero. With a wry expression she answered, 'Of course. The two of you make an admirable pair.'

'I wish I knew quite how you meant that remark. There are times when I feel as though you are not too pleased with me.'

She felt her cheeks grow warm. What a blessing he didn't know that she was fascinated with him to the point of foolish adoration. 'Nonsense. You are merely imagining things, sir.' With that comment she turned to completing the sculpture.

She worked silently for a time, refusing to dwell on the hopes for her future. At last, after a few final deft touches, she stood back, comparing Sir Edward with the likeness she had created. Quite good, if she did say so. She knew she was the toughest judge of her talent, believing that there was always room for improvement. 'Done.'

While Victoria turned to place her tools and all her other impedimenta into the small carryall she had brought with her, Sir Edward strolled over to view the sculpture.

'You feel this captures the true me, then?'

'Yes,' she answered uneasily. 'At least, as I see you. Every artist has a different vision of a subject.' She could feel his dark eyes upon her, assessing her as he often seemed to do.

'Interesting.' Edward studied the head Victoria had done. Was that really how she saw him, that impossibly handsome fellow with the noble nose, imposing forehead, and sensual mouth? Egad, it seemed an idealized, highly romantic creation. Certainly better than the image he viewed in the looking glass every morning when he arose. He turned slightly to give her a speculative look.

She picked up her jonquil pelisse, then gazed at him with questioning eyes as he removed the garment from her hands. 'Sir?'

'I would say—just a guess, you understand—that you care for me, if that sculpture is how you view me.'

Victoria looked utterly mortified. 'Nonsense,' she sputtered. 'That is your imagination. Although I am pleased that you like the representation, for I'd not wish you to detest it,' she added.

'You deny an attraction for me?' He drew closer.

Victoria backed toward the open doorway. One hand clutched her iris pendant; the other reached for her pelisse.

'We must talk,' he said, deciding he had best alter his approach. He had no desire to frighten her into flight.

Victoria stopped her retreat at his soothing voice. She said in a cautious voice, 'Yes? An arrangement for the night?'

He grasped at the proffered straw. 'Indeed.' Egad, but this was becoming a bit sticky. He wished he knew how she felt regarding him. If he proposed, and upset her with his speech, he could destroy the fragile thread that bound them. Yet he wondered if it might not be the best thing to do. If only he knew. He did not want her to think he would propose out of duty, but how to convince her?

'Might I suggest that we attend a party, or perhaps the theater this evening, all together? Let everyone, particularly the villain, see that we have no worries.'

'I cannot speak for my sisters, for Julia was sadly out of curl, and Elizabeth was not in plump current either.'

'But you would go with me?' He hoped he did not sound like a green lad begging a favor from a lady he admired.

'I shall.'

She was foolish beyond permission to go with him to wherever it was. It would be far more sensible for her to remain at home, or better yet, go only with her sisters and avoid all the gentlemen they cherished too much. Yet, even her pride could not prevent her from grasping a chance to enjoy his company while she could. What a blessing he did not possess that bit of information.

So that evening found her dressed in a sea-green crepe gown with a vandyked border around the hem. Dainty sleeves that fell in points revealed more of her arms than they concealed, and the neckline dipped low. She wore a double strand of pearls around her neck and hoops of pearls in her ears. On her head she had wound a clever concoction of pearls and twisted satin in and about her hair.

Evenson beamed an approving smile on his lady when she gracefully descended the stairs. At the foot, she paused, then asked, 'Is either of my sisters about, Evenson?'

'They retired to the workroom just a bit ago, miss.'

Feeling enormously elegant in her dainty Roman sandals of the very latest design, Victoria whisked herself down the hall. She peeked around the door, then smiled with hope. Her sisters argued as they frequently did.

'I say we should.'

'Should what?' Victoria demanded nicely.

'Skip the lace caps, at least until we are very old and decrepit,' Elizabeth pertly said in reply.

'I shouldn't worry about that at this point. Who knows, someone special may come along to steal your heart, and before you know it, you will be married with a baby in your arms. I wish you both were going with me this evening.'

'Are you worried? I should think you would not come to harm with Sir Edward to protect you,' Julia said wistfully.

'It is rather nice to have a gentleman who is strong and protective, is it not?' Elizabeth added, her eyes staring off into space.

'Indeed,' Julia murmured, exchanging a look with Victoria.

Seeing that it was hopeless to persuade her sisters to join her, Victoria returned to the entry in time to greet Sir Edward when he entered.

She was vastly pleased with his reaction this time. He seemed properly impressed with her appearance in the sea-foam crepe. She hoped he did not suspect she desired to impress him. 'I trust I shall pass for whatever you have in mind?' she said hesitantly, not fishing for a compliment, but hoping he might give a hint as to where they were to go.

'I feel sure that the Duchess of Rutland will be awed, my dear.' He bowed low over her hand, then escorted her to his town coach, seeing to it she was comfortable before they took off.

'We fly high this evening.' Victoria was reasonably comfortable with the upper regions of society, not but what she did not qualify for such a position. Her antecedents were impeccable. However, she had become accustomed to the slightly less rarefied atmosphere at Lady Tichbourne's conversaziones. She found she enjoyed the discussions there on interesting topics far more than the usual gossip found at balls.

'Not really, the invitation sat on my desk, and I thought it useful. Anyone who is anyone will be there, and we shall be much in evidence. Leighton has promised to keep an eye on the house while we are gone. Your sisters will be quite safe.'

Victoria recalled what Lizzie had said about how nice it was to be with someone who was protective. How true.

The ball was utterly fantastic. The decor was incredibly lovely, all in peach and cream, in the best of taste. Victoria bent to sniff one of the peach roses, inhaling sharply. 'How lovely.'

'I'm pleased you like roses, my dear,' murmured Sir Edward. 'I do as well. Pay attention, now; look about you with discerning eyes.'

Faintly annoyed with him, Victoria glanced about as he guided her through the throng of people. 'I see the usual people. Even Mr Padbury is here this evening. I wonder if he has his drizzling box along with him.' At Sir Edward's raised eyebrows, she explained, 'It is a lovely tortoiseshell thing and has interesting little spools upon which to wind the gold and silver thread.'

'Ignore the man, for I think him somewhat a mushroom. Concentrate on the others. Smile as though you haven't a worry in your head. In fact, it might be an interesting idea if you were to look at me as though you cared for me. It would cause talk. Could you manage that?'

'Why? Do you fear someone has dug about and discovered the windmill episode?'

'Rather.' He reached into his coat pocket and drew out a small packet. 'Look at this, then smile at me as though you adored me. It will require acting, I know, but try.'

'It is challenging. I shall give it my best.' His eyes teased her as she met his gaze. Bestowing a brilliant smile on him that made him positively blink, she then turned to the packet. Inside was a small drawing . . . of a windmill.

She continued to smile, saying through clenched teeth. 'That hardly means what I think it might, does it?'

'I am afraid so, my dear,' he said, drawing her closer to him. very much fear that we had best announce our engagement if we wish to thwart the blackmailer, or whatever he wants.'

'I thought he wanted a cipher, or the list, or whatever we had at the point he learned about the papers.' Victoria was all at sea. Things were not going quite as she anticipated this evening.

'Smile,' he commanded as he bowed to Lady Chatterton.

Victoria gave Lady Chatterton a supercilious look, then smiled on a young girl who was obviously in her come-out and looked frightened to death.

'What was all that about?'

'Later.' Victoria smiled until she thought her muscles would freeze permanently into position. She listened as Sir Edward dropped broad hints to all and sundry that the charming lady at his side would soon be his bride.

Victoria seethed with frustration as she realized that she would have to retire from society far sooner than she had expected, for the breaking of this 'engagement' would be more than a nine days' wonder.

'I believe we can leave now. If there is a soul at this ball who does not know about our impending marriage, he is not worth the effort.' Sir Edward began to lead her toward the door.

'We shall dance once first, I believe,' insisted Victoria. 'I do not contemplate going into enforced retirement without a final waltz.' Ignoring his quizzical look, she turned to the dance floor with mixed emotions.

They whirled about the room, graceful, ever revolving in the new and rather scandalous dance. Victoria stored up the feel of his arms about her, his closeness. He bent his head so as to appear to be whispering sweet nothings to her.

'You dance this well.'

'Thank you,' she murmured in reply, gazing up at him with the famous Dancy smile pinned to her lips. Could her heart be shattered? It felt so terribly crushed and broken.

14

'It will be a miracle if I have a strand of hair on my head after this affair,' Victoria complained. Seated at her desk, with Sir Edward far too close for her comfort, she tried again to solve the enigma of the encoded list, if that indeed was what was on the page before her.

'You smell like a garden of lilacs this morning,' Edward replied. This non sequitur dropped into the stillness of the room with the impact of a large feather.

Wisely ignoring this bit of nonsense, Victoria rose from the desk to walk back and forth at some distance from where Sir Edward sat at ease, watching her from beneath hooded lids.

'We get nowhere,' she cried in frustration. 'How dreadfully clever of him, whoever he is.'

'Perhaps we ought to turn our attention to something else for a bit, like the windmill episode?'

Victoria stopped her pacing. Wary of this handsome man, she faced him with courage. 'About last night. . . .' She had searched her mind for the best way to bring the subject up, and this might be as good as any. 'You cannot be serious about this marriage business?'

'But I am, my dear,' Sir Edward replied. 'I

know you feel something for me, and it can improve, given time. Neither of us courts the rebuff of Society.'

'Utterly absurd.'

'Perhaps for you, but what about young Elizabeth, and the lovely widow, Julia? Do you wish to risk their alienation from Society?'

'We have covered this before.'

'And you are still mixed-up.' He rose from his chair, then crossed to her side, took her chin in his hand, and gazed at her with determination. 'Come, let us take my head to the foundry. We can discuss this at greater length on the way, and in the privacy of our carriage.'

'Very well,' she said faintly, wondering if his touch had this effect on other women. She felt something like a puppet, meekly following his will. Of course, her knees were weak and trembly as his hand caressed her face, and the puppet was stiff, rigid, moving precisely.

Victoria fled the room and hurried up the stairs while Edward slowly strolled to the entry area, nodding politely to Evenson when that gentleman came in from the kitchen.

'I am sorry that you were disappointed last evening, Sir Edward,' the butler offered in a rare bit of conversation.

'I have a feeling that he will strike tonight. See to it that the servants are silent. I do not want a screaming woman turning the whole thing into a fiasco.' Edward exchanged a knowing look with Evenson, who bowed his head in awareness what silly wigeons maids could be.

'Indeed, sir. May I say that I am most pleased Miss Dancy has a companion? She misses her brother very much, for he's a fine lad, and they were very close.'

'You may. And I was unaware of that closeness.' Edward wondered if young Dancy would expect to be approached with an offer of marriage for Victoria.

Edward's inclination remained the same—to get Victoria to the altar as quickly as possible. Waiting was driving him to the brink of distraction. Also, he knew full well the harsh treatment that Society could mete out for one who overstepped the boundary established for proper conduct. Victoria, by his rescuing her from the carriage accident, and then spending two nights with her in that lonely windmill, had gone far beyond what Society allowed. That someone else knew of this and now threatened their future made marriage imperative. Coupled with her venturesome behavior, sculpturing the heads of prominent gentlemen, she was even more vulnerable.

He cherished her far too much to wish her to be humiliated by the tabbies and prattleboxes. And they would gleefully tear the beautiful Miss Dancy, the woman who led such an unconventional life, to bits and pieces.

Upstairs in her room, Victoria searched her wardrobe for the jade pelisse. Her maid entered with the desired garment over her arm, having just sponged and pressed it.

Within minutes Victoria had slipped it over her simple green sprigged jaconet and had set her bonnet carefully on her curls. Gathering up her reticule and York tan gloves, she left the room in a preoccupied daze.

As she neared the bottom of the stairs, she was met by Sir Edward, who gazed at her with what seemed to be decided fondness, if she was any judge. But how did he really feel? Did he act thus merely to make her feel better about what had occurred?

All the while she had been in her room, her mind had whirled round about in the same struggle that had been going on for hours. Could she yield to his persuasion? No matter what her personal feelings might be, she truly did not wish her dear sisters to be ostracized from Society. And, she supposed, Sir Edward would be a most agreeable husband, from what she'd observed of the man.

He escorted her to his phaeton while her mind feverishly mulled over a way to discover how he truly felt toward her. She'd not force him to wed her, Society or no.

The footman brought the bust out to the carriage, and Victoria insisted upon holding it before her, even though it was painstakingly wrapped so no damage could come to it on the journey.

The horse clopped along, and Victoria braced her feet so she could retain firm hold on the parcel, as well as herself.

'Now,' Sir Edward began, 'I firmly believe we have no choice but to wed. To this end, I propose our marriage. Will you accept my offer, Victoria?' he said most properly.

She looked at that aristocratic profile; the imperious nose, noble brow, and that sensual mouth. 'Do I have an alternative?' She knew the answer, but hoped he might think of a way out of this coil. He was terribly clever; she had seen that time and again. He also set her on fire with his touch, put her senses reeling, and in general caused havoc with her thinking process. She no longer trusted her own judgment.

'Would it be so terrible? A compromising situation in the beginning, perhaps, but we seem to deal well enough together. Many a marriage has a worse foundation.' He glanced at her before returning his attention to the street ahead.

They were traversing an unpleasant part of the city, and it appeared to bother Sir Edward that she went to this area often. The buildings were sturdy brick—not all that old—but the streets teemed with drays and wagons, people of the lower orders who were coarse in language and of vulgar ways. She had not allowed it to concern her in the past.

Victoria mulled over his words. She had to admit that he was right in his assessment of contemporary matrimony, for she knew many marriages of the *ton* were arranged, that the couples scarcely knew one another, and what they did know often repelled them. At least she and Sir Edward appeared to get along reasonably well. Most of the time.

They reached the foundry, and Sir Edward walked around the carriage, using his cane to clear debris from his path. By the time he reached Victoria, he frowned with dismay.

'This place lacks a certain something, I should say,' he commented in a prodigious understatement.

She repressed a smile. 'It is not so bad, really, and it does have Mr Greene. He is the wizard who turns my wax heads into elegant and enduring bronze. Come,' she pleaded, with a smile over her shoulder as she daintily stepped over a brick while making her way to the front door of the building.

The business was conducted much as usual, only this time Edward observed the process, watching with keen eyes as Victoria ordered things to her wishes with sure knowledge of what she desired. He seemed impressed. Mr Greene also bowed to Victoria's orders. They were not questioned in the least, an unusual occurrence in this day and age when men ruled and ran nearly everything.

When she accepted Edward's arm to leave

the foundry, he appeared at a loss of words. He tucked her into the phaeton, then drove off toward the center of London in silence.

'A penny for them,' Victoria said at last.

'I wondered what our children will think of that head in years to come,' came his audacious reply.

'You *are* taking a lot for granted, are you not?'

'Give over, Victoria. Think of it this way . . . we can work together, plotting and planning, and have a good life in the process. I intend to send off a notice to the papers immediately. Which church do you attend? I shall have the banns posted at once, for there is no need to wait. You undoubtedly would like your brother to be here, but we have no notion as to when he will return, or if a message sent to him will even reach him in time. The decision must be yours. But think of him. Make the wrong choice, and you could harm his chances for a respectable marriage as well. You know how scandal can stick like cold porridge to those near and dear.'

Victoria studied him as they neared the park. He wound through the arch of greenery, although she ignored the lovely trees and flowers to be seen on a fine spring day. 'I expect you are correct. I attend St George's, but perhaps we might be married in the evening?'

'I want no breath of anything out of the

277

ordinary for our wedding. No hasty visit to Doctor's Commons for us, my dear. We will have a church wedding with banns and everything,' he went on, as stubborn and firm as a rock on the subject. 'I want to see you in white silk and a lace veil down your back.'

'As you wish.' She would let him win this small battle. Indeed, she would be far too concerned about any number of other matters to be worried about the ceremony. Not even her gown or the other particulars occupied her concern. She was determined to make him fall in love with her, and the sooner the better.

A flower seller had established herself at the edge of the park, offering a variety of blooms for sale. Sir Edward drew the carriage to a halt, then beckoned to the girl. He bought three bunches of fragrant spring flowers, handing them to Victoria before setting off for the Dancy house again.

Victoria inhaled the scent with pleasure. At least her husband would be thoughtful. Until. . . .

'I don't know what is going on in your mind, but forget it for a time,' he ordered. 'We have a full day ahead of us.' He drew the carriage to a halt before her home. 'Part of me wants to proceed with a special license and marry you at once, now, the sensible part realizes that we must wait.' He reached out to caress her face, realizing that he exerted some sort of effect on her—how much, he wasn't sure. But he needed everything in his power to convince her that their marriage was a necessity, for many reasons.

Again he wondered if he ought to confess that he had fallen madly for her. It wasn't the thing for a gentleman to do nowadays. Would she laugh at him?

He had begun the process that first day, when he undressed her in the windmill lest she catch a dreadful cold, or worse. He had been improper. She was aware he had slipped her wet clothes from her, to prevent an illness. But, he rebutted the imaginary confrontation, he had not taken near the liberties he had desired. Both then and now she captivated him. Then, he had grown in interest, fighting it when he thought her a spy for the French. Yet she said nothing, and he wondered how to persuade her.

It would be with great pleasure that he would make Victoria Dancy his.

Shaken by the intensity of his softly spoken words, not to mention that gentle and evocative touch, Victoria darted a cautious glance at him, then left him to enter the house, her preoccupied air surrounding her like a cloak. He was being sensible? But what if he wished otherwise?

She found Julia in the morning room, sitting quietly with the girls playing near her. They babbled in their incomprehensible way, while Julia half-listened, her mind obviously elsewhere.

'Trouble?' Victoria wondered how her sister would accept the news of the coming wedding.

'I was merely thinking about what Lord Temple said yesterday. He is taking the miniature down to his mother in the country and will be there for a time, then return to London. He offered no clue as to what he wants to talk to me about, but, oh, Victoria, I shall see him once again.'

'Oh.' Victoria sank down upon a chair and stared at Julia, her mind in a spin. Never had she seen Julia look so entranced by anything. If Lord Temple had an improper proposal to make her sister, Victoria would personally shoot him.

'What about you? Sir Edward took you to the foundry this morning?' Julia caressed Tansy's curls when she came to lean against her mother's knee.

'We are to be married, Julia,' Victoria announced with not a jot of finesse. 'He received a packet that contained a drawing of a windmill, just like the one in which we took refuge. I thought and thought of a way out of this coil, but after last night I realized there is no way. Sir Edward paraded me from one end of the Rutland ballroom to the other, proclaiming in his offhand manner that we were about to stroll down the aisle.'

'But, that is wonderful.' Yet there was a hint

of doubt in her voice.

'I shall marry a man who is compelled to wed me because we have spent two nights together—with me unconscious part of the time—and our main affinity is a shared fascination with ciphers.' Her laugh was decidedly dejected.

'That is not at all unusual, love. At least, the lack of common ground,' Julia offered with the wisdom of one who has listened to countless hours of shared confidences from her married friends. 'If you are clever, you can build on that.'

'Truly? That sets my mind at ease, I suppose.' Victoria leaned back in near-collapse. She felt tense with worry, worn with fatigue from hours spent awake in the night. His kisses had stirred her to want more of them, and she longed to slip down the hall to her own room, to again know his passion. From what little she knew, a wife was not supposed to possess such yearnings. Perhaps she was more suited to the role of a mistress?

'Do not worry about Elizabeth and me. We shall do quite well, you know,' Julia assured her quietly.

'I would invite you to live with us, but I have not mentioned the matter to Sir Edward. And anyway, there is no sign of Geoffrey on the horizon, much less a wife. However, I feel sure you both would be welcome in our home, if needs be.'

'Heavens, intrude upon a newly married couple? That would be most unkind, my dear.' Julia chuckled at the image of a highly irate Sir Edward when confronted with relatives on his honeymoon.

'But welcome, all the same,' Victoria insisted. She was frightened of her emotions, and she would gladly receive her sisters as a buffer.

'We shall find our little house if it becomes necessary. Perhaps we will visit Aunt Bel for a time, after your wedding.'

'Oh, Julia, what am I going to do?' Victoria wailed, suddenly overcome with the enormity of the situation into which she had been plunged through no fault of her own. She stared bleakly at the array of flowers that lay in her lap.

'Persevere, my dearest. Persevere.'

The day wore on. Elizabeth accepted the news of the coming wedding with surprising tranquillity.

'I hope I shall have the privilege of attending you,' she said timidly, quite unlike the usual Elizabeth.

'You and Julia are the only ones I care about,' Victoria declared.

'We shall wear aquamarine,' Julia said in a decisive manner.

Even the thought of her favorite color did not bring a smile to Elizabeth's lips. Victoria and Julia exchanged worried glances.

'Fine,' Elizabeth said. She knelt on the floor to play with Rosemary, allowing her niece to pull ribands and tug curls with impunity.

'Victoria,' Elizabeth inquired suddenly, 'who do you suppose sent that drawing, and did they really intend blackmail? Or was something else contemplated?'

'I wondered the same. It is the outside of enough when a couple can be forced into marriage merely because of a chance circumstance. It is not as though we plotted the thing, or I set out to trap the man. Nor him, for that matter. And why threaten us with what is now old news?' She well knew that such a matter could hang over a woman's head for years, but it seemed so vastly unfair that she had to rail against it.

'Think back. It had to be someone who knew of your whereabouts, when you were due to return home, and that you were delayed. That person would have had to have access to a good bit of information. Who?' Elizabeth turned to look earnestly at both her sisters.

'Well, we chatted with any number of people at the conversazione after I returned. Could we have permitted a word then without realizing it? And there are the people in the war office who know that I had been in Dover and was delayed on my way home. Perhaps the traitor lurks within?'

'I bumped into Lord Leighton near the war office,' Elizabeth commented.

'Surely you do not believe he has had anything to do with this?' Julia exclaimed, openly shocked.

'Well, he pops up at the oddest places, and he has sought me out a number of times for no particular reason I can see. And he was at the war office, as I said.'

'Oh, Elizabeth, I hardly think he would be a traitor. Sir Edward appears to think quite highly of him.' Julia glanced from Victoria to Elizabeth and back again.

'It might be that he finds your charms irresistible,' teased Victoria.

'Rubbish,' Elizabeth declared fervently. 'I suspect he is up to something. And,' she continued, 'I hope you will not try to hoodwink me again like you did when he stayed the night in the library.'

'He shall be there tonight, dearest,' Victoria cautioned, not wishing a repeat of the previous eruption.

'I shall take great care to keep my distance, in that event. I mislike being teased. That is for children.' Elizabeth raised her pretty nose, then turned as the door opened to admit a young maid carrying a bouquet and a missive.

'Miss Dancy, these just came for you.'

Victoria accepted the flowers and the note, dismissing the girl with polite thanks.

'What does he say?' Elizabeth inquired
284

pertly.

'Lizzie, have a care,' Julia scolded.

'It is nothing more than written notification that he has arranged for our wedding at St George's; the first of the banns are to be called next Sunday. And the announcement shall be in the *Morning Post*.' Victoria looked at the bouquet of spring flowers, gorgeous French lilacs, then sniffed their sweet perfume.

'Is that all?' Elizabeth mocked. 'I should hope that if I ever marry, my husband-to-be would be more lover-like than that.'

'Elizabeth, enough!' Julia said, her temper snapping. 'You are well aware this is far from the usual wedding.' She took note of the expression on Victoria's face, then went on, 'Besides, Sir Edward has a million things to do, I am sure. He will be here this evening, along with Lord Leighton. Please try to remember that there is far more at stake here than what is on the surface.'

'Yes, little sister,' Victoria added. 'How many weddings can you recall that have come about owing to a matter of state? Other than the royal ones?'

Elizabeth pointedly turned her back on her sisters and resumed playing with the twins.

After sharing a concerned look at this uncommon behavior of their sister with Julia, Victoria shrugged, then quietly slipped from the room, taking her lilacs with her.

The day did not get better. Victoria wondered what would happen if she simply disappeared, and contemplated a trip to Portugal to seek out Geoffrey. The impossibility of the task brought her consideration to an end.

Late in the evening she took refuge in her temporary bedchamber, making certain first that her nightgown and all other things she might wish were removed from her room.

The house grew quiet and, as Victoria snuggled beneath her covers, her mind wandered down the hall into her room. Would the intruder return tonight? Sir Edward appeared convinced that he would.

She turned over, trying to find sleep. Her eyelids kept flying open at the least hint of sound. At last she gave up, pushing herself up in her bed and stuffing an extra pillow behind her.

Dared she light a candle? Perhaps not, for these muslin curtains would reveal the light. What was happening along the hall? Had Sir Edward met with Lord Leighton? Who was where? And what if Sable interfered, or barked at the wrong moment, or was hurt?

She scrunched down under the covers, contemplating the problems that might arise.

Was that a creak in the hall? She could stand the suspense no longer. Quietly she threw back her covers, then carefully rose from her bed, ignoring the slippers she had used earlier. She would need to use her bare feet to find the way beyond a doubt. Grabbing her favorite blue robe, she hastily tied it about her, then crossed to ease open the door to the hall.

Silence.

She stood for several minutes listening, wondering. Then she began her soundless inch-by-inch advance upon her room. She knew every squeak in the wood floor, every lump in the carpet, and all protrusions into the hall. She avoided touching the doors along the way.

Her heart thumped madly, and in the silence of the house it sounded like the pounding of a horse on a woodland path. Hands damp with anxiety and nerves stretched more tautly than ever in her life, she continued on her noiseless course.

Then she heard a faint scrape of wood—the very slightest of sounds—and she remained as a statue, silent and still.

Nothing. It seemed as though her heart stopped while she waited, wondered.

Then all the world broke loose. A shot rang out, followed by sounds of scuffling. A piece of china crashed to the floor, and a fleeting thought was spared for her precious Dresden water pitcher.

When Sable yelped as though in pain, Victoria could stand it no longer. She dashed to the bedroom door, alone, for all the others had been warned to stay in their rooms.

Throwing open the door to her room, she could see little, in spite of being somewhat accustomed to the dark. Two figures wrestled near the window. Sable could not be seen, but she heard his whimpering and winced when he yelped again, quite obviously kicked by someone, most likely the intruder. Sir Edward would never knowingly harm the dog who so obviously adored him.

She took a step inside, wishing she knew how to help. She had grabbed a large wooden toy before leaving her temporary room, and now raised it, only to lower it again. What if she hit the wrong person?

Then she saw a flash of metal in the faint light from the window. 'Look out!' she cried, afraid that Sir Edward would be shot, possibly killed.

Bang! The reverberation of the gun seemed loud enough to bring down the ceiling. Victoria ran forward, unable to remain by the door. She paused at the corner of her bed, trembling, yet determined.

Finally she struck out, missing her target, to her frustration.

The intruder turned, dashed to the window, vaulted over the edge, and was gone.

'How did he do that?' Victoria whispered.

The second figure, whose silhouette she knew to be Sir Edward's, did not come to her, but rather dashed after the intruder, and in minutes had also disappeared over the sill.

Silence once again.

Victoria ran to the window, to discover ropes dangling over the side, and curious little metal clips at the window edge. Staring out into the poorly lit night, she could see nothing. Where had Sir Edward gone? Was he all right?

She lit a candle, bringing it to the window to examine the scene more closely. Evidence of the scuffle lay all about her. She glanced out of the window again, worried and fearful for the man she loved. Dear God, she prayed he'd be safe.

Sable whimpered again, and Victoria was at his side in a flash, upbraiding herself for her lack of concern for her pet. Blood seeped from a wound. She frantically hunted for a cloth, then cleaned the area before applying a pressure pad against it. The dog looked up at her with beseeching eyes, and Victoria settled herself on the floor, cradling his head in her lap.

'Victoria? What has happened?' Julia rushed into the room, followed by Elizabeth.

'We heard the shots. Gracious, this room looks upside down,' Elizabeth declared softly, as though afraid that the villain lurked somewhere nearby. 'Sir Edward is gone?'

'I fear for his life,' Victoria said, sweeping a glance over her room. Her beloved Dresden pitcher had been smashed to bits, and other belongings were scattered about the room as though a storm had churned it up.

'Sable has been shot. Send for Sam, if you will. There is nothing we can do now but care for the dog. Sir Edward and whoever he chased have gone. I heard the horses gallop off down the street.'

'Sir Edward did well to keep his horse close by tonight,' Elizabeth said.

'Indeed,' Victoria whispered, turning again to stare out of the window. Somewhere in the night Sir Edward pursued someone, and his life was most definitely in danger.

'How curious,' Elizabeth said, bending over to pick something up from the floor. 'A gold thread. I wonder what that came from? Perhaps your shawl?'

Victoria stared at the thread, shimmering in the candlelight. She owned no shawl, or anything else, for that matter, that had that sort of thread in it. But she knew where she had seen the like before.

15

'Perhaps I may be of help, Miss Dancy.' Lord Leighton entered the bedchamber, swiftly walking to where Sable curled up, half-draped across her lap. With great care he went over the dog, determining its injuries.

His hands were oddly gentle for a man, it seemed to Victoria as she observed him. Watching with worried eyes as Leighton examined the large pet, she found herself torn. Part of her felt she must tend her devoted poodle; the other part wanted to dash after Edward. The sensible part of her took over when Sam stepped hesitantly into the room, pausing by the door before striding over to the injured dog.

'Bad, is he?' Sam queried in a compassionate voice. 'Let us see.' The two men conferred together, totally ignoring Victoria, who sat beside them numb with all that had occurred the past hour.

'I think it best if we take the animal to the stable, miss. It gets along fine with the horses, and we can tend it best there.' Sam bobbed in her direction with a semblance of courtesy.

Drained beyond belief, Victoria reluctantly nodded. As much as she wished to remain by her pet, she knew full well that Sam could do what was necessary for now. She would rest, then assume the job of nursing the dog who had served her with such faithfulness.

'As you say, it is most likely for the best.' She watched them gently carry the dog from the room, using a small rug that Elizabeth thrust at Sam for a sling. When their footsteps had faded away, she pulled herself up, then walked to the window to examine again the curious metal pieces that clamped inside the window surround.

'I wonder if they are the sort of thing that is used by alpine climbers?' Julia said as she peered over Victoria's shoulder.

'Clever.'

'Everyone is clever in this but us,' Elizabeth said, her disgust obvious.

'I suppose we were simply too close to the situation,' Victoria murmured, wondering if she would ever be able to sleep this night. Where did he ride in the dark of the night? Would they head out of London? She wished she knew.

'I propose a lovely cup of chocolate, and Victoria may explain just why she was in this room when the shots went off. You might have been killed, love,' Julia reprimanded her gently. She gathered her sisters, then urged them from the bedchamber and down the stairs to the morning room. Within minutes chocolate was brought, having been anticipated by the cook, whose room was directly over Victoria's, thus she had heard the ruckus.

'I could not endure the suspense,' Victoria said after polishing off the hot chocolate. 'The house was like a tomb, and I wanted to know what happened.' At the accusing frown from Julia, Victoria shrugged, adding, 'My future husband was in there, likely to get killed if that intruder was handy with a gun.'

'For someone who did not wish to marry

him, you have done a changeabout.' Elizabeth added, more softly, 'Dear Victoria, we might manage without you, but I should never like to try.'

The sisters embraced and wiped the traces of moisture from their eyes; then, while Julia and Elizabeth straggled up to their respective beds, Victoria sought out Lord Leighton in the stable.

'Is there nothing we can do? The runners, perhaps? A message to the war office? I feel so helpless.' She paced up and down in the stable, heedless of her disheveled attire. Only when assured that Sir Edward would handle all himself, and not welcome interference, did she consent to go to her bed.

Victoria fell into an exhausted slumber. The house remained still until a late hour of the morning, when she woke. She felt disoriented for a moment; then all returned. Unable to do a thing about Sir Edward, other than worry, she hastily donned a simple muslin gown, then dashed down and out to the stable.

Sam looked up as Victoria paused in the doorway, her eyes huge with worry, ringed with fatigue.

'How is he?'

'He'll do well enough.' Sam relinquished his place by Miss Dancy's pet when she dropped on the clean straw to run a sensitive hand over the dog.

She gave a wobbly chuckle as a tail thumped a trifle weakly, and Sable's eyes met hers with their customary look of devotion. 'Yes, he'll do, at that.'

Ignoring breakfast, Victoria remained with Sable for some time, stroking the soft curly coat with gentle hands, soothing the dog, until she saw that it slept and appeared more comfortable.

When Sam returned, Victoria met his questioning look with relief. 'You have worked wonders, Sam.'

' 'Twarn't me. His lordship that was here did the most. Removed the bullet as neat as could be, and sewed up the wound like a sawbones.'

'How splendid. One never knows what others can do. I trust he has gone home to his bed?'

'Indeed, miss. Said to tell you he'd talk with you again later.'

When Victoria returned to the morning room to report Sable out of danger, Elizabeth merely sniffed at the account Sam had given of Lord Leighton's skill.

'I should like to know why he remained downstairs. We might all of us have been killed in our beds. He was in the library, was he not?'

'Two floors below and behind a heavy door. I doubt he heard much, and then, Edward may have had an agreement with him to stay where he was. You do not know.'

'More's the pity.'

Julia and Victoria exchanged speculative looks; then Victoria plunged into the other matter that concerned her greatly.

'That gold thread you found—do you still have it, Elizabeth?' Her sister rose to retrieve the snippet of thread from where she'd tucked it last night. 'I gather you recognize it?'

'Yes, unfortunately. Since Sir Edward is gone, there is little to do at the moment. But I shall keep my eyes and ears open, you may be sure.' She took the thread with her to her desk, placing it carefully upon one of the papers she had used for scribbling possible solutions to the cipher.

She spent the day alternating between her desk and the cipher, and tending to Sable. Although the wound looked nasty to her, it was soon obvious that the dog responded well to the treatment it received. By that evening she admitted that she could leave the house and attend a small party given by some friends, at her sister's insistence. Appearances must be kept up.

'I will not have you sinking into a green melancholy, my dear,' Julia scolded with affection.

'That would never do,' Elizabeth added with a grin.

The party might have been small, but it was select. The cream of Society gathered at the exclusive Harton House that evening. The girls had been delighted to receive invitations, and Victoria was glad her sisters had prevailed upon her to attend; she'd not have wanted to spoil their treat.

Everyone present had to know the details of the sudden engagement announcement, twitting Victoria on the absence of her betrothed. Unable to reveal where he had gone, she merely alluded to an unanticipated trip, for that was certainly the truth, and made the best of things.

Surprisingly, Elizabeth came to Sir Edward's defense with a stout encomium that astonished Victoria.

'He is wonderfully clever, and enormously kind, you know. I believe Victoria the most fortunate of women to have been captured by him.' She fluttered her fan in a flirtatious manner while making it plain that her dearest sister had been the one besieged.

The following days dragged by in much the same fashion. Between the hours she spent caring for her pet, Victoria accompanied her sisters to the shops.

The delivery of a cryptic note from Sir Edward revealed little beyond that he was giving chase, and requesting that she carry on. Victoria complied. She did not really care to purchase the trappings for a wedding, yet she felt it necessary to pretend. Gossips being what they were, there would be spiteful sniping if she were not seen out and about buying all the frills and furbelows deemed necessary for a bride. She felt a fraud. Her mind dwelt on Sir Edward, not this nonsense.

Lady Tichbourne accosted Victoria while she peered in a Bond Street window at an elegant, but probably expensive, bonnet that was the height of fashion.

'My dear, wherever is that betrothed of yours? He should be doing the pretty with you. What is a betrothed for, if not to carry parcels?' Victoria had to smile at that bit of silliness.

'Do you marry at St George's? And by banns or special license?' Her gaze pierced the shell encircling Victoria.

Here Victoria was on firm ground. 'Sir Edward insists on banns, my lady. I shall have Julia and Elizabeth to attend me, of course.'

'The wedding?'

'The first of the banns is to be read this coming Sunday.' Then, turning her face toward the window, Victoria said, 'Is that not the most becoming bonnet? I expect it is shockingly dear.' Her hand crept up to finger the iris locket, seeking comfort from the miniatures within. It nestled nicely beneath her mantle, atop her round gown of soft blue merino.

Lady Tichbourne followed suit, and began a discourse on the wickedly high prices of the day.

One thing Victoria noticed as she went about her days was that while she did not see Sir Edward, neither did she observe Lucius Padbury.

Lord Leighton did appear, chat briefly, then would drift away. He twitted Elizabeth, but there was not the least sign of an attachment. It could be noted that she might not speak to him, but she followed his form with what she thought to be surreptitious finesse.

Sunday morning the three Dancy women dressed with more care than usual, then repaired to St George's for the morning service. When the second lesson had been read, it was immediately followed by the reading of the banns.

'I publish the banns of marriage between Sir Edward Hawkswood, baronet, of this parish, and Miss Victoria Dancy, spinster, of this parish. If any of you know cause, or just impediment, why these two persons should not be joined together in holy matrimony, ye are to declare it. This is my first time of asking,' the curate announced in his most carrying voice. It echoed through the church with a resounding firmness.

These intimidating words were followed by what seemed to Victoria an enormous silence. She glanced nervously about her, wondering if perhaps there was someone who knew heaven-only-knew-what about one or the other of them. She could see why many women chose to be absent at this formidable event. Some were even superstitious about it, refusing to hear the banns read lest it bring bad luck.

There being no response to his query, the service then proceeded as usual. Victoria tried to concentrate on the sermon, but had little success.

'I should like to know where Sir Edward is now,' Elizabeth whispered as they slowly filed out of the church following the service.

'I presume he is chasing the man who entered the house,' Victoria replied with a semblance of calm.

'He could get killed doing that,' Elizabeth cried softly, then clapped a gloved hand over her mouth in dismay as she saw her sister turn pale.

Lady Chatterton drifted up to where the girls waited for Sam to collect them. 'My dears, how lovely to see you. Will the wedding take place right after the banns have been read?' she gushed to Victoria.

Victoria couldn't fail to detect Julia's sudden stiffening, and recalled the account given of the previous meeting between this lofty woman and her dearest sister.

'Yes, we intend to have a simple ceremony, with my sisters in attendance. Friends and neighbors, you know.'

'I had no idea that Sir Edward was in the

line for a wife,' Lady Chatterton gushed. 'Every chit in Town has been after him this age.'

'Perhaps that is why Victoria is to marry him.'

'Indeed?' Lady Chatterton was forced to meet Julia's gaze; a novel experience, for Julia looked at her with calm, resolute eyes, not in the least intimidated.

'You see, Victoria ran away from him, rather than chased, and Sir Edward was compelled to pursue her. I fancy there are some men who prefer to do the hunting.'

'Truly.' Frost descended over the elegant woman's face and she flounced off in a decided miff.

'Do you think that was wise, dear?' Victoria said as Sam maneuvered the carriage up to where they waited.

'I will not have her think I am a mealymouthed toad.' Julia glared with unaccustomed fervor at the departing figure, then chuckled. 'That was not well done of me, was it? Particularly after divine services!'

This sally was followed by general laughter, and they returned to the Dancy house with lighter hearts. If Julia was concerned about having made a firm enemy, she revealed none of it.

However, Victoria continued to worry about Sir Edward. She wished he might send her another note, or something to let her know he was well and safe. He rarely left her thoughts, and her hours were anxious ones.

*   *   *

Edward surveyed the occupants of the tavern at Folkestone. Not a familiar face in the lot. His prey was deucedly elusive, and far more clever than Edward had given him credit for being.

His trail had led Edward past the memorable windmill—the miller returned, from what he could see—into Barfreston, then down to Dover and along the coast. Edward fully expected to shadow his man for as long as it took, but he hoped capture would be soon. Hythe came next, followed by Dymchurch, and Old and New Romney—*New* Romney dating from somewhere in the thirteenth century, he thought, and scarcely new.

Damn and blast—he ought to be in London with Victoria, not haring about the countryside, following a man who should be a snap to catch, but proved a slippery fellow. About as appealing as an eel, too. Still, Edward wished to see where he fled, and who his contacts might be, prior to apprehending him.

Edward left the tavern, then remounted his tired horse and rode off down the miserable excuse for a road. Small wonder the mail coaches refused to run west from Dover. This track looked fit for nothing more than the cart that took mail into Dover for transfer to the London mail.

He wondered what Victoria was doing, and this contemplation occupied him for some miles along the coastal route to Hythe. This was all smuggling country along here, he recalled, making a note to be well indoors come night. With no moon this evening, who knew what might happen?

On the outskirts of Hythe he paused to survey the area. The town was no longer a major harbor, but the sea still lapped against the smooth shingle shoreline, with innocent-looking fishing boats straggling along the beach. Through the town ran the Royal Military Canal, built as a barrier against the anticipated attack by Napoleon, which had never come to be—as yet.

Edward suspected that Napoleon had finally realized his forces were no match for the British navy, turning his attention to Austria, a far more agreeable task for him.

The first inn came into view and Edward dismounted, tossing his reins to a likely lad, then went inside, thinking this sorry work. Not a familiar face here either. He headed for the innkeeper with a coin in his hand.

*   *   *

'Do you know, I have had another request for banknotes. Only these are to be Austrian,' Elizabeth said in a quiet voice, glancing about to ascertain no one was near. She still felt they could trust no one, not even servants of some standing.

'Clever, how they send these along through the various banks. I wonder if they don't transmit a bit of news the same way?' Victoria said, looking up from the pair of heads she was doing. She had promised Julia for an age to sculpture the twins, and felt this a good time.

'I daresay our surveillance work is not well done. *I* would plan things differently,' Elizabeth declared.

'Well, I do wonder. Geoffrey complained of a severe lack of maps when they entered Portugal. Thank heaven he is fluent in Spanish and French. He was able to get about like a native, drawing hills and rivers to his heart's content. Although I expect we ought not know such things, for he wrote about that in code. As he pointed out, Wellington is a cagey sort, and plans most carefully.' Victoria watched as Elizabeth began to copy the Austrian banknotes with remarkable skill, her burin deftly cutting the design into the copper sheet.

'I think Geoffrey is a spy for Wellington,' Elizabeth whispered, although there seemed no need for such care.

'It is possible. They are well into Spain now, and Geoffrey is in the thick of it, by all accounts. We hear so little. 'Tis frustrating.' Victoria turned her attention back to the wax models. 'I can see him out on his horse, checking the lie of the land, chatting up the *alcaldes* to learn as many French secrets as possible. He always was one able to charm the bark off a tree. What a family we are, and I shall marry another.'

'What will you and Edward do when the war is over and there are no more ciphers to solve?'

'I have asked myself the same question time and again, and the answer has never popped up before me.' Victoria gave her sister a troubled glance.

'I fancy you will think of something.' Julia gave a slight chuckle, then concentrated on her work.

The following Sunday the banns were read a second time, and Victoria felt distinctly uncomfortable to be sitting in her pew with no sign of a betrothed in sight. What would happen if Edward failed to materialize by the date set for the wedding? She would undoubtedly have to claim an indisposition and head for Aunt Bel.

The following evening they chanced to meet Lord Leighton at one of Lady Tichbourne's gatherings.

'I trust your dog is better,' he said to

Victoria after greeting the three of them.

Victoria had noticed the way Lord Leighton had darted an amused glance at Elizabeth, who in turn was making an elaborate attempt to appear oblivious of him. 'Indeed, sir. I believe you are a magician with animals, for Sable is as good as new. And I feel sure I have your skill to thank.'

'Happy to be of service. No word from Hawkswood?'

She lowered her voice and replied, 'Little, so far.'

'I had hoped to talk with him, but I have received an urgent message to go home. My father is unwell and the doctor deems it important that I travel as soon as possible. I leave at first light.'

Elizabeth gave him an arrested look, a revealing one from Victoria's point of view. How sad for Lizzie. It appeared Lord Leighton liked nothing more than to tease, and Elizabeth betrayed a deeper interest.

He remained to chat a brief spell with Victoria, assuring her that Hawkswood ought to return shortly, that he was one to get his man.

After Lord Leighton departed, the girls decided to leave as well. Elizabeth looked vexed and Julia looked bored. Victoria had no great desire to remain, and was pleased to head for her bed.

Lord Leighton's words returned. Would

305

Edward find his man, and soon? She loved the dratted man and missed him dreadfully, not to mention those fiery kisses that reduced her to a heap.

Restless and unable to settle to sleep, Victoria slipped on her robe and went down to the library and her desk. Once the place where her father had worked on his study of linguistics, it now housed all the helps Victoria used in her efforts to decipher the codes written by others. It was a simple matter to put a message into cipher, or code. To solve a coded message sent to someone else was much harder, especially if one did not possess the key to that particular code.

She recalled the gold thread, ran back up to her room to fetch it. Perhaps it would inspire her. She walked along to Julia's room to ask her a question.

Once inside, she waited while Julia tiptoed to the other room to peek at the girls. On the dressing table was a collection of pretty missives, the top one written on cream paper in blue ink with a familiar hand. Victoria had been staring at that particular writing for some time now, and would have recognized it anywhere. She picked up the short note, looking at the formation of the letters rather than at what was written.

'I did not know you were given to reading another's mail, Victoria,' Julia said coldly.

'You know that I am not. How came you by

this?' The letter was not signed properly, only a scrawl that might mean anything. Victoria studied her sister with narrowed eyes, hoping there was a simple explanation for this.

'Oh, Lucius Padbury requested sometime ago that I go for a drive with him. Actually, I was about to throw it out. Why?'

Victoria shrugged, suddenly uneasy, and unwilling to reveal her suspicion. 'May I have it for tonight?'

'Take it. The man is no longer about anyway. I have no use for it.' Julia made a dismissing wave, barely concealing her curiosity. The sisters were not given to prying, however, and she knew that Victoria would tell her what it was all about in due time.

Victoria nodded. Then, her original question long forgotten, she returned to the library and her desk. She placed the two pages side by side. It most definitely was the same hand. Lucius Padbury. Of all people to be a spy, she'd not have picked him.

Yet he had been around all the time, sitting quietly in the background with his drizzling box and fabrics, or whatever. One tended to forget he was there, which was precisely the sort of man who made an admirable spy, if one needed one. And what had been said in his presence? She thought for a few moments, becoming grim as she considered the matter.

How Mr Padbury had managed the invasion of her bedroom, Victoria did not know, but he had obtained information elsewhere, and it had slipped from his hands into hers. That was what he sought. Had she at one time dropped a remark about keeping papers in her room? It was possible, for she did keep a few there—but not where Lucius Padbury had hunted for them.

She continued to study the two pages, then made a startling discovery. The letter she had taken to be a G was instead a C. It was small wonder that she had not been able to solve the mystery of the cipher! Drat that man's wretched scrawl. Neither she nor Edward had caught that slight lack of a tail on the G, a serious error indeed.

After lighting several more candles and calling for a pot of strong coffee, Victoria returned to the desk and renewed assault upon the cipher.

*　　　*　　　*

Edward cautiously crept up the stairs in the small Dymchurch inn. A man matching the description he had given of his quarry supposedly reposed behind the second door down the hall.

It had been a tiresome trek, with rain that had soaked him to the skin, wind that had seemed to cut through his bones like a knife. Spring could be lovely in the country. Here it seemed to be harsh and unwelcoming, or was that merely his mood?

The floor creaked, and Edward paused. Then he continued on his way, for the man had shown no indication that he felt himself trailed. His path had been remarkably straight once he left Dover. Could it be that he believed he had thrown off any follower from his track? Edward's smile was grim. The villain was due for a shock, if that were the case.

Easing along the hall, Edward paused to listen by the second door for a time, before testing the doorknob. It yielded to his touch, and Edward blessed the small inn that could not afford locks that had keys. His man, so confident and assured, had not thrown the bolt on the door.

'Well, well, if it isn't Lucius Padbury. Fancy meeting you here in Dymchurch, of all places. What a small world it is.' Edward opened the door wide, facing his man with nerves and muscles tensed, ready for anything. His pistol, primed and loaded, covered the genial gentleman who stared at Edward as though a ghost had suddenly appeared.

'I say, old chap, not the thing to point a pistol at a friend,' Padbury blustered.

'No, it isn't. But then I wonder if you *are* a friend, Padbury. If you were such, what were you doing in Victoria Dancy's room not long ago? And in the middle of the night, too? I have shadowed you from there to here for nearly two weeks now, hoping to see where you would end up. It has been a most curious path, my good man. I am interested to hear your explanation. My patience is over. I have more necessary things to do. I believe you have a great number of answers to questions I long to ask. Won't you be seated?' Edward said with a false show of courtesy.

The shorter man, confronted by a steely gaze, not to mention that very lethal-looking pistol, slowly sank onto a plain wooden chair. It had slats that dug into his back, and the rush seat was coming apart. Of this he seemed unaware.

'I insist I do not know of what you speak.'

'I feel it may be a rather long night, in that event.' Sir Edward sighed dramatically. 'But rest assured that you shall answer all my questions in the end, my friend.' The sarcastic note in Sir Edward's voice appeared to frighten Mr Padbury, for he shrank against the chair, wincing as a slat dug into his spine.

'Now, to begin. First of all. . . .' Edward waved the gun in Padbury's direction and commenced his interrogation.

*　　　*　　　*

Victoria rubbed her face while she paced her room. Through the windows she could see the first light of day. She had worked all through the night. But it was worth it.

Locked in the small library safe were the deciphered results of her efforts . . . the list of names of those who sympathized with Napoleon and worked to further his victory.

The names on that list shocked her. Men in the highest of places: Parliament, the war office, even one in the Horse Guards itself. Since it was at the Horse Guards that the Depot of Military Knowledge was housed, it was no small wonder that this list had been guarded and put into the most difficult cipher Victoria had ever encountered.

She would sleep for a time. No one could make any sense of what she said until she felt more the thing. Later she would go to her superior at the war office, maybe demand to see the secretary of war himself, and present her translation. This was highest treason, and she wondered what would be done. How did one deal with traitors of this level?

16

'I do hope you have an explanation for this,' mumbled Victoria, rubbing the sleep from her eyes and glancing at the clock on the mantel with a disgusted look.

'But it is nearly eleven, and you cannot be a slugabed all day,' Elizabeth protested. She drifted across the room to pull open the draperies, then the blinds.

'I want you to know that I have had all of six hours' sleep, my dear.' Whirling about, Elizabeth gave her sister a startled and most curious look. 'Why?'

'I broke the code last night.'

Elizabeth crossed to sit on the edge of the bed, fixing Victoria with eager eyes. 'Tell me how you did it, for I was beginning to think it hopeless.'

'Actually,' Victoria began, easing herself up, then stuffing another pillow behind her, 'it was Julia who helped, although she was not aware of it. I found a letter she was about to discard—one from Lucius Padbury.'

'I do not see what that mild man has to do with anything,' Elizabeth inserted.

'Do you wish to hear or not?' At her sister's silent nod, Victoria continued. 'I recognized the handwriting as the very same as on the page I have been trying to decipher. And I also found that a letter I had assumed to be a G was in actuality a C. The wretched man has terrible handwriting. Once I found that mistake, the rest began to fall into place.'

'How clever of you,' Elizabeth said with enthusiasm and no trace of envy in the least. 'Who would have suspected that Mr Padbury had anything to do with spying?'

'I cannot say as to that, for this was merely a list of men.' It had been more than that, but Victoria felt the fewer who knew the whole of the matter, the better. She pushed back her covers, then rose from her bed. 'I feel able to contend with the day after some sleep. I found that once I began work, I simply could not stop.'

Elizabeth gave her a dubious look. It was difficult for anyone who was not fascinated with codes and ciphers, and solving such puzzles, to understand what compelled another to spend long hours over them.

'What now?'

Victoria walked to the wardrobe to choose a special gown to wear for this important occasion. It was not every day she solved such a challenging cipher.

'I shall dress, eat something, then pay a visit to the secretary. I can only hope that by solving this, I shall redeem our part. For you know it is possible that Mr Padbury shamelessly eavesdropped, and construed much from our conversations.'

'He seemed like such a harmless little man. And to think that Julia might have accepted him!' Elizabeth exclaimed in horror.

'That is a blessing, although I believe she could have handed him the mitten under the circumstances.'

'Cried off? Regardless, that does not have a pleasant sound to it.' Elizabeth considered the possible results.

'No, it does not. Now, shoo, so I may wash and dress in peace. You may inform Julia of the wonderful help she unknowingly gave me.'

After the door closed behind her younger sister, Victoria paused to look out of the window at the delicate clouds, tinted pinks and grays. Somewhere south of London, unless she missed her guess, Edward was chasing Lucius Padbury. What happened if Mr Padbury shot Edward, rather than the other way around? She shut her eyes against the painful image, willing it to go away.

Well, she mused as she washed herself from the Dresden bowl that was all that remained of her pretty set after the fracas that had torn her room apart, that would be one solution to her dilemma, although appalling. It would be difficult to have a wedding without a groom.

Her cream jaconet gown, trimmed with knots of willow-green ribands and tiny gold silk flowers, hung in graceful folds down to where the tips of her new willow-green leather slippers peeked from under the hem. An enormous piece of luck had brought a pretty paisley shawl to her attention when she had strolled through Harding and Howell's. It precisely matched the gown. With her willow-green gloves and a rather nice bonnet trimmed in the same shade, she felt ready to face anything she might find . . . even Lucius Padbury, if necessary.

As to the man she was supposed to marry, she wondered if she would ever see him again. The mere notion tore at her heart. Then, dismissing all melancholy thoughts from her mind, she resolutely marched down the stairs to the dining room.

'Victoria,' Julia said, rising from her chair at the table, where she nibbled at her noon meal, 'I found two other missives from Mr Padbury. Foolish woman that I am, I had kept these for the pretty sentiments. Would they help you to prove beyond a doubt that he is the man involved?'

Suspecting that it cost Julia a great deal to hand over something slightly intimate, never mind that such pretty words were written every day, Victoria nodded gratefully.

'The more evidence I have in hand, the better. Not that I anticipate trouble, mind you.'

'Do you wish company?' Elizabeth said from the far end of the table where she picked at a salad.

'Not in the least. Sam will drive me.' Victoria placed her gloves down, and prepared to eat a small meal before taking her leave. Sable, who had padded in behind his mistress, gazed at her with reproachful eyes, sensing he was to be left at home.

'Lizzie, I am sorry Lord Leighton has gone to the country,' Julia said hesitantly.

'Fine,' Elizabeth declared, looking at them rather ruefully. 'When I consider what the gossips said about that man, it is the outside of enough. 'Tis a good thing he merely taunts me, nothing more.'

Julia and Victoria exchanged dismayed looks.

'Do you mean to tell me that you based your opinion of Lord Leighton on what the *gossips* are saying? Did it never occur to you, my precious widgeon, that they might be jealous of anyone he bestowed his attentions upon? He is handsome, well-to-grass, and heir to an earldom that has been efficiently managed. In short, he is not only very plump in the pocket—no small matter when it comes to choosing a husband—but also highly eligible in every way. In addition, he is a very nice person.'

'You needn't read me a scold. It scarcely matters when he treated me like a sister.' Elizabeth placed her fork on her plate and stared at the table with trembling lips.

'You ought to have turned your attention elsewhere, if that is the case,' Julia reproved her.

At which Elizabeth pushed aside her plate and flounced from the room, saying over her shoulder, 'I believe I shall make an extended visit to Aunt Bel when all this wedding fuss is over. I wish to get away from London, that is certain.'

'Oh, dear,' Julia said with a sigh, 'I believe I have hurt her feelings. Only, you know how she is about things.'

'She is young and pretty, and unlikely to go

into a decline. If I know Elizabeth, she will find something at Aunt Bel's to occupy her time quite well.'

'Maybe a nice young man?' Julia said with hope.

Victoria smiled, then turned her thoughts to the meeting at the war office. It would be an enormous relief to have this responsibility off her shoulders.

Once she finished eating, she swiftly went to the library, after informing Evenson to summon Sam to the front door. From the small safe she extracted the papers to be handed over, then paused, staring at them with a frown. She supposed she was being silly, but they were still in her hands, and she had heard nothing about Mr Padbury. What if he were still in London, say, having doubled back or something? Could he interfere with the delivery of these papers?

Someone knew too much about what went on in this house. How, she didn't know, but she could not take chances.

She undid the pins that held her gown at each shoulder, then folded the papers into a more manageable size and carefully stuffed them inside her stays, between her shift and that crisp white corset all young ladies wore. Her hand brushed against her locket, and her fingers stroked the blue lapis stones a moment. This small victory would avenge her parents, perhaps just a little. Satisfied that nothing could be detected, even if she was scrutinized, she redid her gown, taking care with the pins.

Before another hour had passed, she had stepped into the carriage and begun the momentous trip. When she ordered Sam to head for the war office, it was like taking the final lap of a long journey. Victoria leaned back against the squabs, pleased with her efforts, not to mention her appearance.

Directly across the street a tall thin man eased himself from the building where he waited most days, watching the Dancy household go about their business, and hailed a hackney, ordering the jarvey to follow Victoria. The man was one of those nondescript sorts, not the kind of person you would give a second look at, and dressed in sober gray that blended in with shadows.

The cobbled streets seemed more bumpy today than usual, Victoria decided. Or was it that Sam was traveling faster than normal? The carriage appeared to rock and jounce about, and she began to fear for the pretty bonnet she wore, when all of a sudden the carriage rounded a corner, then drew to a halt most abruptly.

Victoria nearly slid to the floor, and caught herself just in time, grabbing the strap by the door. She brushed down the folds of her pretty new gown and then let down the window to lean out and inquire of Sam what had happened.

'Good afternoon, Miss Dancy,' said a tall thin man with an exceedingly dark complexion. 'If you'd be so good?' He gestured to a waiting hackney. He used his hand, but Victoria quickly observed he held a small, lethal-looking gun.

She reluctantly opened the door, while trying to see if she might evade this man and his odious gun. What did he seek? Could he somehow suspect she carried the papers on her? She schooled her face to reveal nothing of her fears.

Sam stood by the horse, looking as though he would like to wring the stranger's neck. But she knew that if he made a move, he would be shot as quick as a wink. She shook her head as he met her gaze. 'Stay where you are, Sam.'

They had turned into an alley somewhere in the area off Charing Cross. It was a dark, quiet place, and she doubted if anyone would appear if a shot rang out. People tended to mind their own business here, as in most places in London. With thievery being what it was, few cared to interfere.

She took her reticule, into which she had dropped a number of guineas and five-pound notes, thinking to do a bit of shopping later. Now she offered it to the stranger.

'Aha, fancy to bribe me? Not but what I may take it anyways. No, Miss Dancy. Take note I know your name, by the bye. Now, get.'

He gestured slightly, but the very terseness of his move frightened Victoria.

She complied. Quickly walking to the hackney, she climbed up into the dusty interior, holding her skirts away from the straw-littered floor. Glancing about her with distaste, she again resolved to contain her fears. Somehow he must guess she carried the papers or something of value. Above all, she must guard those papers.

'How do you come to know my name?' she demanded of the man who had now joined her.

'You're famous, makin' all them heads that you take to a foundry. I've watched you. You go down to a place where ladies don't usually go.' He narrowed his eyes, surveying her with dreadful intent.

'What do you seek?' She tried to compose her nerves, to be prepared for whatever the man planned. The very idea that she had been watched by this man appalled her. She shifted, then froze. Did the papers nestled between her shift and stays crackle a tiny bit? She hoped than none but herself could hear it, if that were the case.

'Ah, that'd be telling. You just wait, you'll find out soon enough.' He sat back against the soiled cushions and made a very nasty grimace that must pass for a smile.

Victoria barely contained a shudder. 'I had not expected a simple shopping trip to be so hazardous.'

'Then why'd you tell your coachman to take you to the war office? I dunno of no shops there.' The man smirked, obviously pleased with his telling point.

He still held the gun in his hand, and Victoria kept it in sight at all times, no matter where she appeared to look. He aimed it at her. Never did he seem to relax.

'I merely intended to pick up a friend in the area, then go on to Piccadilly and Bond Street.' She ached with the effort to remain unmoving. 'Where do we go?'

'Shut your dubber. Think you're a regular duchess, you do, eh? I ain't answering no more questions.'

Victoria compressed her mouth, then licked her lips with the tip of a very nervous tongue. She glanced out the grimy windows of the hack, unable to figure out where they might be. After ordering her heart to be stout, she studied her foe. Mean-tempered, hasty, and as nasty as they come, she decided. Not the sort to argue with, nor persuade. He'd take her money, and what else?

She trembled, fighting it, and hoping that her tremors didn't show beneath the shawl draped over her shoulders.

The hackney drew to a halt.

'Get out, and don't forget my little friend,' he said, gesturing with the gun in his hand. He let out a mirthless laugh that sent chills down

Victoria's spine.

Gathering her skirts about her, she carefully made her way from the vehicle, making an assessment of the area without appearing to do so. They were in a warehouse section, dingy multistoried brick and wood buildings rising all about them. The alley was narrow and stinking, and she doubted if much daylight ever found its way to the ground. From the distance, the cacophony of hawkers and the clatter of traffic reached her ears. No one would hear her cries, should she call for help.

A door, badly nicked, brown paint peeling from it, stood in the middle of the wall on her right. She was not surprised when told to open it. Obediently she moved down the alley, then tugged at the door, which seemed to be stuck. 'I cannot.' She sounded helpless and frustrated even to her own ears.

Breath suspended, she hoped she appeared composed while she tied her shawl tightly about her. She felt to make certain her reticule was snugly about her wrist, then turned to face her captor, edging back as he drew closer to reach for the doorknob.

'Little weakling, eh? I s'pose most females of your ilk are.' Again that mirthless, chilling laugh.

Victoria was thinking furiously. There were no handy weapons, but she espied a pile of bricks nearby. She sidled another step away from the man and the door.

'Well, don't seem no problem ta me in the leastways.' He flung open the door, which creaked ominously. If it was used so little, it meant that few came in and out, and that meant there was little hope Victoria might get away, once on the other side of that door.

In a flash, she bent, grabbed a brick, and, thanking her adequate height, used both hands to knock the man over the head. She struck a second time as she edged past the door.

He staggered but did not go down. She hit the surprised man again. Her effort was enough so that she could push him inside the building, using all her strength, then push the door shut. She devoutly hoped that the thump she heard was the sound of his falling body.

But now what? Where could she flee?

Running madly down the ally, she chose to go left, seeming to recall that was the direction they had come. She darted in and out, eventually holding an arm to her aching side as she ran.

'Here, wot's this? A lady running? That's a laugh.'

Ignoring the gibe, Victoria again turned a corner, then darted in and out of various lanes, hoping to lose the man she felt sure would be on her trail.

Then she walked, as swiftly as she could, feeling she attracted less attention that way. If only she were not dressed in such conspicuous clothing. She was as out-of-place here as a chimney sweep at a Carlton House dinner.

How could she continue? She paused for a moment, leaning against a building to catch her breath.

'Trouble, miss?' An older woman wrapped in layers of shawls over a colorless dress approached her. Victoria paled as she considered who the woman might be. She appeared enormous and threatening, not the least comforting, as her words intended.

'None,' whispered Victoria, then fled, barely escaping from the grasping hand that had shot out from beneath that cascade of dirty shawls.

Stumbling on the uneven cobbles, wet here and there with puddles of nameless dark liquid that smelled rank and horrid, she injured her ankle. It ached something fierce, throbbing with pain. She rounded another corner, wondering if she might be going in circles, even as her bonnet flew off to bounce up and down on her back.

And then she saw a hackney. Dashing up to the jarvey, and most thankful it appeared to be a different man, she made a grab at the door. 'Whitehall, please.'

''Ere now, 'ow do I know you 'ave the price? You don't look like you'd 'ave twopence to rub together.'

Victoria glanced down, horrified to see her

gown was splattered, her shawl askew, and knew her hair must be a sight, what with her bonnet hanging down her back. Wasting precious moments, she opened her reticule and pulled a guinea from it. 'Get me there in a trice, and this is yours.'

Seeing the color of gold, he nodded and motioned her inside. He flicked a rarely used whip and they dashed off as he made his best effort to get that piece of gold. Such never came his way. His poor horse had never been so urged to speed, and it fortunately did not take umbrage at its treatment, in the surprise.

While they careened across London, Victoria attempted to rectify her appearance. First she combed her hair, a difficult task without a looking glass. Then, carefully replacing her bonnet, she tied the ribands in what she hoped was a fetching way. Her shawl might be straightened, but there was nothing she might do about the splattered gown. It was ruined. They would owe her for this, she thought grimly.

When she stepped from the carriage, she realized that she was close to safety, and took a calming breath. Dropping the guinea into the outstretched hand covered in a grimy glove, she then hurried up the steps and through the door.

It was fortunate that the young man on duty recognized her face, for she was certain her garb shocked him. She hobbled up another flight of stairs and down a hall, ignoring the people she saw along the way. Truth be told, she was so intent, it's doubtful she even noticed them.

The clerk in the outer office gasped as Victoria entered, then limped near his desk.

'Miss Dancy?' He half-rose, staring at her with amazed eyes.

'As you see. I have some important papers for the secretary. I do hope he is in?'

'He's in a conference with a gentleman. If you will wait here, I shall inform him you have something for him.'

Victoria turned her back on the door, wondering how in the world she could retrieve those papers from where they nestled! That was something she'd not figured on.

'Follow me, Miss Dancy,' came a reverent voice from behind her.

She whirled about, bowed her head graciously, and tried to behave as though she did not appear to have been dragged through a hedge backward.

'Miss Dancy, Percy said you appeared to have some trouble. Nothing serious?' her superior queried.

'No,' she replied thoughtfully, approaching the desk with her decided limp. 'Not unless you consider being abducted at gunpoint and then dashing for my life across the alleys and byways of London a problem. Otherwise, it was an uneventful trip.' She took a step toward the desk, then, her knees a trifle weak and her ankle giving her the very devil of an ache, she sank down on the nearest chair with a faint sigh. Like the other chair drawn up to the desk, it had a high back, and she found it extremely comfortable.

'Good grief!' the secretary declared. He glanced at the person in the other chair, then returned his attention to Victoria.

She was far too exhausted to take notice of who else was in the room. Indeed, perhaps it might be better were she to ignore the man. Yet she knew he would not be there now were he not considered safe by the secretary.

'I have solved that matter that has eluded us for so long,' she said. 'If I might have a bit of privacy, I shall regain the papers from their place of safety.' At his mystified nod, she left her chair, turned her back, and removed the pins from one side of her gown. It was easier to pull the papers from their hiding place than it had been to stow them.

'There,' she declared triumphantly, turning again to face her superior once the pins had been replaced. She handed him the well-creased and faintly lilac-scented papers, placing them so her solution lay on top. Julia's letters were on the bottom, should confirmation be desired.

She again seated herself on the high-back chair, then watched with eager eyes as the import of what she had discovered sank in.

His changing expression told her all.

'Egad, but I cannot fathom this all. Unbelievable! Here, Hawkswood, have a look at this.' He glanced from one to the other. 'I believe you two do know each other.'

Victoria gasped as she turned her weary head to see Edward staring at her. His face looked oddly pale, and she wondered if he had been hiding out in a dark room while gone. He rose from his chair, taking a step toward Victoria, then realized the secretary still proffered the papers to him, and accepted them instead of going to her side.

It took all his willpower to read the papers. He knew the information was vital to the country's security. But dash it all, his Victoria had been through a hellish time. She needed cosseting far more than he needed to read these wretched papers. Then he began to realize the importance of the names on the list as the first caught his eye.

'So it *was* a list. How did you figure it out? What cipher worked?'

Brushing her fatigue away, Victoria smiled, then revealed, 'I spotted a letter while in Julia's room—I brought several along for comparison. When I read the first, I realized that I had mistaken the C for a G. His handwriting is so dreadful, it is a wonder I could read any of it. Anyway, once I had determined that change, the rest came fairly easily.'

'How many hours?' Edward demanded, suspecting it was not quite so simple as all that.

'Perhaps seven,' she admitted.

'Amazing,' he said, while narrowing his eyes in consideration that she must have been up half the night over this.

'The country owes you both a great debt of gratitude,' began the secretary.

'Padbury?' burst out Victoria, wanting to know if the man still went free.

'I trailed him from your home to the south, finally to Dymchurch. The last I saw of him, he was on a boat headed toward Australia. Not until I had wrung out every secret he possessed, however. He had a man watching you for a long time. That fellow was the one who learned of the windmill. Padbury knew of the iris connection.'

Sinking back in her chair again, Victoria felt drained, tired beyond belief. Her eyes were wary, wondering if he might now decide to disavow his proposal.

The two men exchanged looks, then Edward spoke.

'I trust the matter in hand will require consultation with someone else?' He motioned toward the door, taking the chance that the older man would understand.

'As a matter of fact, I must. If you would excuse me,' the secretary added on his way from the room, the packet of papers in his hand and a perceptive look on his face.

Neither of the occupants he left behind paid the slightest attention to his departure. Left alone, Edward gently pulled her from the chair and into his arms, whereupon Victoria promptly dissolved into tears and wound her arms about him as though she feared he might disappear again.

'I feared for your life; you were gone so very long and I heard nothing from you but that scrap of a note,' Victoria sniffed. 'I love you so dreadfully, you see.' She took great comfort from the reassuring thud of his heart, then sniffed again, accepting his offer of a spotless white handkerchief with which to blot her tears.

'I aged ten years when I envisioned what you must have gone through on your way here today. My dearest love.' He tilted up her face so that he might have the kiss he so earnestly desired.

Her fatigue evaporating for the moment, Victoria cherished his words, welcomed his embrace—especially the kiss she had feared never to know again. His hands skillfully roamed the soft gown beneath her shawl, drawing her as close to him as was possible. No thought went to the possibility that someone might enter the room.

When at last he paused to give them both a breath, he murmured against her cheek, 'I cannot fathom why I insisted upon banns. I think it would be far better to wed this moment. I want you in my arms and bed far too soon, I fear. I missed you quite dreadfully.'

Victoria chuckled, an endearing little sound to his ears. 'I confess I did wonder if you were going to give me the mitten, my love. This is Friday. The third and last banns will be read on Sunday, and then we can be married without delay. All is in readiness for our wedding.' She bestowed a loving look on her adored husband-to-be.

Her locket with its lapis-lazuli stones set to form the blue iris lay outside her gown in plain sight. Edward looked down at it and frowned.

'Did Bathurst insist you wear this?' He gathered the locket in his hands, his fingers brushing her skin as he did.

'Yes.' She trembled, very aware of his touch, even though fleeting.

'I was to wear it until the case was solved. I was torn, for the iris reminded me of the French, and how they murdered my beloved parents. I placed their pictures inside to carry over my heart, to remind me why I did all that I did. Now my job is finished, and I could remove this locket. Yet it is what brought us together, I suspect.'

'I saw it while we were in the windmill,' he admitted. 'I decided to follow you, become acquainted, for I well knew what that symbol meant, and your activities were highly suspicious, my love. You cannot know how relieved I was when I found we worked for the same side.'

'No more so than I,' she confessed.

He gathered her closer, the blue-iris locket forgotten, then claimed her lips again after murmuring, 'Our wedding will be none too soon.'

*   *   *

Hence, the following week, friends and neighbors were treated to the sight of the elegant Miss Dancy, dressed in lace-trimmed cream crepe with a pretty veil hanging down her back, and the most handsome Sir Edward Hawkswood, attired in a smart blue coat, gray pantaloons, and a white piqué waistcoat of the latest design, at the altar of St George's Church while the bishop performed the marriage ceremony. Behind them Julia and Elizabeth fondly watched as their dearest sister became united in wedlock with a man they admired.

It was highly doubtful if either of the pair before the altar took any note of those assembled.

Lady Chatterton sniffed as she viewed the joyous couple. 'Shocking,' she whispered to her good friend. 'It is not good *ton* to be so adoring. And whoever heard of blue irises in a bridal bouquet!'

Her friend, as she watched the couple exchange their vows, then kiss most tenderly before disappearing into a side room to sign the register, merely shook her head. It was quite obvious that here was a marriage truly made in heaven, and the couple so blessed were only to be envied.

A smiling Julia and Elizabeth waved off the carriage carrying a deliriously happy couple. That the sisters held vague dreams of their own was not known to others.

Inside the carriage that sped south from London on the way to their ultimate destination of Switzerland, the pair of lovers were wrapped in each other's arms, saying little. If one had heard the words 'At last, my love!' it would have been all.